DEMON'S KING

HIGH DEMON SERIES, BOOK THREE

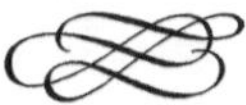

CONNIE SUTTLE

Print Second Edition (2018)
Print ISBN: 1-63478-065-5
Print ISBN-13: 978-1-63478-065-0
eBook ISBN: 1-93975-906-4
eBook ISBN-13: 978-1-93975-906-1

Published by:
SubtleDemon Publishing, LLC
PO Box 95696
Oklahoma City, OK 73143

Cover art by Renee Barratt @ The Cover Counts

To Walter, Joe, Larry, Lee, Dianne, Sarah and Mark.
Thank you.

ACKNOWLEDGMENTS

As always, this book is the result of collaboration. If it weren't for the support of my editor, my cover artist and my beta readers, it would be less than it is. All mistakes, as usual, are mine and no other's.

About the Author:
Connie Suttle lives in Oklahoma with her husband and a conglomerate of cats. They have finally banded together to make their demands, which has proven disconcerting to all humans involved.

You may find Connie in the following ways:
Facebook: Connie Suttle Author
Twitter: @subtledemon
Website and Blog: subtledemon.com

High Demon Series:

Demon Lost

Demon Revealed

Demon's King

Demon's Quest

Demon's Revenge

Demon's Dream

God Wars Series:

Blood Double

Blood Trouble

Blood Revolution

Blood Love

Blood Finale

Saa Thalarr Series:

Hope and Vengeance

Wyvern and Company

Observe and Protect*

First Ordinance Series:

Finder

Keeper

BlackWing

SpellBreaker

WhiteWing

~

R-D Series:

Cloud Dust

Cloud Invasion

Cloud Rebel

~

Latter Day Demons Series:

Hot Demon in the City

A Demon's Work is Never Done

A Demon's Due

~

Seattle Elementals Series:

Your Money's Worth

Worth Your While*

~

BlackWing Pirates Series

MindSighted

MindMage

MindRogue

MindMaster*

~

Black Rose Sorceress Series

The Rose Mark

Rose and Thorn

Black Rose Queen

Queen of Thorns and Roses

Future Wars Series

Buffer Zone

Black Zone*

Other Titles from SubtleDemon Publishing:

Malefactor

Transgressor

Underhanded*

by Joe Scholes

*Forthcoming

Tory was hugging me so hard it hurt. I wanted to scream my lungs out. Aurelius was rushing in and Lendill was suddenly there, saying he'd send everyone out that he could spare. Gavril had disappeared. He was seventeen and gone off for his second semester of private school. He'd boarded the Starship—there were records and vids. No records showed him getting off the ship. Queen Lissa had screamed the moment she'd learned of it—everyone suspected kidnapping.

I was so close to getting out of the ASD, too, and Gavril had asked me to spend my first free summer with him at his mother's palace on the beach. Tory had already made plans to be with us, as had Aurelius. Lendill was still attempting to get me interested. I'd softened a little toward him, but still held him at arm's length. Wylend was waiting for me to get away from the ASD before making a serious proposal. He did come to take me to dinner occasionally and had invited me to a ball or two on Karathia. Of course, all my activities revolved around my duties for the ASD. They'd certainly gotten their money's worth from me. Now, Gavril was missing and I wanted to tear something apart. I think Tory knew that—that's why he was holding onto me so tightly. What would we do? Chash couldn't be gone—just couldn't. I wouldn't know how to live without him. That thought brought me to tears.

"Reah, I know how you feel about Gavril. We'll find him if there's any way." Lendill was in front of me now, while Tory held me. He brushed my bangs back from my forehead—my hair was finally the length it should have been—almost to my waist. I kept it braided, but I had opted for shorter bangs.

"Breah-mul, I can't bear to see you weep." Lendill had started using the Wyyldan endearments more than four years earlier, while I was still suffering from what Teeg had done to me. Now, I heard Teeg was still in charge of Campiaa—still running things across the non-Alliance worlds. Word had it he was forming his own alliance. The ASD was watching carefully, but as yet couldn't point a finger at anything he did as illegal.

Gavin, Gavril's father, was in Lissa's bedroom with the Queen, as were most of her seventeen mates, including Karzac. I think it was he who put her in a healing sleep; she hadn't stopped screaming until he did.

"I want to go looking for him," I demanded.

"Reah, you're too close to this. Remember the rules?" Lendill was still stroking my forehead and wiping tears from my cheeks. If we knew any civilian personally who was the victim of a crime or involved in a crime, we weren't allowed to work the investigation. At all. Couldn't even look up information on a comp-vid. That didn't keep me from wanting to go right out and find whoever had done this and make them very dead. After they suffered. A lot. Lendill's words reminded me that Tory and Ry couldn't work the investigation either —they were Gavril's brothers.

"Reah, come to me." Aurelius was there, pulling me away from Tory. "My love, we will find him." Aurelius was carrying me out of the room—we were in Queen Lissa's sitting area, just outside her bedroom. I wondered where Kifirin was. Surely, he might do something about this. He hadn't appeared, however. Not yet, anyway.

"Come home with me, love. We will deal with this." Aurelius soothed me as best he could when he folded both of us to his spacious home on the light half of the planet.

~

Two weeks went by and there was no word. No ransom notes, no terrorists claiming responsibility—nothing. Kifirin had come after three days, locking himself away with Lissa and Gavin. They'd both looked weary and sad after they'd spoken with Kifirin. It made me wonder what he'd said to them. I was afraid to ask. The search was continuing, however, so they didn't think Gavril was dead.

Gavril. He'd been my best friend and confidant through all of this. He'd talked me around eventually over the whole Teeg thing. "Re," he'd said, "I think he did love you. At least a little." I'd looked at Gavril as if he'd lost his senses. "No, I don't think he could fool you that way. You'd have known, don't you think—if he were lying to you?" The earnest look on Gavril's face as he'd peered into mine had me biting my lip.

After thinking about it, I'd nodded. I would have known if he were lying. But then I'd lost out over Teeg's greed; his desire to have Campiaa and every other thing that Arvil San Gerxon had collected over his long life. I had a feeling that Teeg had managed to take over all the Hardlows' holdings as well—he controlled their warlocks there at the end. Just because Teeg had managed to form order out of the chaos surrounding Campiaa didn't mean I had to forgive him, because I hadn't.

I was nineteen and gullible then. Working for the ASD for more than five years had knocked most of that out of me. Lendill had told me once after I'd gotten shot for perhaps the sixth time, that he was thankful for my High Demon ancestry. The scars all went away after a while. Now, I wanted to talk to my best friend about my best friend's disappearance. *Chash, I love you. So much*, I sent out to him. He had mindspeech, but his parents had muted it. Told him he'd have it back on his eighteenth birthday. I didn't know if he'd ever get to celebrate that birthday. The thought made me shiver.

Reah? Lendill's mindspeech interrupted my fearful thoughts. *Reah, meet me in my office, please.* At least he'd added the *please.* I skipped there—I'd been at the pond where Tory and Ry had taught Gavril and me to skip rocks.

"Vice-Director?" Even my voice betrayed my depression. Lendill sat behind his desk. He had three comp-vids scattered across it and another comp-vid communicator strapped to his wrist. He was apparently in constant contact with everybody.

"Reah, we have good information on Zellar." That had me jerking my head up to stare at Lendill. *Zellar.* Just the sound of that name had every member of the ASD seething. Zellar—the rogue warlock who left drained planet cores in his wake. For years, he only worked on worlds outside the Alliance—the ASD had gotten too close to him on too many occasions. Burned him a few times—Ry had almost gotten him once, but Zellar had used the very last of a planet's power and escaped. Ry always insisted that he'd wounded Zellar, though. I thought he could be right—we hadn't heard anything from the murdering bastard in two years.

"What do you have?" Lendill knew that would divert my attention if nothing else would. So many people had starved or frozen to death when Zellar killed their planets. Drain the core, everything died. Usually in an ice age that couldn't be stopped. Employing that forbidden act was like ripping the heart out of a body—without that vital organ the rest had no chance.

"Here." Lendill pushed a comp-vid toward me. "The only hope I have is Tory or you, and Lissa is terrified of any more of her sons leaving the planet right now. That leaves you, Reah." Lendill was right —Zellar's power, no matter how great it was, couldn't touch me or my High Demon mate. He might get to us using physical means, but that wasn't Zellar's style. Besides, I was hoping he wouldn't discover what I was until it was too late and I had his throat in my hands. I don't think Lendill or Norian would complain if I only brought Zellar's body back.

Lendill rose and came around his desk while I read through the information. One of Lendill's ASD operatives had spotted an irregularity on Kareed. Kareed was definitely non-Alliance. In fact, it was hip-deep in what some were calling the Campiaan Alliance. Our Alliance, officially named the Reth Alliance thousands of turns ago, was now commonly referred to simply as *the Alliance*. Everybody knew what you were talking about. Now, Teeg's machinations might cause that to change. A tiny curl of smoke came from my nostrils at the thought of Teeg—betraying, reptanoid kidnapping bastard that he was.

"I can't tell you how sexy I find that," Lendill took the comp-vid from my hand and lifted me onto his desk. He wiggled his way between my legs and gave me a kiss. "I want you to go after Zellar, *cheah-mul*. Bring him back to me, alive or dead, *deah-mul*. I love you, *breah-mul*." He'd said it out of order, but the meaning would never change. He'd called me his heart, his soul, his breath. Those words were the Wyyldan declaration of love. I didn't stop him when he carefully unbuttoned the top button on my blouse. Bending his head and brushing his dark hair against my lips, he kissed my collarbone. Another button opened, another kiss was laid. I hoped he didn't have cameras inside his office. I didn't hold him back this time. The desk was the perfect height for him and I wondered if he'd planned it that way. Tory and I had the linking. Aurelius had the vampire's bite. I don't know what Lendill had, but the moment our bodies were joined, there came a pleasure that suffused my entire being. Tory and I, with the linking, fed off each other's desires until it was frenzied. Aurelius gave me a slow fire that built to a mind-bending climax. This—I couldn't even put words to this. I only wanted Lendill to give me more of it. When he did, he was whispering my name against my lips—*Reah, Reah, REAH!*

We ended up on Lendill's sofa—he wasn't satisfied with just once. I was more than thankful that he had a private bath adjoining his office. The shower inside was small but serviceable. We both made use of it before dressing.

"Reah, we're not allowed to marry until you're officially out of the

ASD—you know that." Lendill kissed my neck as I buttoned my blouse. "But I'll ask the question a second time, breah-mul. Will you marry me?"

"If Tory and Aurelius agree." I turned in his arms and leaned my forehead against his chest.

"I'll work on that." His voice rumbled in his chest. Suddenly, I huddled against him. Loving Lendill had taken Gavril out of my thoughts temporarily. Now they were back. Somehow, he knew. "We'll find him, Reah. No effort will be spared." Lendill lifted my face for a kiss. "I love you. Don't ever forget that. The moment your conscription is over, I'll take you to meet my father. He's wanted to meet you for a while, now."

"Your father is still alive?" I asked. Yes, that surprised me.

"Very much so. We don't talk often, but we do talk. Now, go and make arrangements to travel to Kareed tomorrow. Do this for me, Reah. Do it for all of us. As long as Zellar lives, he will be a danger to every world across the universes."

I nodded against his chest and pulled away. "Reah, you are *tirlandar'miri*—beautiful beyond words," Lendill whispered

"What language is that?" I'd never heard that phrase before.

"It is the language of my father's race. Go now, Reah, before I change my mind and pull you back. I have no desire to let you walk away from me."

I left him. Yes, I would have liked to stay. I would also like my heart to stop thumping painfully in my chest whenever I thought of Chash. *My Chash.* I wanted to weep as I skipped the rest of the way to the suite I shared with Tory. Most of my clothing was there. I pulled two eight-days' worth from my closet, wiping tears away as I tossed it into a standard-issue black bag.

All ASD agents had at least two sturdy, black bags for travel. They looked much the same as many other bags normal Alliance citizens used, except they had compartments built in for pistols, knives, throwing stars, even rifles. Any other kind of weapon could also be accommodated, as long as its length wasn't greater than that of the bag itself. My knife and pistol went into the bag—I seldom carried anything else.

My knife saw more use than the pistol did, too. Aunt Glinda—Glindarok, the High Demon Queen, had sent it to me for my twentieth birthday. I didn't know where she found it, but it was extremely sharp and never lost its edge. She and I still didn't talk. I'd done my best to understand—or at least to overlook it. I overheard Tory whisper to Ry once that the knife was probably Grey House work, but I didn't know whether to believe that or not. The knife was made in black metal of some sort and had no glint or gleam if I chose to use it at night. It had turned out to be more than useful. Now, I only wanted it at Zellar's throat.

Tory and Aurelius were there to say their good-byes the following morning—I'd spent the night in Tory's bed. He didn't want to let me go, either. I gave him the best kiss I could, asked him to keep me updated on Gavril and skipped away.

"Pretty." The drunk I sat beside at the bar attempted to paw my hair. For the third time. I had my knife-point at his throat in less than a blink. The drunk moved his hands and turned away from me. The bartender gave a slight smile in the dim light and went back to washing glasses. Stuffing the knife into the sheath clipped to the leather waistband of my pants, I went back to my drink.

Alcohol doesn't have the same effect on me anymore—Tory and his father, Gardevik, had done a lot of teaching during the past four years. I was informed that a High Demon doesn't come into adulthood until age twenty-two. Garde had grinned when he'd shared that information. Under the laws of Kifirin, the High Demon's world (named after Kifirin, the god) no female was allowed to legally mate until that age. Tory (and Aurelius) had gotten ahead of things. Teeg—well, I didn't even want to think about him. With High Demons, once adulthood is officially reached, alcohol, anesthetics, pain medications

—all had limited effects. Now it took nearly four times the amount of alcohol that would make any normal humanoid drunk just to get me tipsy.

"Want another?" The bartender tapped the bar in front of my glass. I'd chosen what Ry and Tory called a bloody Mary. The alcohol was named Sardof on Alliance worlds. They called it the same here, too.

"Sure." I drained my glass and pushed the empty toward him. The bar was connected to the hotel where Zellar was supposedly staying—I'd been given his alias and the room number, even. Now I was watching the door into the hotel from my barstool, hoping that Zellar would come in soon. I didn't want to sit there drinking all night in case the bartender had a limit on the number of drinks he could serve to one person.

"I haven't seen you here before." The bartender slid the fresh drink across to me, accompanied by two napkins and a dish of mixed nuts. The drunk beside me had his hand in the bowl before I could decide whether I was hungry. Now I wasn't about to touch it.

"Just got here today," I sighed. "Came here to meet a friend, but he hasn't arrived yet." I was lying to the bartender, but it might keep his interest at a minimum. He seemed nice—the bartender, that is. I got his kind of attention a lot. If I could have disguised myself, I would have. Ry could put a disguise on anyone without blinking. Except a High Demon—if they didn't want one. I didn't want one. I could have worn a wig and makeup, but wigs made my head itch and makeup made me feel as if I had hotcake batter glued to my face. I hated it. Lendill knew not to send me anywhere that required anything of the sort. Therefore, everyone saw me as I was.

I dressed terribly most of the time while on assignment—people tended to stay away if you looked destitute or crazy. Not tonight—I had my black leathers on. Mid-summer had come and it was hot on Kareed, so the top was sleeveless and laced up the front. The pants were tight except around my boots—I had another knife and a small pistol hidden there. Kareed allowed weapons, if they were worn on the outside in full view. I was breaking Kareedan law with what I had in my boots. Of course, I was breaking Kareedan law just by being there. They didn't allow Alliance citizens to set foot on Kareedan soil. Probably why Zellar had chosen the planet to begin with.

Zellar walked in while I was sipping my drink and eating the stalk of celery the bartender had planted in it. A young couple came in right behind him. Couldn't have been more perfect.

"There he is, that cheating scum. I should have known he was seeing someone else." I muttered my accusation loud enough for the bartender to hear. I slapped several Kareedan marks down on the bar and went to follow the couple who walked right behind Zellar.

We rode up the elevator together—Zellar hadn't chosen a seedy hotel. He'd paid for the best. I wondered if he were working for someone or living off funds gained from past jobs. The couple got off the lift before I did. Zellar allowed me to get off the elevator first. I'd gotten a room on the same floor; I'd flirted with the desk clerk to do it but it had gotten me what I wanted.

The rooms on the fourth and top floor were huge, the doors facing a bank of windows on the opposite side of the hall. I slipped my key card into the slot two doors down from Zellar's room and went inside, putting my back to the door when it closed and listening carefully for Zellar's door to shut. When it did, I was out of my room like a rocket and kicking his door in. What happened then I didn't have any explanation for. Not until later, anyway.

Lendill, Tory and Aurelius watched the pirated vid-feed in horror. The hotel where Reah was staying had been bombed. At the moment, only Lendill knew that the room where the blast originated had been Zellar's. Assignments were generally kept secret from the others, unless they were on the same assignment. None of them had been able to reach Reah through mindspeech.

Journalists on Kareed were saying it was a ranos grenade. Aurelius placed an arm around Tory's shoulders—Tory was sitting, Aurelius standing. Tory thought of Aurelius almost as a father figure—Aurelius was old as a vampire and had that effect on others. Gardevik burst into the room. Tory stood and went to his father. Aurelius sat in Tory's vacated chair with a sigh of disbelief.

"Just one blow after another." Norian Keef, Director of the ASD walked in. "Do we have any agents in the area? Lendill?" Norian grabbed Lendill's arm.

"Two," Lendill had to bring himself back from the horror he was seeing on the vid-screen. "I've already sent them. They'll have something for us soon."

"Let me know as quickly as you can. Do you need something? Anything?"

"I need to know that Reah is safe," Lendill choked up.

"Do this first." I barely understood the words; I was in too much pain. There was more—a sharp stabbing pain in my collarbone. What were they doing to me? I couldn't see, something covered my eyes. "Now," the voice was soft as it continued, "normal painkill and anesthetic won't have much effect. Don't give too much—it could harm her."

"But she has broken bones. Her ribs are crushed, three vertebrae are cracked, one leg is broken in two places, the other leg in one. One arm broken, one not. Skull fractures—honestly, I have no idea how she still lives." That was a second voice, talking with the first voice. I moaned.

"Make sure she stays alive," the first voice said. "I'll help this time." Fingers touched—cool against my forehead—followed by pain-free darkness.

Fever came with my next waking. I must have been restrained—I couldn't move. That frightened me, even in my feverish state. I was too weak and in too much pain to struggle. I still couldn't see and knew somehow I'd been blindfolded. Somebody didn't want me to see anything. They wanted me to live; I remembered that much from the previous waking but little else. Who had me? They couldn't be friendly, I knew that much.

"Shhhh," fingers against my hot forehead. Darkness came. Again.

~

A slight sound woke me next. I still couldn't move or see. I must have made some sort of noise—the second voice was back. "Only changing the bag, pretty girl. We have to feed you, you know."

What had they done? Placed a feeding tube? How bad off was I? I moaned. "I didn't mean to upset you. Just stay calm, all right? Gods, you're so beautiful." I felt a tugging around my torso—second voice was cleaning the area around the tube and placing a fresh dressing. I wanted to weep. I wanted him to take off the fucking blindfold. I wanted to be anywhere except where I was.

Could I send mindspeech? How could I tell Tory, Lendill or Aurelius where I was? *Auri?* I sent. *Tory? Lendill?* Only silence met my weakened sendings and I failed to get any response. The effort, too, was taking its toll. Second voice continued his ministrations—he was bathing me now, his hands expertly wiping my body with a warm, soapy cloth. My ribs and the surrounding area were so tender I wanted to scream when I was washed there. "It'll be over soon—over soon," the voice crooned. Could I trust that voice? He'd left me blindfolded—I couldn't. I didn't even try to speak to him. He might ask questions and I was in no shape to keep him from getting what he wanted just by exerting a little pressure against my aching ribs. My breathing became ragged as he worked; pain was waking all over my body. The singsong "It'll be over soon," came again. I whimpered and endured it.

~

"How soon can she be moved?"

"Tomorrow, if you do it your usual way. Make sure you have a secured place for her—she's staying awake longer now."

"You think I haven't already thought of that?" A snort followed that statement. First voice was speaking. Something worried me about the voice, but they'd given me painkill earlier. Drugs were second voice's choice if he didn't want me to be awake while he did whatever he was going to do. I imagined he had to give a lot of it—a normal dose wouldn't do. He probably had to experiment at first, just to get the amounts right. Now I wanted more than anything to allow the drug-induced sleep to come, but fought it to learn whatever I could.

"You're not going to hurt her, are you?" Second voice sounded worried. Another snort but no answer this time. I had no idea what that meant and it frightened me. I hadn't carried any ID other than the false one Lendill had sent with me. They couldn't know I was ASD. What did they want with me? That thought raced around a track in my brain with no way to stop it or turn it aside. And they hadn't said where they were moving me. I hadn't felt this helpless since I was small and Edan had beaten me, breaking a wrist and cracking ribs.

"You should be asleep," first voice said; the fingers against my forehead followed.

"Make sure it's secured—we don't want anything happening. The boss will be pissed if she manages to dislodge the mattress." That's what I woke to—another place. I was sure of it—it smelled different. They'd moved me while I slept. Since I had no concept of time or where I'd been before, I knew even less now. The blindfold was still in place and I was still restrained. At least three were working around my bed—I could hear them moving, cursing softly and breathing.

"Careful," the one who'd mentioned *the boss* said from my left. That statement was followed by the sounds of a buckle fastening and more soft cursing. I tried sending mindspeech to Lendill and the others but there was still no reply. Could I skip? Was I strong enough? It took full concentration to do it. A healthy body would be a plus, but that might not come for a while, if ever.

I still had no idea why my captors had kept me alive or what they wanted from me. I gathered my wits about me and made the attempt to skip. Nothing. I was still right where I was with my attendants securing me to a bed somehow. "Watch the bag." The voice came again. It sounded vaguely familiar, but I still couldn't place it. With my wits addled as they were, I wasn't surprised. My mind could be playing tricks on me, too—I knew that.

"All done," one of my attendants heaved a relieved sigh. I heard them walking out and then the sounds of an iron-barred door closing. I knew something of where I was then; I'd heard that sound many times over the past few years. It was the sound of confinement. I was in a prison cell.

"I think we can remove the feeding tube this afternoon." Second voice was back. I hadn't heard from him for several days. Someone else had come to bathe me in between. Someone with gentle hands, although they never spoke. Those hands always stopped if I whimpered with pain, giving me a moment to deal with it before beginning again.

"Then we'll have to remove the blindfold too, if we expect her to feed herself." First voice was also back. He didn't sound happy.

"She will be weak—she may not be able to lift her hand at first—you've kept her restrained. We should have been exercising her more."

"Don't tell me my business. I know what I'm doing."

"Of course. Sir."

"Call me when the tube comes out. I'll let you remove the blindfold at that time. We may get some feedback from our prisoner then." First voice walked away.

"Taking the tube out won't hurt much, don't worry about it," second voice soothed. At his words, I decided to try my voice. I hadn't spoken for a very long time.

"What does he want?" My voice cracked—my mouth was too dry.

"I don't know the whole of it, and I couldn't tell you anyway. He has forbidden it." I wanted to ask if they were going to hurt me. Ask what they knew about me to keep me like this. I didn't. I knew better.

I had to be patient. Right then, I had very little in the way of patience. I would have to work on that.

"Pretty girl," second voice went on, "I have to ask you now not to hurt yourself if we remove the restraints. Can you do that for me? You won't have control over your muscles at first, and you're still in casts —your arm and both legs, anyway. We'll have to wrap your ribs better once the feeding tube comes out. I know it hurts to breathe." A hand stroked my forehead.

"Name?" I asked.

"He won't allow me to tell you. Mine or his." I tried to swallow but my mouth was too dry. "Here." He swabbed my mouth with a moistened applicator. That helped. "We have an IV line in too, to keep your fluids up. We'll remove that at the same time."

"Should have let me die," I whispered.

"No." Second voice whispered back. "The target did get killed. The boss said finding you afterward was the biggest bonus he's ever gotten."

Was he saying Zellar was dead? Was that what he meant or was there someone else? "Of course all of Zellar's little apprentices are out there now and we have to hunt them down." Second voice sounded extremely angry about that. At least I knew that Zellar was dead, but what was that about apprentices? How many were there? Would they do what Zellar had done, draining worlds until they died? That frightened me and my heart rate and breathing increased.

"I didn't mean to upset you, sweet girl. Calm down, all right?"

"You don't know that I'm sweet," I rasped.

"No, I don't know that," he chuckled softly. "I do know you're the prettiest thing I've seen in a long time and the boss will kill me if I lay a hand on you other than to treat your wounds." He moved around for a while before leaving. "I'll be back in a few ticks," he promised. The sound of the iron-barred door opening and closing came next. I heaved as much of a sigh as my ribs allowed.

～

"IV out first," my right hand felt the tug as the line was pulled out. The hand was wiped with cold disinfectant before a bandage was laid across the wound. "Not much bleeding, that's good," second voice said. "Now, for the feeding tube." He rustled around the bed, unhooking the bag, I imagined, just by the sound of it. A click—the line had been closed off. Didn't want the contents of my stomach all over everywhere, I suppose. "Now, we take the stitches out," a snipping sound and then the tugging came. Removing the stitches didn't hurt much at all. The tube coming out did. It caused a muffled shriek to escape—I hadn't been expecting it.

"It's over, we just have to cover up the small wound," second voice said. He did so, wiping off the wound and covering it with more bandaging. "You'll still have to be bathed for a while until the wound heals and the casts come off. The scans look good, though. Should be a few days at most."

"I want to wash my hair." My voice sounded like one sheet of sandpaper rubbed against another.

"I know, pretty girl. We'll see about that."

"Don't fucking call her that." First voice had arrived and was watching. Second voice was silent. I cringed.

The restraints came off next. "Try to raise your right arm," second voice said. I tried. That was the best that could be said. I got it off the bed but I shook with the effort. "Grip my fingers." I gave the best grip I could. It wasn't much. Second voice moved to the other side of my bed and did the same with my left hand. My arm was weighed down by the cast, although it was made of the lightest materials. I did better at squeezing his fingers on that side.

"Now the blindfold," first voice demanded.

"Now the blindfold," second voice repeated. I learned it was grip-fastened in the back so I wouldn't have to lie on a knot in the fabric. Second voice pulled it away and I blinked, unprepared in the sudden light. Even though it was dimmed, it still hurt my eyes. They watered while I worked furiously to get my sight to clear. I peered into second voice's face. It wasn't a bad face and he was smiling at me. He looked to be around forty turns or so, had dark-brown hair, hazel eyes, a nose that was a bit large and a dimple when he smiled. I couldn't bring myself to smile back at him.

"We'll let you try to eat in just a little," he assured me. He wasn't going to tell me his name. Well, I wasn't going to tell him mine either. Things might have gone well if first voice hadn't stepped into my line of vision. It took everything I had to rip one of the restraints from the bed rail and fling it at him, screaming the entire time.

CHAPTER 2

"Let me go, you stinking pile of shit," I shouted at Teeg San Gerxon. Of course, I was weeping and hanging precariously off the bed while I did it. My muscles no longer obeyed me and the pain of moving with cracked and broken ribs was unbearable. I learned then that my back, too, could bellow its displeasure.

Second voice was shouting for help and Astralan, the warlock asshole, was there to help in only a blink. Both got me back on the bed —with second voice fussing the entire time while Teeg stood off to the side, watching with hooded eyes and absolutely no expression on his face. Once I was back on the bed and arranged to second voice's satisfaction, Teeg came to the bed again. "Done with your little outburst, Reah?" I didn't answer him. "And I don't intend to let you go. While you voided the adoption with Arvil, we are still married. I never set that aside, you know. You'd have learned that if you hadn't skipped away from me the last time."

"Oh, boo-hoo," I said, turning my face away from him. "Send me back to the Alliance—they don't recognize your marriage contract there. See? Problem solved."

"I could have set it aside here. I decided not to."

"It's too late for me to sign a pre-nup."

"Reah."

"Teeg, don't even try. You get everything you want? Do you?"

"You're harder, now."

"You can bet your ass on that." Working for the ASD had done that. Dealing with what he'd done to me before had done that. Now he was back to torture me again.

"Can you still cook?" Astralan asked.

"Astralan, go ahead. Do your best sorcery or whatever the hell it is that you do. I dare you." I turned my head back to glare at the warlock. "How's Teeg treating you? As well as the Hardlows?"

"Not even a comparison," Astralan grinned.

"We had everything set up to take Zellar down inside that hotel room, Reah," Teeg crossed arms over his chest. That chest was just as wide as it was before. "But the Alliance sends in one of theirs. It couldn't have turned out more perfect. They hand you right back to me, when I've been looking for you for years." I pointedly ignored the fact that Teeg was just as handsome as he ever was.

"Sure, you looked for me. And Elves are real, too," I muttered. I didn't add that if I were in better health, I might consider breaking his perfect nose with a single punch.

"You might be surprised," a smile tugged at Teeg's mouth.

"What do you want from me, Teeg? Am I a hostage? You intend to beef up your bank account by selling me back to the Alliance? Force them to do something they don't want to, just to get your way?"

"Oh, I have a project in mind." He nodded at my assessment, his dark eyes giving nothing away. "But I want your help to track those fool apprentices Zellar trained first. They could be anywhere. I've hacked into the ASD records, Reah. I know you still don't miss. You're going to help me take those fuckers down before they destroy what I've tried to build."

He meant his new alliance. I realized that quickly. "Still building things, Teeg?"

"Trying to—yes." Long, well-shaped fingers raked through dark hair.

"Uh-huh." I handed him one of Queen Lissa's best, unusual phrases.

It stopped him for a moment and he blinked curiously at me, attempting to determine what I meant, more than likely.

"I also know you have other mates. I suggest you cooperate with me or I'll put a price on both their heads." That statement made my chest hurt. It made me want to cry. "You didn't take him, did you?" I could barely get my hand up to wipe away the tear that fell.

"Take who?" Teeg was staring at me.

"Nobody," I muttered.

"Maybe we did, then." Was he using what I'd just given him or did he have Gavril? I was shaking.

"You're upsetting her." Second voice had my wrist in his fingers, checking my pulse.

"You mean Gavril, don't you?" Teeg sounded smugly satisfied. How had he gotten that name? I'd never said it to him. Neither had Ry nor Tory. An ASD agent never gave the enemy a target to go after. Teeg knew he'd hit the mark when I didn't answer. "We have him—we just didn't realize he'd be important to you in any way. We were going to present other demands to Le-Ath Veronis. Is that where you live, Reah?" Teeg was digging into my ribs verbally. It hurt. My breathing quickened.

"Do not hyperventilate," second voice issued the command. My body ignored him. Astralan helped get me sitting up in bed and my head down as far as it would go. "Get the quickshot!" Second voice shouted. I struggled; they gave it anyway. I was out in no time.

"It went better than I thought—I think she'll cooperate now," Teeg sighed and rubbed his forehead.

"Why can't you just do what you normally do or have your wizards do something?" Doctor Jes Wurfl asked.

"Because of what she is. Besides, you have no idea how effective she can be against Zellar's clones."

"What is she, then? How can she have any effect against one rogue wizard, let alone half a dozen or more?"

"Have you ever heard of High Demons?" Teeg gave Jes a pointed look.

"Those are myth," Jes scoffed.

"Not myth. That's what my wife is—High Demon."

"Is she really immune to wizardry?"

"Every bit of it. She's going to get rid of the scum in the Campiaan Alliance. Then we'll use her as a bargaining chip with the Reth Alliance. Have them recognize us as an equal. There's a lot at stake here, Jes."

"Could she have killed Zellar?"

"She would have. All she needed was to be within arm's length. He would have died before he knew she'd cut his throat."

"She's that cruel?" Jes' hands went to his throat.

"No. Not cruel. Just well-trained and efficient," Teeg sighed. "She's been forced to be what she is. Besides, what sort of death would you wish for Zellar? He killed your home planet, Jes. She would have given him a quick death. He wouldn't have felt the bite of the blade, I don't think. It would have been merciful."

"But we blew him up with a ranos grenade."

"The grenade was the only thing we had to penetrate his shields, my friend. If I'd known Reah was coming after him, I would have sat back and watched the vid-feed for years to come."

"You had cameras there, didn't you?"

"Yes, and I wasn't watching, someone else was. They didn't recognize Reah, I did. When it was too late. Now we have to get her back on her feet and in fighting condition before I can take her hunting."

"Do you really have the one she asked about—what was his name?"

"Gavril?"

"Yes."

"Oh, yes. I have him all right." Teeg jerked his head toward his study door. Jes knew the conversation with his employer was over.

~

"I want to hear from Gavril." I'd had time to think about this. How could Teeg stoop this low? How? He'd seemed such a good man when I'd first met him. Before he became what Arvil and the Hardlows had been. Teeg had come by to supervise the washing of my hair—had brought in a hairdresser, no less.

"Then stay quiet and let Treesa do your hair. Behave yourself and I'll move you into a suite." I was still locked in my cell. I don't know what Teeg thought to accomplish; I was still as weak as a newly-hatched nestling. My mindspeech still wasn't working and several attempts at skipping only gave me a terrible headache.

"You're telling *me* to behave myself? Child-snatching jackass," I muttered. I wasn't expecting Teeg to burst out laughing. Treesa pulled my wheeled chair up to the portable shampoo bowl and went to work.

"This is your natural color?" Treesa asked. I wasn't about to ask her the same thing—she had green and purple streaks running through the black of her hair. Her fingernails matched.

"Trust me—it's natural." Teeg was still chuckling.

"Nobody has hair this color," Treesa muttered as she washed my hair.

"Reah does." Treesa knew not to push Teeg. She washed my hair several times; it had been a while since it had been clean. Then, under Teeg's watchful gaze, Treesa combed it out and dried it. I asked to have it braided, Teeg refused. "I want it down, just as it is," he demanded. I wasn't able to braid my hair with the cast still on my left arm, so he got what he wanted. What *I* wanted was to hit him before it was over. Treesa took her equipment and left.

"I meant what I said about a suite," Teeg said. "I'll move you into one when you promise not to misbehave."

"Get me a message from Gavril so I know he's all right and you'll get it," I muttered. Ever since I knew that Teeg had Gavril, I woke from my sleep hyperventilating. What was Teeg hoping to gain from Lissa or the Alliance? What?

"I'll have a message for you tomorrow." Teeg walked out. The doctor was walking in almost at the same time.

"I think we can get these off in the next few days," he tapped my arm cast. "You can call me Jes—Master San Gerxon said I could give you my name." The doctor had run the scanner over the breaks in my arm and legs to check on their progress. "How are the headaches?"

"They'd be better if I knew my friend was all right," I muttered.

"He said he'd bring a message tomorrow. He usually keeps his word."

"What I want to know is how easy he finds it to kill." I did want to know that. Would Chash survive Teeg's blackmail? It frightened me to think about it.

"That is something you shouldn't be worrying your pretty head over." Jes plumped the pillows on my hospital bed. "I can bring a vid-screen for you—you can watch vids if you want. Or, I can bring you a comp-reader. We have several here with just about anything you want to read loaded in."

"Comp-vid?" I asked.

"Not unless I want to die."

"Ah. Do you?"

"No."

"Can I have both?"

"A vid-screen and a comp-reader?"

"Yes."

"Of course. You just can't tire yourself out. Go ahead, tell me I sound like your mother." Jes was looking at me hopefully.

"I don't know what my mother sounded like. She died when I was born."

"Ah. Well. I'll go get those things for you." Jes pointed through the doors of my cage. That's what it was—a cage inside a larger room that held nothing except my bed. A few windows lined one wall, but all of them were covered in privacy film. I could only see muted light and nothing else.

Jes brought both promised items when he returned, followed by someone else; a woman in her thirties and likely a servant.

"This is our cook, Ardalin," Jes introduced the woman. Ardalin carried a drink with a straw in it. Until then, I'd been getting clear broth to eat. It was bland and certainly wasn't anything I would have made for myself.

"Thank you," I took the drink from the cook. She didn't look happy to me. Perhaps Teeg was forcing her in some way, too. I rested the glass on the arm of my wheeled chair until I could lift it to take a drink. It consisted of berries blended with fruit juice and was quite decent. I was hoping Jes would leave the glass with me—I wanted to fling it at Teeg's head the next time he came in, but Jes took it with him after I was done. I was tired of using the small, fizzy teeth-cleaning tabs too. Jes brought one every morning and every night.

I settled in to read a book I'd picked out, falling asleep eventually with the comp-reader on my stomach.

"Shhh, go back to sleep, sweetheart." Reah's eyelashes were dark against her pale skin. Teeg worried over the dark circles under her eyes. He'd taken the comp-reader out of her hand and set it aside, almost waking her. She wasn't recovering as fast as he'd like—the ranos grenade had hit her full-on, blasting her through the window opposite Zellar's room and onto the roof of a nearby building. Anyone else would have died. Reah had come very close.

This wasn't supposed to happen. Zellar had practically disintegrated in the blast and he'd held a shield around himself. They'd found bits and pieces of him. Teeg's heart had almost seized in his chest when he'd seen Reah on the vid-screen, kicking in Zellar's door. Astralan had folded him to Kareed; Teeg had almost been crazy after watching Reah get hit.

Now that she had her voice and senses back, all she could do was fight with him. He'd hurt her more than he'd intended. His hope had been that she'd forgive him a little when he found her again. Now his ring was missing from her finger and he wondered what she'd done with it. He'd sealed his fate with her for the moment, telling her he'd taken Gavril. Teeg brushed silky white hair away from Reah's face. "My pretty baby," he crooned softly.

~

"Here's what you asked for." Teeg handed the comp-vid to me. I almost wept at the image on the screen. Chash was there, holding up a similar comp-vid with the day's news from an Alliance world. The date was clearly visible at the top of the news video.

"Is he safe? Are you treating him well? Is he scared?" I wiped tears off my cheeks. I wished there were a way I could get this to Lissa and Gavin. More than likely, they were still terrified for their youngest child. Teeg decided to be awful about the whole thing.

"That's none of your concern," he snapped. "Do I have your promise—not to do anything stupid and not to harm anyone inside my home? You won't escape, I've already seen to that. We did an implant, Reah. Right here." Teeg pointed to a spot on his collarbone. "It's inside the bone, Reah, and Jes tells me the bone has formed around it. No more mindspeech or skipping unless I turn this off." He held a small transmitter in his hand. I stared at him, completely speechless. "I told you I hacked your records. Two years ago, in fact." How could he be so hard? How?

"I want to kill you," I muttered.

"You're still my wife, Reah. I have the papers to prove it. Where's my ring?"

"If I thought you wanted it back, I wouldn't have tossed it in the ocean on Le-Ath Veronis." I had. I'd asked Aurelius to take me sailing and I'd dumped the thing the moment we couldn't see land any longer. Who knew where it was, now?

"I'll get you another ring."

"I won't wear it. You see this?" I turned the comp-vid around so he could see Gavril's image. "As long as you have him, I won't wear it."

"Don't make promises you can't keep," Teeg warned. I wanted to tell him to go fuck himself, but then he might take back the promise to let me out of my cage. He looked angry and frustrated, his dark hair rumpled, a deep frown marring his handsome features. "Jes, release the brakes on that stupid bed and bring her." That's how I got a ride to the old bedroom that Teeg and I had shared. That now seemed a lifetime ago, with a different person. He'd taken my freedom away and kidnapped Chash. Now he wanted to get me another ring. Logic no longer seemed a part of him.

"Now, Reah, I'm going to offer something else if you promise to do what Jes tells you. I need you back on your feet and ready to fight Zellar's spawn quickly before they scatter so far we'll never find them." Teeg had allowed Jes to transfer me to the bed. He'd called a servant to push my hospital bed out of the spacious suite. More than anything, I wanted to hobble to the bathroom and soak in a tub of hot water. The casts were still on so that was out of the question.

I wasn't about to ask him what he was offering now. I didn't need to; Farzi and Nenzi walked into the room. Teeg knew which buttons to push. This had upset me more than anything, when he'd taken Farzi, Nenzi and their brothers away. I'd been planning to take them to a jungle world that held little population so they could live as they pleased. Two of Teeg's warlocks had folded them away at Teeg's bidding. I still wanted to slap all of them for that.

"Farzi? Nenzi? I was sobbing now. Nenzi rushed in, Farzi right behind him.

"Be careful of her broken," Jes' words went unheeded as Nenzi nearly flung himself on the bed beside me, hugging me as hard as he dared. Farzi sat next to both of us.

"Our Reah," Farzi reached out to touch my hair. "Your hair quite long now."

I sniffled and wiped tears off my face. "This was how it was supposed to be. Before it was whacked off to make me look like a boy. Farzi, are your brothers all right?" I wanted to ask if they still lived—all of them—but I was afraid to.

"Our brothers do fine." Nenzi answered my question, pulling my head against his shoulder. "Nenzi misses Reah. Teeg says he cannot find. Now she is ours again." I didn't upset Nenzi by telling him that Teeg had kidnapped me. Gavril, too. I brushed Nenzi's dark hair off his forehead instead.

"Nenzi, I really missed you. And Farzi and all your brothers."

"We not find another good cook," Nenzi smiled at me.

"But Ardalin is here," I said.

"She isn't the same," Farzi pointed out stiffly. That told me right then that Ardalin didn't like the reptanoids. Only their eyes were different—on the surface of things, anyway. No reason to mistreat my people.

"Ardalin is superstitious," Teeg cleared his throat.

"Then send her to one of your many casinos," I snapped. "There is no reason anyone should mistreat Farzi, Nenzi and the others."

"I was hoping you'd help interview potential replacements." Teeg lifted an eyebrow at me.

"Uh-huh. And go take care of rogue wizards and help you with whatever you want to blackmail the Alliance over. My schedule is full, Teeg."

"Reah, not fight with Teeg. Please?" Nenzi's eyes were begging.

"Only for you, Nenzi." I hugged him with my good arm.

"Should have brought him in, first thing," Teeg muttered.

Two days later, with Nenzi, Farzi and six other reptanoids looking on, I got my casts off. My skin looked pale and shriveled when they were removed. "Now you can take a shower, but you probably need help," Jes said. He looked hopeful but Teeg, who was also there, frowned. Jes didn't offer his help. Farzi and Nenzi ended up helping me. They held me up when I didn't think I could stand and I washed myself. I don't know why I didn't worry about them seeing me naked but I didn't. I'd seen all of them naked before, when they'd turned to lion snakes. Nudity was completely natural to them, and held no embarrassment. Honestly, I thought of them as family. Perhaps they saw me the same way.

Farzi helped wash my hair—I wasn't thrilled about Treesa coming in again. Teeg, though, was there when I came out of the shower, dressed in the robe Farzi had helped me slip on. Nenzi was still fussing over me when Teeg picked up the comb and wordlessly started working on my hair. I tried to fend him off, but he stopped me with a sentence. "Gavril will be better off if you let me do this." Was he threatening both of us? I shivered at the thought. Teeg went back to working on my hair. When he finished combing it out, he lifted strands of it to his nose.

"It smells wonderful," he murmured. "Reah, your friend will be fine as long as you treat me well. Treat me as you did before, Reah. When you loved me, still."

I wrapped my arms around myself and rocked a little. What did he want? To go to bed with me?

"No, Reah, you're still recovering. I won't expect that just yet." Teeg got up and walked out of my bedroom. Farzi and Nenzi stared after him.

"Reah, he not harm you—I know this," Farzi sat on the bench beside me.

"Farzi—he's already brought harm. Here." I touched my chest.

"Reah, Teeg not—he not do—he not mean," Nenzi couldn't think of the words. I couldn't really tell if he were saying that Teeg wasn't mean or if he didn't mean it. Either way, I silently disagreed.

Both of them helped me into bed. My legs were still shaky and I felt worn out just from bathing. Jes had said he was starting rehab the next morning. I hoped I could get to sleep so I'd be rested; Teeg wanted me on my feet quickly. More than anything, I wanted to contact Lendill and let him know that Zellar was gone but his trainees might be scattered and already causing havoc. If any of them knew what they were doing, they could already be passing their secrets off to others. It was a frightening prospect. I wanted to get that remote away from Teeg, but Gavril's life might hang in the balance.

"Sleep, our Reah," Farzi turned out the light and he and Nenzi silently left my room.

"You can make it." Who knew that Jes could be such a slave driver? I walked down the hall to the elevator and then to the kitchen with little or no help. I think I was drenched in sweat and trembling by the time I got to the kitchen. Ardalin and an assistant were there cooking breakfast. Ardalin was making a great deal of racket, banging her pots and pans. She wasn't much of a cook if she treated good cooking utensils that way. The eggs she served me were terrible and I found bits of shell in them. I picked it out and ate what I could. Teeg came in with Astralan and the other three warlocks.

"Reah, I hope I get to eat one of your meals again someday," Astralan grinned. Well, he'd just made my life worse, as far as Ardalin went.

"You know," I said, pointing my fork at him, "I ended up on a non-Alliance planet once because the master cook for the Governor of the Realm was so jealous of me he locked me in an escape pod during a drill and reprogrammed the thing. I think if Ardalin had an escape pod, I'd be on my way back to the Alliance right now." Ardalin stiffened at the mention of her name. Well, I wasn't about to get killed or nearly killed again because of my cooking skills. I hadn't failed to notice how Ardalin looked at Teeg when he came in or the fact that he got the best of what she was serving.

"You cooked for a governor?" Stellan asked.

"The Governor of the Realm on Tulgalan. Do you know who Addah Desh is?" Ardalin perked up at the mention of that name. She knew if the others didn't.

"I know he owns the best restaurants on Tulgalan," Stellan was smiling at me.

"My birth name was Reah Desh. Addah Desh is my grandfather. I thought he was my father for the longest time, but as it turns out, my oldest brother raped my mother and then he and his mother arranged for my mother to be killed when I was born. My older brother turned out to be my father. Is that fucked up or what?" I was telling Teeg my family history if he hadn't gotten that from hacking into my records as he said he did.

"Addah sent me to Edan when I was eight because he had DNA tests run, proving that Edan was my father. Edan, who should never be allowed to have children, beat me from the moment I arrived. He broke several bones and sent me to the hospital many times when I was between the age of eight and seventeen. When the Alliance conscription notice came, I was more than happy to get away from my abusive family. By that time, I'd made Desh's number two famous for my cooking, though Edan took all the credit. Too bad that all went straight to hell the moment I left. Ardalin, these eggs are awful. If you don't serve good food, it's your own damn fault." I slid off my barstool and hobbled out of the kitchen.

～

"Now, that sounded like a master cook talking." Celestan guffawed. Jes was staring after Reah, wondering if he ought to follow her.

"Ardalin, I think you just got insulted by the best cook I've ever seen, and I've been from one end of the universes to the other," Galaxsan pushed his plate toward the gaping woman. "If you'd tried, she wouldn't have said a word. Reah doesn't miss. Not while shooting or while watching people. If you were interested, you might have learned from her. Too late for that now."

"Then I quit," Ardalin ripped off her apron. Secretly she was hoping Teeg would call her back. He didn't. She stalked out.

"Make sure she gets out of the gate and tell the guards not to let her back in," Astralan was already on his communicator.

"She served eggs with bits of shell on Reah's plate; I saw her picking it out," Jes offered.

"Fuck," Teeg rubbed his face with both hands.

"I'd like to learn from anybody whose last name is Desh," the assistant said timidly. Teeg lowered his hands to look at the man.

"Her last name isn't Desh anymore—she had it legally changed to Nilvas. And since she's still married to me, her last name is officially the same as mine." Teeg stood. "I'll take your offer to her and see what she says."

～

I hadn't gone back to my suite—I'd gone to the pool at the back of the house instead. I'd had to lean against the wall and rest a time or two—Teeg's palace, formerly Arvil San Gerxon's, was huge. Now I sat on a chaise, trying to get my breath back from so much exertion. That's where Teeg, Jes and the warlocks found me.

"Ardalin quit," Teeg said, sitting on the chaise next to mine. The sun was already bright overhead; I had to shade my eyes to look at Teeg.

"I'm sorry if I cost you your cook."

"You didn't—she did this to herself. If she hadn't quit, I would have fired her."

"You should have done it long ago if her food is that bad."

"Would it mean anything to you if I told you I was punishing myself by keeping her?"

"Teeg, that makes absolutely no sense at all." I turned my head; the light was easier on my eyes that way. I was dressed in pajamas and a robe—that's all I had to wear. I didn't like wandering around the house like that, but I didn't have a choice.

"Think about it, Reah. Ardalin's assistant wants to learn anything he can from you. As soon as you can sit up and give him directions, he'd appreciate it. As would the rest of us, I think. Five turns of bad food is enough."

"Where are you keeping Gavril?"

"Reah, don't ask about that. He's safe at the moment and he has no complaints."

"Will you take a message to him?" I was afraid I'd choke up.

"I'll relay a message."

"Tell him I love him and I'll do whatever I can to keep him safe."

"Reah, I," Teeg stood, looking uncomfortable. "Get on with your exercises. I have things to do." He walked away from me, the warlocks right behind him.

"We'll get clothing for you," Jes had worked with me all morning out by the pool. I walked. I stretched. I lifted small weights. He let me rest between sessions. Teeg had told him to push me. Jes was pushing. I ached all over by the time he was finished.

"You can get in the spa naked—I'll send someone out for clothing this afternoon," Jes said. He might have hoped I'd crawl into the hot water naked. I wasn't going to do that. Too many guards and servants wandered through while we were working. I was so stiff as I made my way back to my suite I almost didn't make it through my bath. My breathing was labored as I flopped onto the bed. I was thankful someone had come through to make it up.

"I hear you made Ardalin quit." Someone walked into my room unannounced as I lay on the bed, my good arm thrown across my eyes. Lowering my arm, I stared at another woman. A housekeeper, by the look of things. She had two large pillows in her arms.

"I did. She served eggshells with my eggs for breakfast."

"Then I thank you. Whenever she is mad at anyone, she makes them suffer. I am glad she's gone. Would you like more pillows?" She held the pillows out to me.

"Sure." I rose stiffly and the pillows were stuffed behind my back. "What's your name?" I asked.

"Laree. I've worked for Master Teeg ever since he took over." She was telling me the truth. Teeg hadn't been able to take that talent away from me. I didn't think he could control the demon in me either. If he didn't know I could turn, he might get a nasty surprise if I knew Gavril was all right and I could get to him.

"Well, Laree," I nodded at the woman, "Thank you for the pillows—they make things easier for me."

"You are welcome. Now, maybe we'll have decent food in this place." She walked out of my suite.

CHAPTER 3

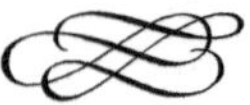

"Don't let it boil, just simmer gently as you stir," I said, watching as Marc made a sauce to go over the eggs. "You'll ruin it if you let it boil. There—see, it's thickening properly. Now, take it off the fire." Marc removed the pan from the heat and set it aside. The eggs were now ready to prepare. We poached eggs, shaved ham, added a bit of this and that, then served breakfast right after the rolls came out of the oven.

"Oh, my goodness." I'd invited Laree to breakfast in the kitchen—the others got served in the dining room. Laree liked what she was eating, I could tell. I'd sat on a stool while I supervised Marc's cooking. He was smiling broadly as the compliments came in.

"Time to get into shape," Jes walked into the kitchen. I wanted to grumble and go back to bed. I was still stiff and sore from the day before. Farzi, Nenzi and the others had shown up for breakfast—I think they didn't care for Ardalin either, and appeared as soon as they heard she was gone. Nenzi offered to carry me to the pool area, but Jes told him I needed to stretch my muscles and build my stamina. I walked with Farzi and Nenzi on either side. Teeg didn't follow. Well, he'd told me the day before he had things to do. Perhaps he was out kidnapping more children.

"Here, this is berries, juice, protein and a vitamin mix. It'll help." Jes handed me a glass around midmorning after torturing me for two clicks. This drink was much the same as the one Ardalin had brought to me, except it tasted better.

"Marc made it." Jes grinned when I asked.

"Then Ardalin should have let Marc do all the cooking," I grumbled, drinking my concoction. "What does he call this, anyway?"

"Teeg calls them smoothies. Don't ask me where the word came from. We always called them jumbles."

"I've heard that term before. Made a few of them, too, as I recall. Mostly mixed with alcohol for customers."

"No alcohol for you—boss' orders. He says the alcohol will slow the healing down." Jes gestured toward the weights and other equipment scattered across the flagstones surrounding the pool. Someone had brought in a treadmill and I was now walking on it until Jes said I could get off. "He says he wants to go out next eight-day. He says you can still be a little weak for the first job or two." Jes was looking away from me, his eyes unfocused for a little while. "You need to get them." He turned back to face me. "Get them, Reah. For me and all the people on my world who didn't make it."

"Need help?" I gimped past Teeg as he stood inside the door that led to the pool. I elbowed him in the ribs at his question and kept hobbling along. "Not bad—that blow would almost be effective," he grinned at me. I shot a dark look his way and kept going. I'd worked harder after Jes said what he did. His entire world dead, because Zellar destroyed it. Now, Zellar's trained vipers were out there, possibly doing the same so they could draw power to themselves.

"Reah? Reah?" Everything was dimming around me so I'd stopped walking, attempting to get my vision to clear. "Baby, don't. Don't pass out on me, sweetheart." Teeg's voice was muted. I don't know if I did faint or just nearly so, but I came back to myself in the kitchen while Teeg and Marc were trying to get me to drink more jumble.

"Just take a sip, baby. Show me you're all right." My cheek was resting against Teeg's shoulder as he held the glass to my lips. "Come on," he coaxed softly. "Take a drink, baby." I swallowed some of the protein-laced juice concoction. "That's right, drink more." He wasn't satisfied until I'd finished half the glass, handing it to Marc before pulling me tighter against him. My face was buried in the hollow between his neck and shoulder. Teeg's fingers sifted through my hair, massaging the back of my head and neck. "Need a cold compress, baby? Will that make it better?" I didn't answer but Jes, who was fussing impatiently nearby (he was the physician, after all) handed one over.

"Perhaps we should let her soak in the spa," Jes suggested.

"No. Reah will not get into that thing and don't suggest it again. She can have a nice warm bath and I'll bring someone in to give her a massage." I raised my head at Teeg's orders. That's what they were—he was definitely being the boss right then.

"Reah, don't get into the spa. A warm bath is better for you." Teeg's dark eyes held concern as they looked into mine. "Don't disobey me, sweetheart. Gavril will suffer if you disobey me."

Teeg was suddenly back to making threats. He'd been so nice, until he'd threatened Gavril. I wanted to get out of his lap. He wasn't having it. "You'll get your dinner in bed tonight." I was carried to my bedroom and settled onto fresh sheets. Laree was taking good care of me now.

When my tray was brought, all the reptanoids came with it, each carrying a plate of food. I had dinner with Farzi, Nenzi, Darzi, Chazi, Perzi, Yanzi, Bekzi and Hirzi. After my bath, which Teeg, Farzi and Nenzi supervised, I brushed my teeth and climbed into bed with two lion snakes. Farzi and Nenzi would be guarding me for the night.

Jes arrived almost as soon as the sun was up. Farzi and Nenzi rose up in the bed in their lion snake forms, their fringed hoods spread out at the potential threat. The hoods disappeared and they lowered their heads when they saw it was Jes. Jes had stopped halfway to the bed so the snakes would calm down.

"Nenzi, you have such a nice pattern," I stroked his neck just below his head. He moved around until his head was just below my chin. A lion snake version of a hug, I suppose. I reached out and ran a hand along Farzi's side, silently thanking him for his protection. Both snakes plopped off the bed and made their way into my bathroom to turn, coming out a few ticks later, fully dressed.

"Go have breakfast, I'll be right there," I promised. Nenzi grinned at me. Farzi gave me a smile and a nod.

"Now, we'll get you up and you won't push it too hard today," Jes ordered.

"I can dress myself," I closed the bathroom door in Jes' face.

"Let me know if you feel faint," he tapped on the closed door. I got my clothes on—someone had gone out to buy for me. I now had nearly a closet full. What I wore mostly while I was getting back in shape was loose exercising outfits. I had plenty of the jackets and pants, with stretchy tops to go with them. Athletic shoes had also been purchased for me, in addition to many other shoes I hadn't even looked at—they were still in boxes.

Following Jes, we took the stairs down instead of the elevator. Jes walked slowly ahead of me, just in case. I told him I was fine. It didn't make any difference; he continued his slow walk down the steps.

Marc made flaky rolls with ham and sauce inside for breakfast while I supervised. Fresh fruit went with that, as did a flavored tea and coffee.

"Now we get decent food," Astralan was having seconds.

"Reah, I don't want a repeat of yesterday," Teeg rubbed the back of my neck after rising from his seat at the table.

"We'll work on that," Jes promised. He and I went back out to the pool and started my exercises again.

"Your walking is improving—you can go for half a click without tiring," Jes was quite happy with our morning results on the treadmill. "The weights are coming along—we did heavier ones today."

"Jes, I noticed we did heavier ones today." He and I were taking a break when Marc brought my mid-morning jumble.

"Your massage is set up for this afternoon, so we'll stop when the therapist shows up."

Teeg and the massage therapist showed up at nearly the same time. I didn't want to get undressed for a massage out by the pool. Teeg made everyone leave. Only he, the therapist and Farzi and Nenzi were there. The therapist was an older woman who worked on my back and legs for quite a while. "You have too many knots in your shoulders," she informed me, working on those even more. "You need to get rid of this stress."

"Don't look at me." Teeg held out his arms.

"Uh-huh," I mumbled while my back was kneaded. "Are you trying to be funny?"

"Maybe."

Jes was right; Teeg was preparing to take me with him an eight-day later. I was feeling better and my stamina was definitely improving. Jes still watched me carefully. Farzi and Nenzi had done their best to hover. They hadn't spent the night with me since I'd fainted, but there wasn't much need. I had dreams, too—unsettling dreams—that Gavril was in danger. Several times, I woke wiping my eyes.

Teeg always said Chash was fine and I didn't want to push him. Now I was stuffing clothing into a bag—Teeg had told me to pack enough for two eight-days. I had no idea where we were going and was afraid to ask. Of course, the four warlocks were coming with us— they were our transportation. It made me wonder why Teeg didn't use them to hunt his quarry. I went so far as to ask him about it one night after dinner, when he sat at the kitchen island while I showed Marc how to make oxberry tarts.

"Zellar was a power-seeker, didn't you know? He could feel power from quite a distance. Why do you think the King of Karathia couldn't catch him for centuries?" Teeg snorted at my question. "It stands to reason that some of his trainees could be the same. Or all of them. Doesn't it make sense, Reah, that he'd only train those who couldn't lead his enemies straight to him?" I thought about that for a bit.

"Yes, you're right," I'd admitted. "He certainly kept all of us from finding him. Until this time. I wonder how that information landed in two places at once?"

Teeg looked at me strangely. "Reah, you just frightened me."

"Well, if what you said before was true, then one of his trainees had to betray him. Didn't they? I mean—he's been dancing away from the best trackers and the finest warlocks for a very long time. Yet now, suddenly, everybody knows where he is?"

"Then that means at least one of them really is trying to take over. I'm sure he had his contacts—those who still used his services and paid well."

"Then one or more of the trainees convinced Zellar to trust them, or they did a little digging and went behind his back. What was he doing on Kareed anyway?"

"No idea." Teeg stood and yawned, stretching his tall frame. "Time for bed, Reah. Come on—you can puzzle out crimes later." He pushed me gently toward the door.

∼

"Aren't you done, yet?" Teeg invited himself into my bedroom.

"You didn't tell me where we were going so I wanted to be prepared."

"Reah, sweetheart, we could end up in several places. I'm bringing Farzi and Nenzi with me, just for you. I didn't want you to feel outnumbered with me and two warlocks."

"You're only taking two?"

"Astralan and Stellan are coming. The other two are staying here with my assistant, to keep things running."

"I didn't know you had an assistant."

"We stay separated, just in case."

"You're not going to tell me."

"And risk getting a good employee killed? No way."

"Well, then, we mutually distrust one another."

"Reah, you're ASD and they probably have my name on a wanted list somewhere."

"And if I said they didn't?"

"I have Gavril, remember. If my name isn't on the list yet, it will be."

"True. Is he all right?"

"Gavril is quite fine. He isn't bored or lonely. He's being kept busy."

"I'm begging you not to mistreat him."

"Gavril will be fine as long as you don't mistreat me or disobey. Understand?"

"Yes."

"Reah, I'm not asking for the universe here. Most kidnappers would be asking for everything you know."

"Is that what you intend to get, Teeg? Everything I know?"

"Reah, I hope you trust me enough one day to tell me freely. Until then, you're welcome to keep the ASD's secrets."

"You think that day will come?" It was my turn to snort at him. A tiny curl of smoke came from my nostrils as a result. Teeg zoned in on that immediately.

"Is that what I think it is? I thought that was impossible for female High Demons."

"Well, it isn't for this one. Go away, Teeg. I have to finish packing." I tossed a jacket into my bag.

Teeg answered me by falling onto my bed and laughing. Hard. He did get up and move my bag for me after I closed it up. He was still chuckling. I pointed toward my bedroom door. He grinned and shook his head.

"Treat me well and Gavril gets treated well." He wanted in my bed. "Come on, Reah. I won't force it—I just want to be in the same bed."

"And I'm supposed to believe you?"

"Reah, I won't force you." He sidled up to me and put his hands beneath my jaw, his thumbs rubbing my earlobes gently. "I know what my Reah wants," he said softly, leaning in to place a kiss on my collarbone. "I know what my Reah likes." Fingers slid beneath the scoop neck of my blouse, caressing bare skin. He nipped my neck gently. I whimpered. "See?" He lifted his head and gave me a kiss, nipping my lower lip with his teeth and then deepening the kiss. "You're my wife, Reah. I won't ever let you go." I knew the truth in his words—he meant them. Is that why I didn't fight him when he took me to bed and loved me so gently I almost wept? I'm not sure I would ever have the answer to that question.

"Where are we?" I looked around the luxurious home—it was the top floor apartment in a very tall building. Marble floors, expensive rugs in beautiful colors, an open space leading to windows, floor to ceiling, along one wall gave me a spectacular view of a city all around as the warlocks landed us somewhere.

"One of my homes," Teeg announced, walking toward a wall and waving his hand across a scanner. I hadn't even realized we'd set an alarm off by appearing as we did. It made sense, though. Teeg seemed to be ahead of everyone in the technology game. I still didn't know where he kept the remote that prevented me from skipping or sending mindspeech. If I could get my hands on that and turn it off, I'd be sending mindspeech to Lendill in less than a heartbeat, telling him where I was and who had kidnapped Chash. I worried about Gavril every day, although Teeg was telling the truth when he said Chash was fine and not being mistreated. He also wasn't lying when he said that if I didn't mistreat him, then Gavril wouldn't be mistreated. Treating Chash well was a good way to keep me in line and he knew it.

"Our bedroom is through here." Teeg took my elbow and led me through a beautiful kitchen that matched the rest of the home, then down a hall that held doors to several bedrooms until we reached the suite on the end. Light surrounded us as we walked in the master suite, with another spectacular view through wide windows. The bed was enormous and covered with expensive fabrics and pillows.

"You bought that bed just for you?" I wondered how many women he'd slept with since I'd left him. I pushed those thoughts out of my head. I had no right to dig at him over that. I had two other mates. Well, three, counting Lendill. Four if Wylend decided to make his move.

Wylend—he was smooth and charming on the outside. Tough as steel on the inside, and once he chose to love someone, that love was fierce and consuming. He loved me, even though he held it back when he took me to dinners or brought me in on his arm at a ball he was holding at his palace. If any money-hungry woman saw Wylend's palace, they'd have pushed for marriage right away. I was content to wait with Wylend until I was free of the ASD.

Karathia still wasn't a member of the Alliance. Well, the Reth Alliance, anyway. Wylend never said, but he was watching the Alliance Teeg was putting together very carefully. Eventually, Karathia would be forced to make a decision. Even I knew that—it simmered around Wylend most of the time, although he didn't think I'd guessed at it.

Wylend had been King of Karathia for six thousand years—had inherited the throne from his father after taking down the warlocks who'd attempted a coup by murdering his father, the former King. Wylend was a powerful warlock and he surrounded himself with powerful warlocks he could trust. Erland Morphis, Ry's father, was one of those and perhaps the best and strongest that Wylend had around him. Ry had inherited his father's abilities plus some, unless I missed my guess. After all, Queen Lissa, who rumor had it was a goddess, was mated to Kifirin the god and was Ry's mother.

"I thought about you the whole time I was building this place," Teeg moved my hair aside to place a kiss on my neck. "The kitchen was built with you in mind. Not too big, not too small, with cabinets and things that you can reach easily. I wasn't thinking when I put Arvil's together. You have to have a step-stool to reach the upper shelves."

"Teeg, what are you doing?" I turned to face him. "The ASD is searching for me and for Gavril. You have to know that. They'll go crazy if they learn you have both of us." I didn't add that Wylend would likely send anybody he had (and that was a lot of warlocks) if he learned that Teeg held me and his great-grandson hostage. Wylend was Lissa's grandfather. Erland was one of Lissa's mates. If that wasn't a double whammy (one of Lissa's terms) against Teeg, then I was a lion snake shapeshifter.

"Reah, where bags?" Nenzi walked in, carrying Teeg's bag and mine.

"Nenzi, you don't have to carry my stuff around, I can do that." I went to take my bag from his hand. I gave him a hug when he smiled and dropped Teeg's bag on the floor. Farzi came in carrying Teeg's other bag. Teeg had two cases—I'd fit my things into one. That was the reverse of how things usually were, but the ASD had taught me to economize.

"We'll take it from here," Teeg smiled at the reptanoids. Farzi pulled Nenzi out of the bedroom.

"They've loved you since they met you, I think," Teeg sighed. "Arvil never knew that they'd have killed him if he'd tried to hurt you in any way."

"They're like my family," I said, walking toward the wall of windows to stare at the cityscape surrounding us. I realized as I said it that I'd handed Teeg another weapon against me.

"I know that," Teeg said, dropping his hands on my shoulders. "I'll never hurt them, Reah. They've been hurt enough in the past. When you offered them love, it was the first time that had been given to them. They soaked it up like a sponge. Nenzi talks about you often. He missed you the most, I think. Now that you're back and he can touch you anytime he wants, he's the happiest lion snake shapeshifter in existence, I think."

"Farzi is more reserved, but I think its shyness," I said. I'd watched him—he always closed his eyes in pleasure when I hugged him or stroked his scales while he was lion snake.

"They love being touched while they're lion snake," Teeg agreed. "It's confirmation that they're not repulsive in that form. That someone loves them, despite what they look like."

"I'm sure they didn't get that growing up," I said. "And that's a shame."

"Well, are you dressed to go hunting with me?" Teeg moved away.

"Hunting where?"

"Up in those mountains." Teeg pointed toward a mountain range I could barely see in the distance. I saw snowcapped peaks, but that was all I could see through the windows of Teeg's top floor apartment. I imagined the apartment took up the entire floor, but I wasn't going to ask.

"I'm not dressed for that." I turned to pull my bag off the floor.

"I'll do that. Jes says no heavy lifting for another eight-day, at least." Teeg lifted my bag easily and dumped it on the bed. I found my black leathers with the jacket quickly and walked into the bathroom to change.

The bathroom was almost as large as the bedroom and held a spa tub that could hold at least ten people. A separate bathing tub only half as large, plus a spacious shower took up one wall. A lengthy vanity with three sinks took up the opposite wall, and the closet took up the rest of the space. "Were you thinking of me when you put in three sinks?" I asked, coming out later with my leathers on.

"No, I was thinking of me. My baths all have two sinks and I use both of them. The third one here is for you."

"That's nice," I muttered.

"Generally, a power-seeker's talent extends about two clicks." Astralan was explaining things to me as we stood inside a tiny cave of sorts on the side of a mountain. We were staring down the mountain for more than two clicks. A compound had been constructed there, but it was mostly covered in snow. Useful if you were a wizard or warlock who could fold in and out. Reaching the buildings below would be next to impossible unless you flew, and then you'd have to be able to spot it from above. That would be an impossible task, since it was probably blocked by spells.

"I can't get you any closer than this—they'll either sense me or I'll set off the power-spotting spell," Astralan added.

"You don't know if they're home?" I stared at Teeg incredulously.

"Reah, it isn't as if we can give them a call on their communicator," Teeg said grimly, staring down at the compound. The clear air around us shimmered as a wind blew across the face of the mountain, stirring up the freshly fallen powder snow on the surface. The snow was blinding in the morning light, so I was thankful we stood inside the darkness of the tiny cave. I shivered, but not from the cold. What was Teeg going to ask me to do?

"Astralan, we'll take it from here." Teeg nodded to the warlock, who nodded back and disappeared.

"You've got them eating out of your hand, now," I muttered. Teeg hmmphed at my statement.

"Reah, they're people. Powerful people, but still people. Did you think only the lion snakes needed somebody to care about them? Money isn't everything, you know."

"Fine. Those warlock brothers are now brother-priests."

"Reah, they'll never be brother-priests." I knew that—brother-priests gave away all their possessions to the poor and then lived among them. They funneled donations to those most in need, helped them keep their housing repaired, scoured cities in search of funds, clothing, food—anything else they could find. Their brown robes let everyone know who they were, in addition to the tattoos on their foreheads. "But they have become decent people. They only needed a nudge here and there to push them in the right direction."

"I suppose they don't fry anyone anymore either," I grumped.

"They only do that when necessary. When is the last time you killed someone who deserved it?"

"About six moon-turns ago. A murderer who was taking children." He'd tried to attack me when I found him. He died swiftly. "Did you find my knife when you found me?" I asked. Thinking about my last kill had brought it back to mind.

"Yes, and I have it locked safely away. Nice work—Grey House unless I miss my guess."

"Difik," I muttered. Teeg laughed.

"Now, we're going down the side of this mountain," Teeg informed me after his mirthful episode had passed. "You're going to turn and carry me."

Staring at Teeg in horror, I huddled against the cave wall at my back. He must have learned of my Thifilatha from my records. If I turned Thifilatha, my clothing would be burned away. If I undressed first, I'd be naked and freezing.

"I know you're still recovering, baby, but this is important. You'll only be cold for a few ticks, I promise. I think the heat from your Thifilatha will melt snow as we go down. I'll carry your clothing—you know your heat won't harm anything that you will it not to harm. That means me, in case you haven't figured that out. Remember, I hold Gavril. If I don't come back, Gavril doesn't live either." Teeg knew I could turn and he was threatening Gavril again. I stalled a little.

"Teeg, the sun is too bright—my eyes are watering just from looking at it from here."

"I have this," he drew out a wide, loosely woven black cloth. "I'll tie it around your eyes when you kneel down after the change. You can see through this and it'll protect your eyes while we travel."

"You've thought of everything," I muttered sarcastically.

"That's how I stay alive," Teeg countered. "Take off your clothes, Reah. Let's get started."

Undressing in subfreezing temperatures was certainly topping my list of things I never wanted to do again. I think my skin was blue in the time it took to remove my top and pants and I was moving as quickly as I could. "Hurry, baby," Teeg urged. He didn't need to, I was already hurrying as fast as possible. I had to step outside the cave to turn, otherwise I would have destroyed it when the change came. At least the cold no longer hurt me when I changed, rising to eighteen hands tall in the bright morning sunlight upon a snow covered mountain.

"Kneel down!" Teeg was shouting as I attempted to shade my eyes against the glare. I realized eventually that he was shouting at me—the wind was telling me things as I listened to it. I had to huddle in melting snow while Teeg tied the blindfold around my eyes. It was just as he'd said—I could see through the loose weave of the cloth and it did make the brightness bearable. Lifting Teeg afterward, we strode down the mountain as snow sizzled and melted around each step I took.

"Hurry, baby." I was shivering again while trying to dress damp skin in tight leather. It wasn't going very well. We stood on what looked to be a back porch area behind the compound—a concrete deck with a short concrete wall around it and a low overhanging ceiling. I'd had to stop outside it and turn, forcing Teeg to haul me over a snow bank and onto the concrete floor. Teeg had to help dress me; my fingers were freezing after five ticks.

Our target didn't expect an attack from this side of the house, and certainly not in the form it came. Who knew if they even suspected High Demons were real? Jes had thought they were myth. He'd asked me many questions while he'd worked at getting my strength and agility back. Some I'd answered, some I hadn't.

Teeg had an electronic card in his pocket. All he had to do was swipe it around the locked door leading onto the concrete patio and there was a beep before the door opened for us. I knew to be quiet as we walked inside—Teeg held a ranos pistol in his hand as we cautiously made our way through a storage room. He walked ahead of me—barely—as we made our way through the entire compound, room by room, building by building. The compound consisted of a five-sided collection of buildings with a central roof covering all of it. The roof was constructed of reinforced steel and built to withstand the snow that might fall upon it. A slow-melter worked to keep the snow at a manageable level and also provided water for the compound—we found the control box for it and the rest of the compound inside one room in the second building. The entire place was empty. Teeg holstered his pistol.

"Now what?" I asked.

"We make ourselves at home until they come back." Teeg was

grinning. I just shook my head at him—it sounded like colossal foolishness to me.

"And what do you intend to do if we can't handle what shows up?" I had my hands placed strategically on my hips.

"I have this," he pulled the transmitter that made my skipping and mindspeech useless from an inside jacket pocket.

"How many pockets does that thing have?" I reached a hand toward him.

"Nope, you don't get to explore right now," he grinned, pulling the transmitter beyond my reach. "Let's see what they have to eat in the kitchen."

The kitchen and six bedrooms were all inside the same building—the fourth one we'd explored. All were connected through a tunnel that ran underneath. At least the inside of the compound was warm enough. Teeg said the snow outside helped insulate everything. Sunlight collector poles painted white covered the top of the compound, too. We hadn't seen those until we'd gotten very close. Everything was solar-powered. I found food in a freezer and prepared a meal. I was tiring, though, and cleaning up the kitchen afterward took the last of my strength.

"Lie down, baby." Teeg led me to a comfortable sofa in the media room. Our rogue warlocks hadn't denied themselves any comforts.

"This was Zellar's hideout, wasn't it?" I asked as I curled up on the sofa.

"We think so, yes," Teeg nodded. "Sleep for a while, Reah. I'll wake you if our residents show up." Teeg leaned in to kiss my forehead as he knelt next to the sofa. He was rubbing my belly gently as I fell asleep.

"Erland." Wylend looked up from the message he'd received to watch his best and strongest ally's face as he handed the news to him.

"My King?" Erland decided to go formal.

"Erland, I want you to look at this message I received. I can't trace it to the source—it has been blocked. Tell me what you think." Erland accepted the comp-vid from the King of Karathia.

King Wylend, greetings, the message began. *I am contacting you to arrange a meeting. As you know, I am forming an alliance, which many are calling the Campiaan Alliance. It is my hope that you will consider joining. I think many things can be arranged to our mutual benefit. I am attempting to make this alliance a mirror of the Reth Alliance, but as you likely know, it will be a long road. So far, I am making slow but steady progress. Things are gradually coming in line with the placement of laws and such. I will contact you again soon to learn your feelings on this. I know you have been doing research already.* The message was signed *Teeg San Gerxon.*

"So he knows we've been snooping," Erland handed the comp-vid back to Wylend.

"I would know," Wylend agreed. "Is there anything new on Reah or Gavril?"

"Nothing since we got word that two bodies were hauled out of that hotel—one in pieces, the other still intact. The word I got from the ASD source was that the second was still breathing when they hauled it out—it was held inside a stasis gurney."

"Then Reah may still live." Wylend set the comp-vid aside.

"Gardevik seems to think his son would know if she'd died—his Thifilathi would be grieving if she had. So far, Tory's Thifilathi is fine."

"Then I might wish for such a barometer," Wylend sighed. "Did I make a mistake waiting? Erland, tell me I was not the greatest fool you've ever seen."

"My King, you are not a fool. Reah herself saw the sense in this, I think. How many potential captors might have gone looking for her before this, if they learned you were mated? This was wisest, Wylend. She has nothing to give them now. Not where you're concerned."

"What are they doing to her—if they have her?" Wylend's eyes watered.

"My King, we will find her and she will be whole." Erland went to hold Wylend's head against his chest.

~

"Mom, what did Kifirin say to you? About Gavril?" Tory couldn't stand it any longer—he had to know. He'd been hit twice—first with Gavril's disappearance and then with Reah's. His Thifilathi knew Reah still lived, but in his humanoid form, Tory fretted and worried.

Lissa lifted her head from signing her name on the comp-vid with a stylus. She looked haggard—Tory saw the dark smudges beneath her eyes.

"He says we'll see Gavril again one day, but he will not be the same." His mother's words stunned Tory; he sat down heavily on one of the chairs Lissa kept at the front of her desk.

"How? How will he not be the same? Are they hurting him? What are they doing to him?"

"Baby, I don't know," Lissa let her head drop onto her desk. "Kifirin won't tell me and my superiors tell me I can't interfere." She raised her eyes to look at Tory's face. "We have to wait. That's what Graegar says."

"You talked to Graegar?" Tory breathed a sigh. Graegar was one of the five Larentii Wise Ones. They held their doings secret most of the time. Their abilities, too, were a closely guarded secret by all the Larentii race. All Tory had was whispered conjecture and speculation.

"I talked to Graegar and Garegar." Garegar was Graegar's son and also a Wise One. Seldom did two appear at once in the same place and they were always accompanied by their protectors. "Garegar agreed with his father." It was Lissa's turn to sigh deeply. "We wait. This has hurt Gavin more than I can say."

"Mom, he never expected to have a child. Now, somebody has taken the one he did get. With you."

"Yes. Connegar and Reemagar are watching both of us. If they didn't place the healing sleep, we wouldn't sleep at all, I don't think."

"See, if you dovetail the joints, they fit together better and you don't need nails." Gavril watched as Dormas finished cutting the pieces of a cabinet drawer. The one who'd taken him had set him down in

Dormas' large shop. Dormas was now the one who held him captive. Gavril had been warned; that Reah could die if he didn't do as he was told. Therefore, he stayed with Dormas and learned carpentry.

Dormas had every tool imaginable, modern and powered, but he was teaching Gavril how to do everything by hand first. That's how Dormas had learned. He only worked at night—he owned a very large construction firm on Mharbool. Mharbool had a thriving vampire population—they worked at night, allowing the humanoids to work the days. Dormas was five thousand turns a vampire and had learned all his skills by working with his hands. He still enjoyed his work, though he currently built high rises rather than simple huts.

At first Gavril had found it difficult to stay awake at night—he'd been used to doing everything during the day and sleeping at night. Now he was getting better at staying awake until dawn. It was still close, though, and Gavril was blinking sleepily as Dormas snapped the two dovetailed pieces together.

"Time for bed," Dormas smiled at Gavril, tousling his hair. "Come, we'll get you a light snack before we sleep." Gavril followed Dormas out of the workshop.

CHAPTER 4

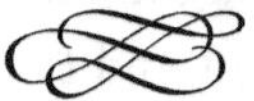

*O*ur unknowing hosts didn't arrive the first day. Or the second. Teeg had succumbed to sleep the first night after making sure the transmitter was safely tucked inside his jacket and delivering a threat against Gavril. I wasn't about to do anything that might jeopardize Chash. Teeg knew it. He couldn't have devised a more foolproof plan. I let him sleep until he woke, puttering around the place and eventually preparing a simple meal plus dessert—our targets didn't have much in the way of cooking skills and relied on prepackaged food.

"That smells good." Teeg was behind me, his arms around my shoulders.

"It's the best I can do with what I have. Somebody should teach these people how to shop for food." Teeg got a steak cooked the way he liked it (rare) with the best sauce I could put together using what was available. He still enjoyed his food.

"Teeg, what will we do if they don't show up for days?" I flopped onto the sofa—we'd both used it for sleeping. I was tired of wiping myself off with a wet cloth—Teeg didn't want either of us caught in the shower if our targets showed up.

"They'll be along." I don't know how he knew that, but he seemed sure of himself. I started to call him the all-seeing, all-knowing, but I didn't. That had been a joke between Chash and me and I was holding my memories of Chash close to my chest. I still had hope that I might see him again someday.

Teeg wanted to make love too, but if we couldn't take a shower, we couldn't do *that*. I pointed that fact out to him. Twice. Our quarry showed up while he was sleeping on the third day and chaos erupted.

"That's what Kifirin said? That we'd see him again but he wouldn't be the same? What the fuck is that supposed to mean?" Ry raked a hand through his hair in exasperation. Tory had waited until Ry had returned from an assignment to share the information.

"No idea. Want to hunt Kifirin down and ask him?"

"He still scares the bejeezus out of me." Neither Ry nor Tory had any idea what bejeezus meant, but they'd adopted the phrase from their mother, who'd employed it often.

"Me, too," Tory agreed. "So I guess we won't be asking Kifirin any questions."

"What does your dad say?" Ry looked at his brother.

"He's not willing to go to Kifirin either. He says that when Kifirin doesn't want to tell you something, he won't. He talks in riddles when he does answer and you sure as hell don't want to ask him for any favors."

"Why would you not ask for favors? I heard the comesuli went to Baetrah all the time to ask for something." Ry was frowning at Tory.

"Yes, but they weren't asking *directly*. That's what Dad says. You ask for something directly from Kifirin, well, he remembers. Forever."

"So?" Ry still didn't see where the conversation was headed.

"So he points out to you at a later date just what sort of mistake it was to ask for what you asked for. And then he still remembers past that. Like it's an unforgivable sin or something."

"Well, we should have known. He *is* Lord of the Dark Realm. Not like the light side, where people ask for things constantly with no fear of retribution."

"Opposites," Tory nodded. "That's the way it was made, to balance."

It might have been perfect, made sense and allowed us to do what we came to do if all three of them had arrived closer to each other. Instead, they landed in three separate spots inside the media room, forcing Teeg to shoot one warlock before he could cast a spell. Then Teeg was standing beside me, an arm around my waist as spells were launched at us by the other two warlocks, creating blasts, fire and explosions. They were flinging them at us blindly, too—Zellar hadn't taught them to remain calm in this sort of emergency. Part of the roof was blown away over our heads, causing snow, water, wood and bits of metal to rain down around us. Teeg pulled both of us down and jerked me out of the way at the last tick.

"Move forward, Reah!" Teeg was shouting as more blasts came, making me nearly deaf for a moment. I went forward, Teeg still glued to my side. He had his pistol in his hand, but the two remaining warlocks had raised shields. The bullets might not penetrate. If they didn't they'd likely ricochet, which could hit either Teeg or me. Teeg was waiting for me to get close enough to neutralize the spells. Then he could shoot them. I wanted my knife—I didn't have it. I knew how close I had to get before my natural shield prevented the spells from activating. A sphere around fourteen hands in every direction. Chunks of the ceiling landed on our heads, causing me to duck. Teeg went with me. We moved forward. Furniture started flying. While we were immune to the spell itself, we weren't impervious to the airborne furniture once it had been set in motion. Teeg got hit with a lamp table. His "oof" as it hit him hard on the right shoulder had me trying to pull him behind me. He refused and kept going. The accessory table almost hit him in the head. We ducked again. The sofa was lifting off the floor and we were still too far away. Twenty-five hands away. That's why we were both shocked when the sofa was dumped onto the floor with a resounding thump, raising dust off the rug when it fell. Our two targets were still furiously attempting to cast spells but nothing was happening. Teeg didn't even spare me a glance; he rushed forward so fast and had two heads knocked together so quickly I barely saw him move.

The warlock Teeg shot with his ranos pistol was dead; the other two were unconscious when Teeg called Astralan on his communicator. Astralan and Stellan appeared only ticks later, metal cuffs in hand.

"What are those?" I asked as Astralan and Stellan placed them around each warlock's wrists.

"They used to make something like this to control vampires," Teeg sounded proud of himself. "These control wizards and warlocks. Handy, huh?"

"You mean they can't use their power if those are in place?"

"That's exactly what it means." Astralan sounded quite sure. I stared at Teeg. He *had* been busy. No doubt it was the same sort of technology that he'd used on the chip in my collarbone. A double-edged sword, in every sense.

"Now, let's go back, I want a bath." Teeg was done here. Astralan folded us back to Teeg's apartment while Stellan took charge of our prisoners. Our two prisoners were waking inside a cage much like the one I'd been stuck in while convalescing. This cage was in one of the bedrooms—Teeg showed me. Farzi and Nenzi were there to watch our two captive warlocks while Teeg and I cleaned up and Astralan went back to destroy the compound. It was a shame Teeg wanted it destroyed—I thought the architecture was a work of genius. Surely, Zellar hadn't built it himself. More than likely, he'd killed the one who had built it and taken it for himself.

"Reah," Teeg hadn't been willing to bathe separately. Now he was kissing my shoulder. Caressing my ribs and hips. "Did they hit you anywhere, sweetheart?"

"Just little bits of stuff hit me," I said.

"You said *stuff.*" We didn't get out of the shower for a while.

"What are you going to do with your prisoners?" I asked Teeg as I set out two plates of food to serve dinner to the two rogue warlocks. The rest of us had eaten already. Nenzi had helped, cutting up vegetables and such.

"Ask them questions. Tomorrow, when they've had time to think about things."

"And then what?"

"I have plans for them."

"You're not going to tell me, are you?"

"No. But I am taking you out for a little while. Then you're going to bed. You look tired."

"Where are we going?" Stellan had come with us as protection. We'd walked out of the building that housed Teeg's penthouse apartment and then to a shopping district just a few ticks away.

"To pick up something I ordered," Teeg said.

"Tiralian crystal, as requested, Master San Gerxon." The owner of the upscale jewelry shop came to deliver the ring in person. My face was burning—if I'd known this was what he was after, I might have dug my heels in and refused to come. I didn't want to make a huge scene so I didn't fight with Teeg about it. I'd told him I wouldn't wear his ring as long as he held Gavril, but if I refused, then Chash might suffer. I didn't have a choice, now. The crystal setting was large and Teeg placed it on my hand there in the shop. Teeg just grinned at my embarrassment and took me out for a protein jumble at a shop nearby.

Teeg's arm was draped around my shoulders and I was sipping my drink; Stellan got ice cream while Teeg let his coffee cool as we walked out again. Teeg drew in a breath two steps out the door, then did something—I don't know what—grasping my arm and Stellan's before we were all flying through the air. I'm not sure how I heard the blast from the sweet shop behind us, but it was obliterated by an explosion. I had no body, no hands and no mouth, else I'd likely have been screaming. I could see all about me as I hurtled through the air, which frightened me. I remembered being carried like this just once before. I didn't know how it had happened the first time. I was pretty sure I knew who was responsible this time.

I watched in shock as we passed right through the wall of Teeg's apartment. "Keep her here!" Teeg shouted to Farzi and Nenzi as I became solid again right in front of the two reptanoids. Gathering Stellan and Astralan to him, Teeg and the warlocks disappeared right in front of me, leaving me with a look of stunned wonder on my face.

"Reah, you are fine?" Farzi made it a question. I whirled to look at him.

"Farzi, what happened? I mean, how did he do that?" I turned to look at the space previously occupied by Teeg.

"We not knowing," Nenzi shook his head. "He only do when has to."

"Somebody blew up the sweet shop." I discovered I still had the cup in my hand. "Did those people get killed?" I was turning in a circle—normally I'd have a comp-vid handy so I could check on things like that. Teeg had carefully kept those things out of my reach. I headed for the door, determined to find out if the young man who'd served us was injured, as well as the other customers in the shop.

"No, Reah. Teeg say you stay with us." Nenzi was blocking the door.

"Nenzi, those people might need help."

"Reah, you have no identification. You stay." Farzi came to stand next to Nenzi. Farzi was right, of course. I had no identification—Teeg hadn't given anything back to me. It may have been lost, too—I had no idea what I'd had with me when they found me. "Teeg will come soon—let him take care of this." Farzi was pushing me gently toward a chair away from the door.

"I will get blanket." Nenzi was offering. Only then did I notice my hands were shaking. Adrenalin, more than likely, but I was worried, too. Had that blast been aimed at us?

"Reah, sit," Farzi pushed me toward the chair. He got me settled into it. "Drink," he tapped the cup I still held in my hand. Nenzi trotted into the room with the promised blanket.

"I'm fine," I said. "Just shaken up. I've been in worse situations."

"Reah will sit with us," Farzi turned to lion snake and crawled on the arm of the padded chair. Nenzi did the same on the other side. Nenzi rested his head on top of mine, Farzi settled on my right shoulder. I was covered in a blanket and lion snakes. Left with no other options, I sipped my drink and worried about the people affected by the blast.

～

"Reah? Sweetheart?" Teeg smelled as if he'd just gotten out of the shower. He didn't have a shirt on when I opened my eyes, so that was probably the case. I couldn't believe I'd fallen asleep after the day and night I'd had.

"You were tired, baby." Teeg leaned in to kiss my forehead. My lion snakes had deserted me at some point. "I sent them to bed. I can handle this part," Teeg answered my unspoken question.

"Why didn't you let me die before—when the ASD firebombed those fields? You wouldn't have had any worries about being Arvil's only heir." That thought had been running through my mind ever since I knew Teeg had been the one to lift me out of the fields being firebombed all around me. He'd then dumped me in the plantation swimming pool and jumped in after me. I felt like an idiot for not connecting the two incidents before.

"Reah, I'll do whatever is within my power to keep you alive. Yes, I needed to be Arvil's only heir, but I didn't rip up our marriage contract."

"To keep me under your thumb."

"Reah, the criminals Arvil associated with would have eaten you for breakfast."

"Thanks for having such faith in me," I snapped, trying to get away from him. "I'm good enough to haul into the fray when wizards or warlocks are attacking, but useless anywhere else, is that it?"

"Reah, I wanted to remove the target Arvil painted on your back. They would have come hunting—for both of us. Right now, I'm doing my best to eliminate the last of those evil-minded fuckers. We've finally gotten them down to manageable numbers. I don't know how the one who attacked us tonight got our whereabouts, but he's no longer a threat. We've eliminated that little problem. I'm officially in charge of his encampment, now."

"You don't know how he knew where we were, yet you ordered a ring from a jewelry shop?" I shook my head in disbelief.

"The shop's owner wouldn't have betrayed us, but that doesn't eliminate all his employees or stray customers," Teeg set my blanket aside and pulled me to my feet. "I'll check on that tomorrow."

"Did the people inside the shop die?" I was back to my original worry.

"Reah, two people died in the blast. Customers near the door. They were aiming at me, baby."

"Does this happen frequently?" I stretched as I walked toward the bedroom.

"Not often now, since we've cleaned out most of my would-be assassins, but there are still a few left. Zellar's rogue warlocks just complicate things." Teeg lifted me and I put a hand around his bare neck. Teeg has very wide shoulders and muscles anyone would be proud of. I leaned my head against his shoulder and reveled in the smell of him. Of course, I wasn't going to tell him that. It didn't matter, he chuckled and I knew he knew it anyway.

"Baby, do you want to come with me while I question the employees at the jewelry shop?" Teeg was waking me with kisses.

"You'll let me come?"

"Yes. And if you sniff out anything from any of them, I expect you to tell me."

"All right." I started to scoot away from him so I could get off the bed.

"No, let's shake the bed a little first."

～

"Harji, you're such a hairdresser."

Teeg and I were interviewing the last two employees at the jewelry store. None of them had known anything, but Harji was asking me questions about my clothing and shoes. His coworker, Mish, was elbowing Harji.

"Mish, honey, if I could look like that in those clothes, I'd never go home to you," Harji teased. Teeg wanted to laugh, I know he did. So did I, but I held back. Teeg had picked out what he wanted me to wear and it turned out to be a low-cut, breast-hugging red silk top with black pants and heeled boots. Teeg's ring was on my finger—he wasn't willing to let me take it off. Dangly diamond earrings rounded out the ensemble. My hair hung loose—if I were out with Teeg, that's what he wanted. I'd given up on trying to braid my hair with him around.

"You'll never have her hair, even if you wear a wig," Mish was poking at Harji again. "Face it, sweetie, you're stuck with me."

Of course, both of them had ogled Teeg, but he was Teeg San Gerxon. You didn't make a big deal out of that to his face. We thanked the owner and walked out of the shop. Astralan and Stellan were waiting for us, but thankfully, no one was waiting to hurl bombs at us today. Teeg pulled me close against his side anyway as we walked along.

"Teeg?" I looked up at him.

"What, baby?" His mind was miles away, I could tell by the slight frown on his face. I was about to bring him back from wherever he was.

"Teeg, what if those two you have in your apartment have some sort of homing beacon or locating chip? We've dealt with that before —well, you know. We have." I didn't want to say ASD aloud on the streets, since I had no idea where we were.

"Then we'd better do a little checking. Astralan?" Teeg nodded toward the warlock, who folded us straight to the bedroom that held Teeg's captives.

"Tell the truth, do you have an implant that will allow someone to find you?" Teeg demanded right away. I didn't know what good that might do, but I was surprised.

"I do." One of the two warlocks—the shortest one—pointed to the back of his neck. Teeg cursed. "Stellan, go get Jes. Now." Stellan disappeared.

Jes spent the afternoon removing a tiny chip implanted in the back of a warlock's neck.

"I have the urge to destroy this, but I'm hoping it will bring somebody right to me instead. They know we're here, they're just waiting for the right opportunity to strike. We got those last night, but now I have a feeling they have friends." Teeg was almost growling. "Astralan, take this to the plantation on Birimera and leave it on my desk. Inform Denast what it is and to be ready in case somebody shows up. Then get back here; we need to go back to Campiaa and ask a few questions of our friends, here." He jerked his head toward the two warlocks.

"You look nice," Jes whispered while Teeg grumbled and paced nearby.

"Thanks." Normally I didn't wear red—didn't like the color much. Teeg obviously did. Nenzi helped me get our bags packed later; Teeg was busy in his study; he and Stellan were closeted there, sending messages, no doubt.

Breszca Loffus stared into her drink glass. Graumil Loffus, her husband and candidate for High Council on Tulgalan, should have skated through the election. Now, some industrious journalist had gone digging into her past instead of that of her husband. The damaging information would be released in the morning. Tulgalan law required that all parties be notified at least one full day in advance of the release of information, if the information could damage the parties in any way. It gave them time to refute the information in case it turned out to be false. Breszca wished she could prove it false. She couldn't. Every bit of it was true. How the journalist had managed to get his hands on the adoption records when they were supposed to remain secret for one hundred turns might remain a mystery.

Breszca hadn't even seen the baby after it was born, signing it over quickly to the state. Someone had adopted the little girl and named her Raedah. Breszca had only been nineteen when she became pregnant—she'd put off getting the birth control chip and then *he* had come along. Breszca had just gone to university and drinking with new friends was her favorite thing to do. Denus was handsome, no doubt about it, and Breszca couldn't help herself when he'd invited her to his bed. She'd gotten pregnant after only two encounters, but didn't learn of that fact until she'd left Denus behind for Alvis. She'd listed Alvis' name as the child's father—Alvis who'd somehow gotten killed in a hovercraft accident. Now, merely the fact that she'd put the baby up for adoption wouldn't have raised eyebrows—it was the responsible thing to do for one so young and unprepared for parenthood. What the journalist had found when he went through the records was that Raedah couldn't have been Alvis' child—the blood types and DNA didn't match.

Breszca couldn't imagine anyone going to that much trouble just to get Alvis' records after learning she'd had the child. Anyone else would have taken the records at face value. If she'd ever wanted to kill anyone, the journalist now topped that list. It was a crime not to report the true parent of a child put up for adoption—not to notify said parent that they had a child in order to give them the opportunity to take it instead of consigning it to state care at state expense. Generally it was a good law and one that Graumil had supported over the years as a magistrate in the capital city. Now, Breszca's past was undermining his bid for High Council by flouting that law. Who knew where Denus was? She hadn't seen him since she'd dumped him in favor of Alvis.

The other things the journalist had ferreted out about Raedah were perhaps even more bizarre, but Breszca wouldn't be held accountable for that. Raedah had married Addah Desh at the age of twenty-one. She'd been his eighth and last wife he'd taken, gotten pregnant shortly after the marriage and died shortly after the birth. Still not so bizarre, until you learned that the child Raedah had wasn't Addah Desh's but his second oldest son's—Edan Desh. Breszca blew out a breath at that name. Edan had frequently been in the news in years past—he'd taken the crown from his father, making Desh's number two the best restaurant on Tulgalan. That no longer held true —Edan was now serving prison time, as was his mother, Marzi Desh. Edan had raped Raedah, then had been found to be the child's father. He and his mother had plotted to kill Raedah with the help of a physician after the child's birth.

The physician had been stripped of his license and had served a shorter sentence—only a few moon-turns—after testifying for the state. Breszca's grandchild had disappeared. The journalist found records that the girl had separated from the Desh family, taking another name. Nobody could get into those records, although the journalist had tried his best. They were sealed and hidden. The journalist informed Breszca and Graumil at the formal meeting they'd had that he was currently tracking Denus. As yet, Denus hadn't been located, but he was determined to keep looking.

Graumil had stalked out of the house the moment the journalist had left with his crew, leaving Breszca alone. Breszca had asked a servant to bring a bottle and locked herself inside her suite. The vids would be all over the news by morning—the journalist had sold the story to every affiliate on Tulgalan. He'd already made enough to retire off Breszca's mistake and looked to make even more if he could find the real father. His daughter was dead but he had a granddaughter somewhere. The journalist was determined to find her as well.

Hild Marolla, noted investigative journalist, sat at his desk and sighed.

He'd hit another dead end. Records of Denus Lithik were scarce—rental records, banking records, things of that nature, were available for a period of six years. No records were found, however, of Denus coming to Tulgalan by conventional means. Or leaving Tulgalan the same way. He'd still been on Tulgalan at the time and could have been notified of the child's birth—no doubt about that—Hild had all those records on his comp-vid. He wondered, not for the first time, if Denus had been an illegal involved in criminal activity.

No work records were available, either, though Denus appeared to have plenty of money. The short time he'd been with Breszca, he'd bought her jewelry and taken her out to the best restaurants. Vid-photos were acquired; Hild had gotten those from Breszca's college friends. They were more than willing to come forward in exchange for money and the notoriety it would bring them. Denus was a handsome man—with dark hair and green eyes. The vid-photos of Raedah showed the same green eyes and unusual, white hair. Rumor had it that Raedah's child, Reah, had looked much like her mother.

Hild grimaced every time he thought about Reah. He had no photographs of her and when he'd tried to dip into her records, someone from the ASD had shown up at his office. That same someone had offered Hild a stretch in prison if he continued to dig into Reah's information. Hild was angry over that—he'd already paid a bribe to a lesser public agent to get what was available. His bribe and the public agent disappeared the following day.

The story would still go public in the morning. The entire Alliance would then begin searching for Denus Lithik. Generally, they weren't willing to let something like this go, and as far as favorite news-vids went, reuniting lost children or grandchildren with their parents or siblings was right at the top. Even though Hild couldn't produce the daughter or granddaughter, he was sure than anyone in the Alliance who found Denus, if he didn't see the vids for himself, would alert him to the fact that he'd fathered a child and still had family out there somewhere.

～

Denevik Lith was having breakfast. The home he had now was a rented mansion—the owner had been forced to lease it and take humbler accommodations when a business had failed. The property was perfect for Denevik—he didn't plan to stay more than a turn or two before moving on. Jusef, Denevik's servant, had served up rolls, coffee and eggs, leaving Denevik to eat at the kitchen island while Jusef puttered around, cleaning up and worrying over the midday meal. Denevik moved often in case Jaydevik Rath ever came looking for him. Or Gardevik, Jayd's oldest brother.

Of the two, he felt Jayd might be the most merciful. Denevik hadn't been on Kifirin since his oldest brother Tarevik had killed Lendevik, their father. He still didn't know if Tarevik had intended for their mother Belarok to die as well—she'd been attacked and raped by two High Demons in their smaller Thifilathi. She'd died, according to his sources, screaming in pain. Denevik could still not get that mental image out of his mind. Now, he was the only one of his brothers who still lived.

Glindarok, his sister, was Queen on Kifirin and ruled alongside Jaydevik Rath, her husband and King. He'd heard that Glinda had birthed twin daughters for Jayd, but they'd gone to other houses. A High Demon female would never come to him, or any children. When he'd failed to see the true plot behind Tarevik's lies, he'd sealed his fate.

"Isn't that you?" Jusef brought Denevik away from his morbid thoughts. Jusef was pointing to the vid-screen in the kitchen. Denevik stared in horror as a vid-photo of himself was splashed across the screen.

"Turn it up," Denevik demanded. Jusef increased the volume.

"Breszca Loffus failed to inform the true father that she was pregnant with his child," the journalist reported. *"Instead, she identified another as the father, who was killed before the child was born. The child was given over for adoption, and little Raedah was taken by an older couple."* A vid-photo of the couple replaced Denevik's image. *"Raedah married Addah Desh at the age of twenty-one,"* the journalist went on. Denevik watched in horror as a wedding picture, featuring his daughter and Addah Desh

was shown. There was no mistaking the long white hair or the green eyes. His daughter looked exactly like his mother, Belarok. He wanted to weep when he learned that his child had died at the hands of others, and then stared in shock when it was announced that he had a granddaughter.

"My sources say that Reah Desh looked very much like her mother, but we cannot find any vid-photos to verify that and we have not been able to research her records. Regardless, we believe she is still alive somewhere and it is our hope that grandfather and granddaughter may someday be reconciled. This is Hild Marolla, reporting live from Tulgalan."

"Jusef, pack. We are going to Tulgalan immediately." Denevik ordered. Jusef was nearly as shocked by the vid as Denevik had been. Jusef was Amterean and had cooked and did for Denevik for more than one hundred turns. He knew all of Denevik's secrets. Except for this one, and even Denevik hadn't known it.

"We won't be going to the news-vids or that stupid journalist. We'll be doing the tracking ourselves, starting with Addah Desh, I think." A curl of smoke drifted from Denevik's nostrils. He knew not to contact anyone who might put his face on the news-vids. If Jaydevik or any of his happened to see his image, then his life would be over. Denevik wanted to see his granddaughter before that happened.

"Go ahead and pack your bags, but you will not be going to Tulgalan." Someone else had appeared inside Denevik's rented kitchen.

"Lord Kifirin," Denevik went to his knees and bowed his head.

"One of the two remaining who know to bow to me," Kifirin remarked, lifting Denevik to his feet.

"Then where should I go? I want to find my granddaughter."

"Then you need to go to Campiaa. But you will not identify yourself to her right away. This is what you must do instead." Denevik listened carefully as Kifirin laid out his instructions.

~

"Reah, I've hired two new people—one will work as a new bodyguard for me, the other will help Marc in the kitchen," Teeg announced over breakfast. He and the warlocks were going back to question the two prisoners. So far Teeg hadn't gleaned as much information as he might like from them, so another round of intense questioning was about to follow. Jes, who was happy to have me back so he could do more rehabilitation, was going to make me do my exercises out by the pool again. The whole thing made me sigh as I sipped my protein jumble. Jes had added a powdered vitamin mix to the protein and berries.

"It will help you recover faster," he'd informed me. I thought things were coming along fine but Jes was the physician. I didn't argue with him.

The two new hires were introduced during the midday meal—the bodyguard was tall, with brown hair and green eyes. The cook's assistant was Amterean. I went to him immediately and took his hand when it was offered. Yes, I thought of Master Morwin the whole time. He still lived on Le-Ath Veronis—Morwin did, though his job as Gavril's tutor had officially ended the moment Gavril had been accepted into the private college off-world. We'd become good friends, Morwin and I. Now I was introduced to Jusef, who smiled at me and wiggled his bushy brown eyebrows. Lenden Stone, the bodyguard, looked sad when I took his hand. I squeezed his fingers—there wasn't any need for that. Teeg seemed to be a good employer. None that I'd seen had any complaints, if you discounted Ardalin. She'd been in love with him and insanely jealous. Mostly insane, though. She was gone. I hoped for good.

"This is my wife, Reah," Teeg had done the introductions. Lenden nodded respectfully to me.

"What is this we are eating?" Jusef took one bite of the yaris fish and closed his eyes in pleasure.

"My wife would qualify as a master cook," Teeg sounded proud. I didn't know what to say. I'd never get the chance to qualify. Not from here. I still had no idea what Teeg's long-term plans were—for me or for Gavril. I wanted mindspeech back so badly I could have screamed with the frustration. Skipping might have been an added bonus. Teeg held both of those things in check with a tiny transmitter.

"This is yaris fish with my own sauce recipe," I said. Lenden took a bite and then blinked at me in surprise.

"Excellent," he nodded, lowering his eyes. Marc had helped me make it; Jes had nearly worn me out with the morning's workout.

"You will teach me this?" Jusef sounded hopeful.

"I'll think about it—it's a closely guarded secret," I smiled at the Amterean dwarf.

"When did you start cooking?" Jes was pushing my knees up to stretch the muscles in my legs.

"When I was eight. Edan shoved me into the kitchen to clean but I was watching one of my other brothers make pastry. I learned pastry making from Ilvan. In between sweeping the floors and doing dishes after I got out of day class, that is. That's when I still thought Edan was my brother." I grunted as Jes pushed my thigh muscles to the limit before letting the leg back down.

"Reah, you couldn't have been bigger than a tick, how did he abuse that?"

"People often do things that others find impossible," I said. As an ASD operative, I'd seen my share of it. The worst had been a crime kingpin who'd forced his oldest daughter into an incestuous relationship and then had children with her. He was looking to have the same sort of relationship with his oldest granddaughter when we caught up with him. Tory had nearly ripped the man's arm off when he'd tried to escape. Lendill and Norian hadn't even turned a hair over that. The criminal had been sent to Evensun. He probably hadn't survived that.

"What about you? I asked.

"I loved my parents," Jes told me. "And they loved me. I wasn't married—went off-world to study medicine and decided to stay. By the time we really understood that my world was dying, it was quarantined. Nobody could get on or off. It died a quick death, Reah. If I could have paid the black-market traffickers, I might have been able to get my family off. I didn't have the money. They're all dead, thanks to Zellar."

"I imagine he has a lot to answer for, if people really do answer for those sorts of things," I said. I was thinking about Kifirin and wondering if he ever involved himself in anything like that.

"The gods are a myth," Jes grumbled.

"Well, hold onto that thought." I patted his arm while he pushed up my other knee.

CHAPTER 5

"I can't believe he let me go without him," I said. Farzi, Nenzi and Lenden were with me as I walked down a pedestrian street filled with upscale shops. I had a credit chip bracelet too, and Teeg had told me to buy anything I wanted.

"He not wish to lose you," Farzi pointed out.

"I not wish that either," Nenzi grinned. I gave him a hug.

"I have no desire to lose sight of you either," Lenden offered. I looked up into his green eyes. They were nearly the same color as mine. Well, he was my bodyguard for the day—Teeg was paying him not to lose sight of me.

"Nenzi needs haircut," Nenzi stopped outside a hairdresser's shop.

"Then we'll get you a haircut," I pulled him inside. Farzi and Lenden were forced to follow. Just to make things look normal, I got my hair washed and my bangs trimmed.

"Where did these scars come from?" My hairdresser had found Tory's claiming marks.

"That's a long story," I said. I wasn't about to tell her anything about them. She shrugged and kept washing my hair. Farzi and Lenden sat off to the side, watching while Nenzi and I were worked on at the same time. It wasn't until we sat down at a sidewalk café later to have a cool drink that Lenden voiced his question.

"Who gave you those marks?" He whispered while Farzi and Nenzi went to the counter for refills.

"I won't be giving that information," I said. I wasn't sure Teeg even knew what they were and I certainly wasn't going to give him more information to harm anyone else I knew. I hadn't gotten any updated information on Gavril either, and didn't know if I were brave enough to ask. Teeg hadn't mistreated me and I hoped that went for Gavril too. I had no idea if Gavril might attempt to escape—he was perhaps the brightest person I'd ever met. I was praying that Teeg remembered he was only seventeen when it came to Chash's treatment.

Lenden didn't push it, but something bothered me about his question. I didn't puzzle it out until later. Nenzi bought two chips containing repair manuals for vehicles. That was the day I learned that Nenzi oversaw Teeg's fleet of vehicles. I was happy for him—it was something he always wanted. Farzi had taken over guest services at the casinos Teeg had inherited from Arvil. He made sure complaints were handled and the staff treated the guests well. He brought recommendations to Teeg if anyone needed to be fired for their actions. The other reptanoids were employed here and there within Teeg's empire. Darzi and Chazi ran the shuttle station. Perzi and Yanzi handled supply requisition. Bekzi and Hirzi supervised the farming now done on Campiaa—before, none had even considered running farms there. Plenty of good farmland lay to the east of Campiaa City. Teeg had brought in equipment and experienced help. Now the farms were thriving and the casinos got fresh fruit and vegetables. I was amazed at how industrious and progressive-minded Teeg had been.

"We still have to import oxberries." Farzi wasn't thrilled about that.

"I have it on good authority that it takes a special kind of soil for those berries," I said. "Word has it that the imports everybody gets from Le-Ath Veronis are only possible because they bought truckloads of soil from the southern continent on Kifirin," I said.

"Otherwise, Kifirin is the only world I know that has the right kind of ground to grow the berries."

"Have you been there? To Kifirin?" Lenden wanted to know.

"No," I answered truthfully. The ASD had always interfered with any plans I might make to go there. Tory intended to take me and show me the palace in Veshtul when my stint with the ASD was over. Gavril wanted to go with us, so we'd made tentative plans. Now, all that might just be something we dreamed about. I missed Tory with an ache in my heart. Aurelius, too. Lendill—we'd barely gotten to know each other outside being Vice-Director and employee. He wanted to take me to meet his father. Now, none of them knew if I were alive.

"Teeg moves us tomorrow," Farzi announced when we finished our drinks. "If Reah needs something to take, she should buy now."

I blinked stupidly at Farzi—when had this been decided? "Farzi, where are we going? What will the weather be like?"

"Hot, where we go. No sleeves best." Farzi wasn't comfortable giving me orders and it affected his speech.

"Farzi," I leaned over and kissed his cheek, "you don't have to worry about upsetting me. I'll still love you, Nenzi and the others, even if I'm mad at the time."

"But Teeg say you be upset about moving."

"Probably, but I'll be upset with him, not you. How's that?" Nenzi was leaning closer to me. "You want a kiss too?" Nenzi grinned. He got his kiss on the cheek. We went shopping for sleeveless shirts and shorts after that. Jes' workouts must have produced muscle I didn't have before—clothes fit tighter so I got different sizes. I certainly had more muscle and definition in my legs now. I bought sandals for all of us, Lenden included, when he said he was coming along. He was surprised that I'd even think of it.

"Well, you need something too, don't you think?" I looked up at him. He just shrugged. "Besides, Teeg's paying." I grinned and flipped the chip bracelet on my wrist.

"Now see, Farzi was supposed to tell you so you'd be over your mad by the time you got back," Teeg said. He was pulling his shirt off to go shower—he was taking me to dinner. Kiasz was going to cook for us and we'd be served in one of the private rooms in the restaurant.

"You wanted me to be mad at Farzi instead?" I had my hands on my hips.

"No, I just thought you'd be calmer if the news came from him." Teeg let his pants drop. The underwear followed. At least he picked up after himself.

"You're not going to tell me where we're going?"

"No. I may not tell you when we get there. You might figure it out for yourself, though."

"Great." I flopped onto the bed, feeling a snit coming on.

"Reah." Teeg came over and pulled me up again. Leaned down to kiss me. His naked body was telling me what it wanted, even if he never said. We were nearly late getting to dinner.

Teelas. That's where we landed. It was hard to wrap my head around the fact that it actually existed. Hot as a desert most of the time; the rains came in late afternoon or early evening. If it were hot enough, the cold rain hitting the hot stones that made up the roadways often steamed and sizzled as it hit. Teelas was a paradox. Tales said that it was created by wizardry of some sort. Lush trees and plants grew in small oases around the equator, where most of the population lived. Of that population, which numbered around ten million, two-thirds held some sort of power. Rogue wizards or warlocks found it easy to blend in, there. Teeg must have gotten information from the two he'd captured, leading us to Teelas. The two captives were already gone when we left for Teelas—I had no idea what Teeg had done with them.

All four of Teeg's warlocks were with us and quite happy to be on Teelas. Farzi and Nenzi had come—the other reptanoids had stayed on Campiaa. Lenden, Jusef, Marc and Jes made up the rest of our party.

"Little girl, do you remember anything about your mother?"

Lenden sat down heavily at the bar that fronted a spacious kitchen inside the home Teeg had secured for us. I handed him an iced fruit juice blend and he sipped it as he watched me prepare other drinks for Jusef and Marc.

"My mother died shortly after I was birthed. I have no memories of her," I said, wondering why he wanted to know. "You can ask Teeg —he probably has more information on that than I do. My father, whom I thought was my brother for the longest time, managed to plot with his mother to get Raedah killed. That's all I know." I could have asked Lendill for the entire file and the court transcripts. I didn't. Edan and Marzi had confessed to their crimes, and that was enough for me. They were still in prison.

"What about you? They didn't treat you very well, did they?"

"That I know more about," I nodded. "I was happy to get away from all of them when the conscription notice came."

"You're an Alliance conscript?"

"She's ASD. She probably won't tell you that, so I will." Teeg came in with Astralan and sat with us at the bar. Marc and Jusef got their drinks, so I started working on something for Teeg and Astralan.

"Can I get a little Sardof in mine?" Astralan wheedled. I looked at Teeg; he nodded benignly. I poured a shot of the clear alcohol into Astralan's drink. I started to pour some into the drink I made for myself but Teeg slapped his hand over my glass. I sighed and put the top back on the bottle.

"What do you do for the ASD?" Lenden was still curious.

"She won't tell you that either. Or the fact that she's High Demon. Or that she has two other mates who are likely going crazy right now, since I have her."

"Thanks, Teeg. *Difik*," I muttered and walked angrily out of the kitchen.

~

"She called you an idiot," Lenden lifted an eyebrow at Teeg.

"I know what difik means," Teeg grumbled, watching Reah walk away from him. He shouldn't have mentioned her other mates—that was likely a sore spot and he was digging into it.

Lenden wanted to tell Teeg how much Reah looked like Queen Belarok, her great-grandmother. He didn't. It wasn't time to tip his hand. He wanted Reah to trust him. Perhaps to care for him as she did those others—the ones with the eyes of reptiles. They were humanoid in every other way and Reah loved them as if they were family. Lenden was family and he wanted to tell Reah that more than anything. *I will be patient,* he told himself. Over and over until he believed it.

"What's wrong?" I sat on a chaise in the enclosed courtyard next to Jes. The house was built in a square shape, with a centralized courtyard that housed a pool and a garden of sorts, comprised of tropical plants. Jes noticed the angry expression on my face and asked the question.

"Teeg. Just—Teeg."

"What did he do?" Jes made to rise from his chair. I motioned for him to sit back down. Jes wanted to be friendly—more than I wanted him to be.

"He won't let me have alcohol. I didn't even get a glass of wine with my meal last night."

"It's not good for you—you're still convalescing."

"Surely a little wouldn't hurt." I couldn't believe Jes was siding with Teeg.

"Reah, just bear with us. All this will go away after a while. In the meantime, you have to keep up your strength in case Teeg needs you to go out with him."

"Oh sure—let Reah get shot at but she sure won't get any alcohol. Which is more dangerous, Jes? You're the physician, tell me." I was grumpy and out of sorts and I knew it. Teeg's dig about Tory and Aurelius had capped off my anger with him. If it weren't for the fact that he held Gavril, I'd have walked out of the house and gone anywhere else right then. I wanted to shout at him for taking my mindspeech away. Shout at him even more about taking my skipping ability away. But more than anything, I wanted to shout at him for kidnapping Gavril and then holding me captive. I was so upset after only a few moments I wanted to weep. I got up and threw my glass of juice against the stone fountain nearby, shattering the glass to tiny pieces. "I hate you!" I shouted. "I hate you!" I stormed out of the courtyard, brushing tears away that I wanted to hold back.

~

"What the fuck happened?" Teeg was there within ticks, taking in the shattered glass and Jes' stunned expression. "What did you do to her?"

"I?" Jes had his fingers at his chest. "I didn't do anything. She complained that you wouldn't let her drink, sat down for a few moments, got up, threw her glass against the fountain, shouted *I hate you* twice and then ran off crying. I did nothing."

"She was shouting at you? That she hated you?"

"No—I got the idea she was talking about you." Jes leveled his gaze at Teeg.

"Fuck." Teeg started to go after Reah. "Clean this up," he said to nobody in particular, waving a hand vaguely toward the shattered glass and took off down the corridor leading to the bedrooms.

~

"Reah, I can break this door down if I have to." Teeg's muffled voice came through the locked door.

"Go ahead," I shouted. "Break down the door. Do whatever the fuck you want, Teeg. That's what you do!" I shouted back at him. I heard him cursing through the door. I might have shouted at him again, or thrown something at him if he'd come through the door any other way. As it is, he performed his invisibility trick and walked right through it instead.

"Now, Reah, care to tell me what this is all about?" His arms were crossed over his chest as he materialized in front of me.

I was sitting on the side of the bed—it was the spot I'd chosen to do my crying. Now he was interrupting me. "You," I stood and jabbed a finger into his chest, "are the one who brought up my mates, like they mean nothing to me. That Gavril means nothing to me. That you get to do whatever you want with me and that's supposed to be all right. It's not all right. You never tell me anything, yet you go off and tell everybody everything about me, like it doesn't matter." I was really crying now. I didn't normally do that. Was it the stress? I'd been stressed before and hadn't broken down like this. I had no idea what was wrong with me.

"Reah, you're allowing your emotions to get the better of you."

"My emotions are not the problem!" I shouted. Yes, I shouted at Teeg San Gerxon. Would it harm Gavril? I was suddenly terrified.

"Reah, I'm not going to try to reason with you right now—I don't think that's possible. When you're ready to talk rationally, then come and find me." Teeg left the same way he'd come in. I threw the lamp at the door. The base was metal, so only the shade was damaged. It did make a satisfying thump against the door when it hit. The door was dented pretty good too—my strength was coming back.

"Difik," I muttered.

I didn't talk to anyone when I got up the next morning. I made my own breakfast and then went back to bed, huddling there and reading a book on the comp-reader Jes had given me. Nenzi and Farzi came looking for me after a click or two.

"Reah, you getting dressed today?" Farzi asked quietly.

"No." I thumbed the comp-reader, getting to the next chapter in my book.

"Teeg want to hunt rogues this morning."

"Does he?" I kept reading.

"Yes. He say that." Nenzi was nodding.

"Nenzi, if he wants me to know something, then he should have enough manhood to come and tell me himself. I love you and Farzi both. I know Teeg sent you. I'm not speaking to Teeg." I went back to my book.

Farzi and Nenzi looked at one another before leaving my room quietly. Teeg hadn't come to bed with me last night, so I was claiming the room as mine.

"Reah, what is this?" Teeg was there moments later, looking like a thundercloud. I didn't say anything to him.

"Reah, get up this instant and get dressed—we have to go out."

I still didn't speak to him, but I did get up and get dressed. I walked out of the bedroom, Teeg right behind me. Astralan was waiting for us, as was Lenden. Astralan folded us to a building somewhere within the city where we stayed.

"She's not talking," Astralan said after a while. Teeg appeared to have some destination in mind but he hadn't said what it was.

"She'll burst if she doesn't talk after a while," Teeg muttered. I wanted to give him a hard elbow to the ribs. Teeg turned down an alley after we walked for a quarter click. The buildings on both sides were placed so closely together, only a small amount of sunlight found its way into that narrow space. It was quite dark there after leaving the brightly lit street behind. I could see an open courtyard farther down that was brighter, but for now, we walked down a narrow, darkened cobblestone tunnel with stucco walls reaching upward for three or four stories.

I wanted to tell Teeg he was leading us into a trap. With my training and ASD experience, I would have approached from above, just to check if there were any enemies waiting for us around either corner where I couldn't see. Since I wasn't speaking to Teeg, I moved forward until I was even with him. I missed my knife and pistol. No sounds came as we neared the open area in the alley.

Teeg may have been relying on sound to tell him if anyone was waiting there for us. I didn't rely on sound, but I did catch the barest hint of shadow. The sun was just right overhead, so that when the rifle was noiselessly raised, I caught the tiniest bit of darkness cast on the ground. I snatched Teeg's wrist to hold him back. He stopped dead still. I gave him the hand signal that all ASD agents use—the two fingers up that meant hold steady where you are. Teeg didn't move. I looked up the side of the stucco wall—It had gouges in it.

Taking a deep breath, I leapt upward as noiselessly as I could, digging my fingers into the deepest and best chipped out slots I could find. Still making as little sound as I could and hoping that the noise from the street continued, I kept climbing until I had the ledge gripped in both hands. I pulled myself over, sending the *I'm fine* signal down to the others. Then, ducking down and running quietly overhead, I peered carefully downward over the back of the building and into the open courtyard below.

Three men with ranos rifles were backed against the wall waiting for us. Hoping mightily that Teeg knew the Alliance fingerspeech, I ran back until he could see me well enough from overhead. I gave him the signal for three men with rifles and then sent fingerspeech, telling him I thought they were ranos rifles. I had a hard time seeing anything in the darkened alley below, so I hoped he'd gotten the message. I pointed toward the back of the building again, telling him I was going to attack from overhead.

When he didn't move or do anything else, I headed toward the open area again from my high vantage point, lifting two square blocks of stone that a tenant had used to hold a roof patch in place above his apartment. His patches were going to blow away in the hot air that stirred around me, but right then, I needed the heavy blocks more than he did. Stopping short of the back of the building, I peered over the edge to make sure Teeg and the others were coming. They were.

In my physics lessons, I was taught that in a vacuum, two objects, regardless of weight, would fall at the same rate of speed. I was about to see if two very similar objects, dropped at the same time, would provide similar results. Aiming carefully and doing my best to time it with Teeg's arrival, I dropped the stone blocks. Both my targets fell to the ground and I ducked immediately when they were hit; the third man was shooting at me quickly and knocking chunks off the top of the building when Teeg landed a very good hit to the shooter's jaw. He dropped like a sack full of redfruit.

"Reah, come down here please." Teeg was staring at our would-be attackers. He didn't sound happy.

My journey down would have been so much faster and infinitely easier if I could have skipped down. Instead, I had to find more handholds and make my way down slowly. I hopped the last few hands distance to the ground.

"Lenden, would you mind carrying her now? I might be persuaded to swat her ass a couple of times," Teeg grumped. "Astralan, can you carry these back to the house and lock them up?" He jerked his head toward the three attackers. "Ask your brothers to keep an eye on them. Make sure they're not power holders." Astralan nodded and folded the three away. Teeg was still glaring at me as Lenden lifted me up. He carried me carefully as Teeg made his way toward a doorway at the back of the open area. Teeg knocked on a door to the left but there was no answer.

Cautiously he tried the door—it pushed inward as he touched it lightly. It was his turn to use fingerspeech—I learned he knew it well. He told us to tread softly and follow him. We did. What we found inside the home, if that's what it was, was a bloody battlefield.

Six people looked as if they'd struggled before they'd died. Blood was everywhere. I'd seen similar scenes before but this time the smell combined with the sight of the bodies had me gagging. While Teeg went through the place, room by room, Astralan came back with Stellan. While I did my best to hold my breakfast down, Teeg went from one body to the next, checking for any signs of life. He didn't find anything.

"Clean it up," he whispered to the two warlocks. I was feeling more ill by the moment, but I did my best not to show it. Lenden still held me, so I wrapped my arms around his neck and buried my head against his shoulder. He rubbed my back gently as he watched the two warlocks do their job.

We were folded back to the house shortly afterward, and the moment I was set down, I ran. Straight to the bathroom in my suite I went, sliding to the toilet on my knees and losing everything I'd had for breakfast, heaving until there was nothing left. And then heaving past that for a while. Teeg came in while I was coughing up the last bit of my stomach's contents. I wanted to tell him to go away. Shout at him to go away. He didn't. Teeg stayed until the very end, when I could finally let go of the toilet and flop miserably onto the floor. I lay there, curled up and unwilling to move. I might have been moaning, too—I can't say for sure.

"Reah, sweetheart?" Teeg was washing my face with a cool cloth. I shuddered. "How long were you sick, baby? Did you hold this back all that time?" Moaning again, I huddled into a smaller ball. I still felt ill—thought I might have to heave again.

"Shhhh, it's all right, Reah. Come on, let's get your mouth rinsed out and put some clean clothes on. Then we'll put you to bed. Marc will bring something to put in your stomach—it doesn't need to be empty, love." Teeg was stroking hair away from my face—it had tangled while I heaved and was now in a mess. Lifting me off the floor, Teeg did just as promised, holding me up while I rinsed out my mouth with shaking hands. Then he pulled my clothing off and put me in clean pajamas. Marc brought in clear broth and crackers. Teeg sat beside me while I did my best to eat some of it. He got me down for a nap, then. Jes was peeking in the doorway most of that time, but Teeg waved him away.

"Go to sleep, baby," Teeg put his fingers against my forehead and I was out immediately.

Gavril swept up sawdust and wood shavings. Dormas had put him to cleaning up after he'd sanded cabinet doors most of the night. "It always pays to clean up before starting again the next day. Don't ever leave a mess behind," the old vampire advised. "If you work hard the next six eight-days, I'll show you how to varnish what you're sanding." Gavril leaned on his broom for a moment, feeling weary and ready for bed. He nodded to the old vampire and went back to sweeping.

"Sweetheart, wake up, it's time for dinner." Teeg woke me up from an extended nap. My stomach still felt uneasy, as if the slightest thing might set it off again. I brushed my teeth and used mouthwash—my mouth still tasted awful. Teeg hovered while I changed and dressed. He didn't even argue when I braided my hair and tied it at the end with a ribbon I found in my things. I was barefoot when Teeg lifted me and carried me to the kitchen—I still hadn't spoken to him.

Marc and Jusef had cooked—the fowl was good, I just didn't feel like eating much. Teeg hauled me into the media room and pulled me against him, rubbing my belly while we sat there and watched some old vid he'd pulled from somewhere. I huddled against him after a while. He kissed my forehead and let me lean on him while he rubbed and stroked gently.

Teeg went to bed with me, too. He let me walk to the bedroom on my own while he followed close behind. "Just to make sure you don't wobble," he teased. That was an about-face from earlier in the day. I wanted to ask him about the six dead men we'd found. Also about the three he'd taken prisoner. I didn't. Things were unsettled for me at the moment and I was unsure how to handle any of it.

"Reah, are you going to talk to me again? I shouldn't have said that. I shouldn't have. I was upset when you were screaming that you hated me." Teeg was pulling me against him, sliding my body across the sheets until I was snugly imprisoned against him. His dark eyes were staring into mine from very close quarters—he bumped his forehead gently against mine.

"Couples fight all the time," I muttered.

"Reah, I don't like fighting with you. I can't help feeling inadequate against two other mates who aren't holding you hostage." His fingers were gentle against my face, stroking and tracing the line of my jaw.

"Will I ever see them again?" My lower lip trembled—I couldn't control it.

"I'll do my best to make it happen, baby." Teeg crushed me against him. I wanted to ask him if I'd see Gavril again too, but that would truly make me cry. He just held me tighter and rocked me gently, muttering nonsense into my hair.

~

"Well, well. Look what we have here." Erland walked around the two prisoners he held inside a powerlight cage. Erland Morphis was one of three warlocks who possessed the ability to form a powerlight cage. These two would not escape. King Wylend and Erland's son Ry were the other two strong enough to do it.

Wylend was reading the note that came with the two rogue warlocks. Teeg San Gerxon had sent them as a gesture of goodwill. Wylend had been searching for these, but they'd had power-seeker abilities, eluding all of Wylend's special forces. How Teeg San Gerxon had managed to capture them was a mystery. Wylend wasn't going to argue with the results—these two were a part of the small army of rogues Zellar had trained before getting killed.

"Which cores did you drain before you were captured?" Erland demanded of the two. They shrank back from Erland, although the cage provided some protection. They'd thought a powerlight cage was only myth and rumor. They were learning better, now.

"We didn't drain anything—we did pull power away from a few," the shorter one grudgingly admitted. They weren't going to get away from the King of Karathia or his right hand, Erland Morphis.

"Did you not realize that anything pulled from the core will upset a fragile balance? Did Zellar not explain that to you? Of course not." Erland tossed up a hand. "You've killed millions, more than likely, unless they start the exodus now. The climate will fail, plants and animals will die and then the people. Is that what you wanted when you decided to play your little power games?" Erland was dangerously angry.

"Zellar said it wouldn't hurt if you took what you needed occasionally," the taller one snapped.

"There," Erland hissed, "is a reason that this is forbidden spellwork. It kills the planet from the very first tapping. It may take a while to die, but you've opened the drain. All life on those worlds will run out that drain now. It would take more power than you can possibly imagine to make it right again. Tell me the names of those worlds, so we may pass along the information. Do it now."

"What can provide that power?" The shorter rogue asked.

"The Larentii might do it, but as you know, they do not interfere. They will not lift their hands to save what you have destroyed."

"Why wouldn't they save a planet?" The taller one huffed. He'd never seen one of the blue giants, but their abilities were legendary.

"They have made a vow of noninterference, you imbecile. Give us the names of the worlds you have destroyed with your greed and foolishness, and your deaths will be swift and painless. Failure to do so will force me to call my blood warlocks." Wylend examined his fingernails. The two rogues stared at one another inside their cage.

"Roorthi," the shorter one said. "Xordthe. Shillverr."

"What's this?" Tory accepted the envelope from his mother, Queen Lissa.

"Something that came with my other mail—ever since they learned I like paper messages, I get swamped with the stuff. You should hear Grant and Heathe grumble about it." Lissa shoved her strawberry blonde hair behind an ear and went back to sorting through other messages she'd received. All of them had been carefully checked before they were handed to her assistants. One had come addressed to *Torevik Rath, Le-Ath Veronis.*

"How did they get my name and why would they be writing to me instead of you?" Tory's face bore a puzzled frown as he settled on a chair in front of his mother's desk.

"No idea." Lissa sat down, too—she'd been through a lengthy Council meeting already—Aurelius was grieving over Reah's disappearance and Lissa didn't want to put him through the stress of the Council meetings. Aryn had volunteered, but she'd told him that she'd handle the meetings for the next month. She needed to get a better grip on a few items anyway. Lissa watched as Tory ripped up the flap of the old-fashioned envelope, pulling out the contents. Tory drew in an audible breath as he examined what had been sent.

"What is it?" Lissa was around the desk and beside her son in record time—even for a vampire. Tory turned the paper so his mother could see, causing Lissa to draw in a breath. Two photographs printed on paper. Taken separately and at different locations. One was Reah, standing next to a pool in what appeared to be exercise clothing. The other, with very little surrounding him other than a white wall, was *Gavril*.

"*They are safe,*" the enclosed note read. "*They will be returned to you, if you will agree to a meeting in the future. You will be contacted with a time and place.*" No name was signed on the message. As soon as Lissa regained her voice, she was shouting mentally and physically for Gavin, Norian, Aurelius and anyone else who might be listening. Tory, though, touched both faces with a finger. "I love you," he whispered softly.

CHAPTER 6

"There isn't anything. It's like a robot prepared the message and then sealed the envelope." Norian had gotten his team of experts to work on the envelope and the enclosed photographs and message. No fingerprints, no body oils, no residual anything. For all Norian knew, it had been created in a vacuum. It had been a wrench for Tory and Aurelius to hand over the photographs. Lissa, too, wanted the one of Gavril back—he looked to be all right and much the same as he had when he'd left Le-Ath Veronis, heading for the private school he'd attended.

"Could you tell anything from Reah's surroundings?" Aurelius asked. He was grasping at straws—even the Saa Thalarr said something was blocking their ability to *Look* for her and the Larentii had said the Wise Ones had issued a noninterference policy on the whole thing.

"That could be any pool anywhere," Norian grumped. "Perhaps a hotel pool, for all we know." Lendill walked in—Norian had sent a message to his Vice-Director, saying they'd gotten something on Reah and Gavril.

"I didn't get anything from Hild Marolla—he's hit a dead end too,"

Lendill sighed. Lendill had hopes that the journalist might open doors that would be closed to anyone bearing an ASD badge.

"Did you tell him that if he comes across Denevik, that Jayd wants to know immediately?" Lissa asked Lendill.

"Yes. I told him that the Kifirini King wants his subject to come home—all is forgiven," Lendill muttered, holding the photographs of Reah and Gavril in his hands. Lendill had even contacted his father, hoping Kaldill might be able to do something. Kaldill didn't refuse outright, but then elves seldom did that. Kaldill had merely stated that things would likely work out. Lendill had been even more frustrated after speaking with his father.

"Well, this blows my news completely out of the water," Erland sighed as he appeared suddenly.

"What news?" Lissa looked up at her warlock mate.

"Teeg San Gerxon just handed two of the rogues Zellar trained over to us, free and clear. We got information on three worlds that they started to drain. Teeg wants to lure Wylend to the dark side."

"Teeg's not a bad sort," Tory muttered. "Ry and I worked with him before. What if he's really going to put a decent alliance together? Have you thought about that? I know what he did to Reah, but think about it—she'd be in danger there and he might have wanted to send her home where she'd be safe. Of course, that didn't prevent this." Tory took the photographs from Lendill.

"I've gotten reports that a lot of the kingpins on some of those worlds have met with an untimely demise." Norian was smiling at the thought.

"It only makes sense to destroy your rivals," Aurelius pointed out.

"Could be that. But we haven't seen a great deal of crime as a result— in fact all my operatives are reporting downturns in criminal activity."

"That still doesn't help us with the rogue warlock problem. We still don't know how many of those idiots Zellar trained. I wish I could have been there to see him die." Erland clenched his hands, still angry that someone else had gotten to Zellar when he and Wylend had been chasing him for years. The fool had nearly drained Le-Ath Veronis through Gren, a half-fae and one of Zellar's first trainees. Miraculously, things had been set to rights for Lissa's planet, but they couldn't expect the same for any other world.

"What does Ildevar Wyyld think about all this?" Lissa touched Norian on the shoulder. Norian was Ildevar's adopted heir and sometimes privy to what Ildevar thought about things of this nature.

"Ildevar says he's waiting for a request," Norian sighed. "That's it—waiting for a request. He wouldn't give me anything else."

"Talking in riddles," Tory muttered, nodding.

"Reah looks tired." Aurelius had gotten the photographs back.

"And Gavril looks grim." Lissa pointed at her youngest son's face.

"More like determined," Gavin said. Lissa looked up at her mate before slipping an arm around his waist.

"You know they're holding both of them separately because they're using each one's safety to force the other's compliance," Norian grumped.

"I know." Gavin blew out a breath. Of Lissa's four children, the one who belonged to him had been the one kidnapped. Only Lissa had known what toll this had taken on her first vampire mate.

"Erland?" Lissa had an idea.

"What love?" Erland pulled Lissa to him and gave her a gentle kiss.

"Can Wylend contact Teeg San Gerxon? Have him help us look for Gavril and Reah? Would he do that?"

"You know Wylend worries about her too," Erland agreed. "Do we know for sure that she's there—somewhere in the Campiaan Alliance?"

"Hmmph," Lendill coughed into his hand. Norian did his best to look innocent.

"Norian Keef, you never have said just what her assignment was," Lissa's hands were on her hips.

"She, uh, was sent after Zellar. We think that she might have been injured when Zellar was killed. Whoever picked her up after the bombing likely has her now. If they want a meeting with you, breah-mul, then they want something from you."

"But the note came to me," Tory pointed out.

"Then they have your name. Perhaps they got it from Reah somehow. They may be trying to get to all of us through you." Norian was trying to piece all of it together.

"Le-Ath Veronis' policy is not to succumb to blackmail or extortion," Lissa pointed out. "If the note had come to me, then Grant or Heathe would have turned it over to Gavin and Tony, who would have pulled Drake and Drew in, and then the Council would be notified. Instead, they sent it to Tory. Perhaps they knew all of this, somehow."

"Nice way to move completely around the Council and the military," Erland observed. "I'll go have a talk with Wylend—see if he will approach Teeg San Gerxon for a brief conversation."

Teeg turned the handwritten message over in his hands. It had come to the designated spot—a deserted planet that Zellar had drained. Wylend Arden had sent a request, with the promise of a generous reward if Teeg did as Wylend asked—help him in his search for Reah Nilvas and Gavril Montegue. Teeg wondered briefly what Wylend would do if the King of Karathia learned that he was involved in both disappearances. Putting it out of his mind, he penned a reply.

I will do what I can regarding your request, Teeg wrote before sealing the envelope. Astralan would remove fingerprints and any other identifying markers before sending it to Wylend. Teeg sighed as he rose, stretched his lithe, muscular frame and then went in search of Reah.

"Reah, eat something for Em-pah Lenden." Why Teeg's bodyguard referred to himself as a grandfather, I might never know. I was feeling queasy that afternoon, just days after we'd found the blood and bodies inside the house. Teeg and his warlocks had been questioning our three captives, after checking them over for location beacons or chips.

Teeg had certainly learned better on that. Teeg had also brought in the other six reptanoids. All of them were with us now. Teeg said they needed a break from Campiaa. I didn't ask.

"Come on, you'll feel better if you get something in your stomach," Lenden said. "Let Marc and Jusef prepare something for you."

"Reah, do what he says." Teeg walked toward the chaise where I sat beside the pool. If I felt better, I might have gone for a swim.

"I don't feel like eating," I grumbled at both of them.

"It's because your stomach is empty that you feel this way," Teeg grumbled right back. "Do I have to carry you to the kitchen?"

"No, I'll go," I slid off my chair and walked past him. He and Lenden followed me.

"Reah needs something to eat, Jusef," Lenden said as soon as we arrived. Jusef was already there, puttering around. I learned that Marc and Celestan had gone to the market to buy food. Jusef put something together for me—a quick snack of fruit, cheese and crackers with a glass of juice. Lenden rubbed my back while I drank the last of my juice. Teeg watched closely as I finished it.

"Oh, good, you got her to eat." Jes walked in. "I thought I'd find you out by the pool, but I see somebody beat me to this."

"Want something?" Jusef, the Amterean dwarf asked Jes.

"Just the juice," Jes nodded. "I don't have a queasy stomach like Reah. Probably a side effect of all your injuries," he held up a hand when I started to say something. "You're still not fully recovered."

"Thanks for clearing that up," I muttered and slid off my stool. I couldn't decide whether the food made me feel better or not.

"Reah, we'll be moving tomorrow morning, so get your things together," Teeg was behind me quickly, a hand on my shoulder.

"I don't suppose you'll tell me where we're going or what happened with those three men?" I knew they were no longer in the house—the warlocks had likely taken them away.

"Now Reah, you should know better than to ask, now shouldn't you?" Teeg's hand slid down to my hip, squeezing lightly.

I just sighed at his words. Someday, when he wasn't holding Gavril (and I hoped that day would come) I would consider turning and slamming him into a wall a time or two. After I had the transmitter, of course, so I could skip away. If that happened, he might never see me again. Teeg watched while I packed. Then he insisted on watching while I changed into my swimsuit to get into the pool. He even got in the water with me, after removing all his clothing. Honestly, there wasn't a shy bone in his entire body.

"Come on, baby, just relax against me," Teeg urged after pulling me against him. Farzi, Nenzi and their brothers came into the pool with us, all turning to lion snake. Well, it only made sense that they could swim that way. Jes sat on a chaise and watched while eight reptanoids and two humanoids lazed and swam around.

"I'm not sure I've ever seen anything like this," Lenden was chuckling as he settled on a chair next to Jes, a drink in his hand.

"Every one of them would kill for her," Jes murmured.

"I like that," Lenden nodded.

"I wasn't just talking about the snakes," Jes added.

"Even better."

We were in a high-rise again and Farzi and Nenzi's six brothers had been taken back to Campiaa by one of the wizards. Now we were down to Teeg, Farzi, Nenzi, Astralan, Stellan, Jes, Lenden and Jusef. Jusef was more than enough in the cook department, so Marc had gone back with the reptanoids. Teeg didn't stop me from watching news-vids this time so I found out immediately that we were on Shillverr. Restlessness overcame me the moment we settled into the spacious apartment; something felt wrong about it. It wasn't just the apartment, either—it was the whole place. We'd settled in the capital city of Shillvas and the entire news vid had been about some sort of blight on a few exotic plants and changes in weather patterns. The governor's wife was complaining that all her rare orchids were dying. The journalist was poking fun at her in a subdued manner, but I was beginning to feel what those orchids were feeling. Something was wrong with Shillverr.

"Reah, I think we'll need your Thifilatha again," Teeg poked his head in the bedroom door as I was switching channels on the vid-screen.

Not feeling my best at the moment, I hoped he didn't need it right away as I turned the power off and slid off the bed. This, just like Teeg's other apartment, was luxurious. Beautiful artwork, fabrics, rugs, marble and stone throughout, and hand-carved doors going into the master suite. The carvings were intricate and whimsical at the same time—leaves, plants and tiny creatures that hid among the vines and branches. It made me wonder if Teeg had paid to have it done or merely bought it as it was.

"When and where?" I asked, trailing Teeg into the kitchen. Rubbing my stomach, which threatened to become upset quickly, I watched as Teeg settled onto a barstool at the massive island.

"Come here, baby," Teeg beckoned. Not understanding what he wanted, I stayed where I was.

"Reah, come here. Jusef, can you throw a snack together?" Jusef, who was puttering around the kitchen, putting away a pile of food he and Lenden had gone to a nearby market to purchase, nodded to me and began slicing fresh nannas. When I still didn't move, Teeg tried again. "Reah, you look almost green. Love, you need something in that empty stomach. That's what makes you feel sick—it's empty, baby."

His last words came from far away—darkness was already closing around me. I have no idea if I hit the floor or if he caught me before I reached it.

~

"Come on, Reah, it's not that bad," Jes was washing my face with a cold cloth. Sputtering at the dampness against my skin, I woke almost as quickly as I lost consciousness. "You just need to eat more often. That's all."

"Reah, now will you come?" Teeg was grumpy—I could tell that even in my semiconscious state. Lenden was also kneeling beside me —I was on the floor. Jes and Lenden lifted me and helped me walk to the island, where a dish of fruit and a flaky roll waited. Still unsure whether I wanted anything to eat or not, I ate part of what I was given under Teeg's watchful gaze.

"We'll be going to a remote area here on Shillverr," Teeg informed me as I forced myself to eat more fruit. Jusef placed a glass of milk in front of me, plus a small plate of cheese cubes.

Later, I dressed in my leathers again, hoping we weren't going to snow covered mountains to accomplish whatever Teeg planned to do. Astralan was going to fold us to our targeted area, just as before. Lenden was frustrated that Teeg wouldn't allow him to go. Farzi and Nenzi didn't like it either, but Teeg was in charge and he reminded all of them of that fact before Astralan folded us away.

"We need to do this quick," Teeg whispered in my ear as we kept an eye on the remote cabin in a deep vale. Thick woods surrounded the small building, but the solar panels covering the roof were collecting the abundant sunlight beating down on all of us. I was hot in my leathers—Teeg should have given me a better gauge on how to dress for this. Astralan had landed us the prescribed two clicks from the cabin, so it looked tiny from my vantage point, high on an adjacent hill.

"Your smaller Thifilatha should be able to walk beneath most of these trees," Teeg pointed out. Nodding and doing my best to ignore the feeling of wrongness leeching up from the ground and even through the soles of my boots, I swallowed with difficulty. Sunset was coming quickly to this part of Shillverr—I knew that even as Teeg nodded for me to change.

Walking through thick brush and closely growing trees carrying a tall man isn't the easiest thing I've ever done. Teeg grumbled more than once when he was slapped in the face with a tree branch as I lumbered along. Still, he clung to my back tenaciously while cursing softly. I didn't use my smaller Thifilatha often—when I did go Thifilatha—it usually required the larger one. No matter—we were closing in on our target and more and more I was beginning to believe that Teeg was right—these residents were home.

"Go to your larger Thifilatha and take the house down," Teeg ordered just before we exited the forest we'd traveled through. A tiny clearing surrounded the cabin—designed to keep the trees from blocking sunlight for the solar panels.

Well, Teeg could have told me this to start with, only he didn't. I wanted to kick him in the groin for refusing to give me information on this particular assignment. The ASD called it *Need To Know*. I called it callous, rude and unfeeling. Lendill and I had a few arguments about it through the years I'd spent working for him and Norian Keef.

Just for leaving me out of this part of our attack, I left Teeg hanging on a tree branch before going full Thifilatha and kicking an outside wall of the cabin, sending the whole structure falling over in a heap.

"Lendill?"

"Father? What do you want?" Lendill had to work to keep the heavy sigh out of his voice when Kaldill Schaff contacted him via communicator. Lendill leaned back in his chair with a suppressed sigh, waiting to hear what his father had to say.

"If Reah is returned to you, you must marry her immediately. Bring her here and the ceremony will be performed."

"What?" Lendill was shocked by his father's demand. Before, his father had only requested a meeting with Reah. Now he wanted the marriage ceremony? Where had that come from?

"Child, I cannot elaborate at this time," Kaldill's eyes were unfocused—a look with which Lendill was only too familiar.

"But father," Lendill shouted as Kaldill terminated the call.

Teeg had to kill two of the three with the ranos rifle he carried—the two wizards had nearly reached the perimeter of my spell-negating ability. The third had gotten trapped beneath debris from the cabin I'd destroyed and he was desperately attempting to spell his trapped leg away from the heavy beam that pierced part of it. Teeg lifted it off easily and slapped cuffs on the man before calling for Astralan.

Ordering me away from them so Astralan could do what he could to stop the bleeding in the wizard's leg, I walked away from them, still feeling the wrongness through my Thifilatha's bare feet. This world was leaking energy. I whirled swiftly to glare at the wizard Teeg and Astralan were attempting to save for questioning. It made me angry—I knew now who'd caused the energy leak—those three wizards. Now, all the planet's energy would drain from the core if something didn't stop it. I was experienced with pulling energy from somewhere. But where? I couldn't pull it from Shillverr—the planet was already losing it at an alarming rate. Glancing up at the stars appearing overhead, I realized there was more than enough energy there. All I had to do was tap into it. Could I do it, by latching onto the light energy and pulling it to Shillverr even faster from so far away? If I couldn't, Shillverr would die.

Sitting down, I turned my head toward the stars, focusing on one. Stars and suns created energy constantly. They wouldn't miss what I needed now, if I could force it to my will. Closing my eyes, I held the mental image of the star in my mind and *Pulled*.

"Perhaps you should come see for yourself, Norian. They were delivered two days ago." Ildevar Wyyld smiled at his adopted heir.

"But how did they get here?" Norian was bewildered.

"I am not inclined to question at the moment. You have been looking for these for a while. They conveniently have confessed nearly all their crimes." Ildevar walked ahead of Norian, through dark corridors flanking the cells in Ildevar's dungeons. Ildevar seldom used them, unless it was to keep a prisoner until feeding day.

Norian stared and whistled at the three prisoners. He had been looking for these for a while. Thirty years, at least. The last remnants of Solar Red glared at him through the bars of their cells.

"Do we have to report them to anyone?" Norian turned to Ildevar.

"No, they were delivered straight to my dungeon while the note appeared on my desk. We are the only two who know they are here, other than the ones who sent them."

"Are we going to let anyone else know?" Norian smiled at Ildevar.

"Only if that is your wish, child."

"I don't wish."

"Good. I think I'll start with this one," Ildevar gave a nod toward the prisoner in the middle cell.

"When?" Norian was mildly curious.

"Two days."

"Good." Norian turned on his heel and walked away. These prisoners were never getting out of Ildevar's dungeon alive.

"What did she do? What did she do?" Teeg was shouting and fretting at the same time. Reah had done something—Astralan had said not only was Shillverr's energy drain stopped, but the core had been healed somehow. Reah was connected to this, only none of them could determine just how she was connected. Now, she lay unconscious on the grass, still in full Thifilatha.

"We have to get her turned back—we can't leave her like this, Astralan was fretting almost as much as Teeg. Teeg was glad Farzi and Nenzi hadn't come; they'd be having a breakdown.

"Reah, come on baby, wake up. Please. For me. Do this for me, all right?" Teeg was begging. He was about to promise anything to her when she moaned softly.

Waking up flat on my back in the middle of the wilderness while night insects sang in the trees around me wasn't the best situation in which I've ever found myself. "Thank the stars," Astralan muttered from somewhere nearby. Teeg was standing on my left arm, peering into my face. "Baby, change back. We need to take you home so Jes can have a look at you."

"Teeg, I don't feel good." I covered my eyes with my free hand—Teeg was still standing on my left arm; I couldn't move it unless I wanted to knock him to the ground. My stomach was threatening to heave up its contents; if there was anything left to heave.

"I know, baby. Change back. We'll get you home and Jes will fix it. I promise." Teeg sounded upset, for some reason. My mind felt fuzzy—cloudy somehow, and I had to think for a moment before I could recall how to change back. Teeg jumped down the moment things looked to go back to normal.

"What happened?" Jes was fretting the moment Teeg showed up with me wrapped in his arms.

"A little more work than Teeg wanted from her, that's what," Astralan murmured. Lenden was there and looked as if he were going to lift me from Teeg's arms. Honestly, I just wanted to spend quality time with the toilet. When everybody was talking to one another and leaving me out of it, my body decided to react in its own way. I heaved all over the floor, causing Jes to jump aside, Teeg to shout and Farzi, Nenzi and Jusef to quickly search for something to clean the floor.

"All gone now?" Teeg was beside me on the bathroom floor when it looked as if I might stop heaving up nothing.

"Hope so," I muttered. My throat was raw, my insides felt as if they wanted to become outsides and I just wanted to curl up and die somewhere.

"None of that; come on, sweetheart, let's get you up so you can rinse out your mouth."

"Teeg, I don't want to get up." I was hugging myself as hard as I could. Nauseous didn't begin to describe how I felt.

"I know. Lenden?" Lenden appeared in the doorway to the bathroom. "Help me get this one to the sink. We'll get to the bed after that." Lenden took one side, Teeg took the other and they lifted me easily off the floor. I was still trying to curl into a ball, but both of them forced me to straighten and shuffle toward the sink. Lenden propped me up while I weakly brushed my teeth; Teeg went to find clean pajamas for me. I was afraid to ask for a bath—most likely I'd fall asleep in it, anyway.

"You just spent too much of your energy," Jes said when he examined me after Teeg got me into bed. "And I'd like for you to drink a jumble. Jusef is making one now and cursing the rest of us in Amterean while he's doing it," Jes added.

"He *is* cursing in his native language," Lenden walked in, carrying the glass and a straw. "The last I heard, we all have mulch for brains."

"Can't argue with that," I said weakly as Jes accepted the glass and stuck the straw in it for me. Teeg chased the others out, pulled me against him in the bed and proceeded to hold the glass while ordering me to drink. I felt too ill to argue with him, rolling my head against his shoulder and closing my eyes after only a few sips.

"Baby, this will be over before long, I promise," Teeg whispered as I drifted off.

"I still don't know how she did it and there's two more out there, if we got the truth out of those two," Teeg held his head in his hands. "How can we put her through this? How are we going to ask this of her? You saw what it did to her last night."

"But the populations on those worlds will die if we don't do something," Teeg's assistant had come—courtesy of Galaxsan—to discuss things with Teeg.

"Tell me something I don't know," Teeg muttered. "Dee, tell me what to do. And make it something that won't kill her. And me as a result."

"It didn't kill her last night—it just made her weak and ill. What does the physician say? How long will it take her to recover from this?"

"If she starts eating, perhaps an eight-day. Maybe a little more."

"We have little time, unless we want more of these worlds to die. I've gotten intelligence on two other rogues that Zellar trained. Has the one you captured last night been able to talk?"

"Jes is working on him, trying to get him conscious for more than a few moments at a time. What if she's permanently harmed, Dee?"

"What will you do, if that turns out to be the case?"

"If I don't kill myself, Torevik Rath will kill me anyway."

"Em-pah's here." Those words greeted me when I woke—Teeg must have gotten up earlier.

"Huh?" I felt lethargic and weak. My eyes were refusing to open for some reason.

"Come on, little squirrel, let's get you to breakfast." Lenden was lifting me off the bed. Teeg hadn't come in the night before until very late. He'd barely wakened me while slipping in and wrapping his arms around me. Now, he was up early and off somewhere, leaving Lenden to carry me to breakfast. I wasn't going to complain—Lenden wanted to adopt me, somehow. Compared to the one grandfather I knew I had, this was more than different. Addah Desh wouldn't have shown gentleness if someone paid him to do so.

"Jusef, look what we have here." Lenden settled me on a barstool. Farzi and Nenzi came in and they sat to my left while Lenden sat on my right. Jusef served oatmeal with brown sugar and a bit of cream. It was good and helped ease my stomach. Farzi and Nenzi looked worried, but turned their heads away when I tried to catch them watching me.

"Where's Teeg?" I asked.

"Working with the prisoner," Lenden replied. "Little girl, don't worry yourself over that. He's bad and deserves whatever he gets."

"I know," I answered wearily. Jes must be with Teeg, since the rogue warlock had been wounded. Wouldn't do to let the man die before he answered all of Teeg's questions.

"Eat your breakfast. We'll be taking care of you today," Lenden rubbed my shoulders as I went back to my oatmeal.

~

"They split up," Kastalt's voice was shaky but he couldn't help himself —he was answering any question these two asked. The physician had given painkill; that helped some. "They sold the information on Zellar, Nidris admitted that when I saw them last. Didn't matter, we were tired of looking at him anyway."

Teeg knew about that—Zellar had been disfigured nearly forty-five years before.

"The names? Besides Nidris?" Teeg pushed.

"Qwan. Halmus."

"The ones we sent to Karathia," Astralan said softly. Teeg nodded.

"Where did Nidris go? Do you know that?"

"Said he was heading home for a while until he wasn't hunted any longer," Kastalt was fading fast. Teeg looked at Jes, who shook his head. He'd given a higher dose of painkill than should have been given, just to keep Kastalt awake and talking. Kastalt was near death as it was—this was going to finish him off.

"Do you know where Nidris' home is?" Teeg gentled his voice.

"Alliance," Kastalt whispered. "Tulgalan."

"But there isn't anyone with talent on Tulgalan," Astralan denied Kastalt's claim.

"Hasn't been there long. Family," Kastalt grunted with the effort to speak, "moved there twenty turns ago. Hiding power. Hunted by Karathia. All of them." Kastalt slumped in his chair. Jes went to check the pulse and looked up at Teeg, shaking his head. Kastalt was dead.

"Get rid of that," Teeg ordered. Stellan came forward to take the body.

"What now, Boss? We won't get into the Reth Alliance."

"Not in any normal manner, no. We also need more information on Nidris. I'll send a message to Wylend Arden." Teeg stalked from the back room of the warehouse where they'd held Kastalt.

~

"Erland, look at this." Wylend handed him the note from Teeg San Gerxon.

"What is it this time?" Erland was frustrated—Teeg had managed to capture more rogue warlocks in a matter of months than Erland and his spies had managed to hunt down in decades.

"He's asking for information on Nidris. Says he received information from Kastalt before he died that Nidris had received training from Zellar. Says Kastalt told him that Nidris had gone to Tulgalan—that his family had relocated there to get away from us."

"Nidris," Erland almost growled the name. He and Wylend had reason to loathe Nidris Hazlan and his entire family. The one highly placed family who'd plotted to kill Wylend's father and then managed to escape. Wylend and Erland had seen the others executed when Wylend wrestled the throne away from them.

"And now he's draining cores, more than likely," Wylend heaved a frustrated sigh. "Who knows what he might do with the power that will give him?"

"We need to notify Norian Keef," Erland was motivated, suddenly. "If that fool has started draining Tulgalan or any other Alliance worlds, this could be disastrous."

"I will come with you—I haven't seen Lissa in days and my grandson is still missing. I don't know what I might do in her place."

CHAPTER 7

"Wylend and Erland are coming for a visit," Lissa announced as she walked into Norian's office; he'd been going over reports with Lendill.

"Is there a reason we should know this?" Norian looked up at Lissa.

"Yeah. Em-pah Wylend got a message from Teeg San Gerxon. Says that he captured one of those rogues Zellar trained. The note said that one of the rogues has possibly slipped into the Alliance, to meet with his rogue family of wizards, who are reportedly living on Tulgalan."

"You're joking." Norian was standing in a blink. "You don't think they're draining Tulgalan, do you?"

"No idea, but Em-pah seems to think that this particular wizard would do just about anything to keep away from him and his network of spies. Erland says they'll explain that completely when they get here."

"We're here, now," Erland and Wylend folded into Norian's office. "Nidris Hazlan and his family are murdering scum," Erland went on. "The Hazlan clan led the coup against Warlend, Wylend's father and killed him to take the throne six thousand turns ago, give or take. The Hazlans would kill their children if it would get them what they want."

"You can't mean that," Lissa sounded skeptical.

"Already happened, granddaughter," Wylend sighed. "Three of their children were in my father's court at the time. They knew nothing of the coup and were killed right along with my father's guards."

"Expendable, to keep suspicion away from their clan," Erland said angrily. "Warlend didn't suspect them at all, and they hit him like a storm. Zellar was in on the planning, but he was too much of a coward to come and fight with the others. Teeg San Gerxon confirmed his death for us," Erland added.

"How did he confirm the death?" Lissa folded her arms across her chest.

"We got the head. Wylend placed it in stasis and locked it in the treasury."

"You got the head? Gross," Lissa muttered.

"Best way we have of making a positive ID," Erland replied. "It got knocked around a little in an explosion, if I hear correctly. Teeg managed to get it somehow and sent it to us."

"And what does Teeg San Gerxon get out of all this?" Lissa asked, feeling a bit grumpy.

"He wants to meet with Wylend sometime soon. He also wants in on the take-down of the Hazlan Clan." Erland handed the note to Norian. Lendill moved so he could read over Norian's shoulder.

"We should allow it, in my opinion." Ildevar Wyyld appeared in Norian's office. "Hello, child, are you well?" He smiled at Norian. "Lissa," he nodded respectfully to her, "always a pleasure."

"How are we going to work this? Can we just allow someone from outside the Alliance to skip right in and do what he pleases?" Lendill looked at Norian. Erland coughed politely.

"We do it already," Norian jerked his head at Erland's words. Erland maintained his Karathian citizenship, although his marriage to Lissa granted citizenship on Le-Ath Veronis as well.

"Then we need to lay some ground rules," Lendill grumped.

"I hesitate to place too stringent a leash on him—he's managed to capture more rogues in five years than we have in decades," Wylend pointed out carefully. He had no desire to anger the Head of the ASD or his second-in-command.

"Tory and Ry have already worked with him—they have respect for him," Lendill grudgingly admitted. "And he isn't a San Gerxon by birth. Haven't been able to tell just who he was before Arvil adopted him, but we're still doing research."

"What if he succeeds in setting up the Campiaan Alliance?" Lissa asked. "Will they compete with the Reth Alliance?"

"How? They are already self-sufficient," Ildevar pointed out. "They get no legal goods from the Alliance, and we get none from them."

"But the black market thrives," Norian observed dryly.

"As it always will. Think you, child, that it will ever die completely? If the Campiaan Alliance becomes a reality, perhaps we will be able to hammer out trade agreements that will protect both sides while allowing legal trade of what we do desire. Imagine getting Gishi fruit easily and inexpensively." Ildevar smiled indulgently at his heir.

"I'd go for that," Lendill nodded. He loved Gishi fruit and had only gotten it when an illegal shipment had been confiscated in the occasional raid. His father loved it too, and managed to get it now and then.

"And we almost got a promise from Teeg San Gerxon to look for Reah and Gavril if they're out there somewhere. Chances are that rogues have both of them, and since he's hunting the rogues, he might come across them. Of course, he and Reah have some history, but I'm hoping that doesn't keep him from treating her well if he finds her."

"I think he'll treat her well," Tory folded in and put an arm around Lissa. "Sorry, Mom, Ry was listening in and he sent mindspeech. I couldn't help myself."

"Where is your brother? I swear, I should have kept that restraint on him. Now he listens to everything." Lissa sounded grumpy but Tory gave her an extra squeeze and she smiled up at him.

"As I was saying, none of you saw the way he'd look at her. I know he jerked San Gerxon's wealth away from her, but her claim would have been voided anyway, since she was indirectly connected to

Arvil's death. Teeg just managed to separate himself from all that so he'd have it free and clear."

"And now he's building an Alliance," Norian tossed Wylend's note on his desk. "Set up a meeting, Wylend. As soon as possible. If that perverted piece of shit warlock Nidris Hazlan intends to drain Alliance worlds, I want to know about it and I want to send everything we have against him and his family."

~

"Reah, how are you feeling?"

"Awful." I did feel that way. Didn't feel like moving or doing anything else. Jes had already come to see me in Teeg's solarium, asking if I felt like getting a little exercise. I'd snapped at him and he'd slunk away.

"Baby, it has been two days. Surely you should feel better by now."

"Teeg, I don't feel good. I'm sorry." I pulled the cool pack off my eyes and glared at him.

"We need to get you up and around quickly. Whatever you did for Shillverr needs to be done for two other worlds. They'll die if you don't, baby. I already sent Stellan and Celestan to Roorthi and Xordthe. They're in the same shape. We're still trying to figure out how you plugged the leak in the core to keep the energy from draining out, but we need to do it again. Jes says you should be good to go in an eight-day. I was hoping for sooner than that."

"Teeg, are you trying to kill me? Is that what you want? I don't have anything—you're not going to collect insurance money or anything when I die."

"Baby, don't even talk about that," Teeg growled softly. I was too tired to point out that he'd gotten his wealth and position from Arvil's death. If he hoped to capitalize on mine, he needed to think again.

"How is Gavril?" Teeg hadn't given me any information in days.

"Gavril is fine, if a little frustrated. He's learning woodworking," Teeg said. "Not something he planned to do with his life, apparently."

"Gavril is probably the smartest person I know," I placed the cool pack over my eyes again and leaned back in my chair. "I hope he gets away from you."

"He won't. Neither will you," Teeg whispered. "We need you up and around in three days, Reah. Do Xordthe and Roorthi for me and I'll let you see him."

I was up and sputtering, letting the cool pack drop to the floor in a wet sounding plop. "Teeg, don't dangle that in front of me," I wanted to shout at him, only I was still too tired. "Don't promise that and then pull it away from me." I was crying and I didn't mean to do that.

"You love him that much?"

"He's my best friend, what do you think?" I hugged myself and turned away from Teeg. The building housing Teeg's apartment on Shillverr wouldn't support a pool at this level, but he had a beautiful water fountain in the solarium that rippled over natural stone. Water lilies and other plants grew in the shallow expanse. I went to sit on the flat rocks that bordered it, trying to get my tears under control. Would he allow me to see Chash? Would he? It was almost too much to hope for.

"Baby, I see you love him a lot. Hold onto that, all right? Do Roorthi and Xordthe for me and you'll see Gavril. I promise." I nodded, still not trusting myself to speak. "I'll get Jusef to bring something for you." Teeg's footsteps walked away from me.

"I have the answer from Teeg San Gerxon," Erland said. He'd asked Lissa to arrange a meeting with Norian and Lendill.

"Well?" Norian didn't want to waste any time guessing.

"He says he can arrange something in fifteen days. And he says to bring Lissa. Says he'll have a gift for all of us," Erland waved the note Teeg had sent to Wylend.

"Do you think he'll bring more rogues with him?" Lendill asked.

"No idea. But he does have some stipulations."

"Of course he does," Norian visibly deflated. But if San Gerxon could bring in anyone on Norian's wanted list, he would be more than happy to hand over a few concessions.

"Wylend had to think carefully about some of these," Erland said. "But he's willing to allow it, since Wilffox and Wilffin Hardlow pulled their strings and got them into trouble before."

"Who are you talking about?" Norian asked.

"The brothers Starr," Erland said. "Astralan, Stellan, Celestan and Galaxsan. Powerful warlocks who fell in with the Hardlows. Now they work for Teeg and seem to be redeeming themselves. Wylend is going to suspend their criminal status on a trial basis, unless they get into trouble again. He'll lower the hammer if that happens."

"And what does Teeg San Gerxon want from us?" Norian lifted an eyebrow at the warlock.

"To suspend the criminal status of the reptanoids. He says they work for him and they wouldn't have committed any crimes if they hadn't been threatened and mistreated," Erland said. "You know how Reah feels about them."

"She threatened me if I hurt any of them," Lendill snorted.

"Exactly. Teeg wants a clean record for all eight of them, and their names are on this list," Erland *Pulled* a list into his hand and handed it to Norian.

"Who gave out these names?" Norian looked at all eight, shaking his head in confusion. "Does he plan to bring them when he comes?"

"I think so—he wants bodyguards, I think, just in case."

"I would do the same," Lendill muttered.

"Arrange to have Ry and Tory come with Lissa—since they've worked with Teeg before. Where are we meeting him?" Norian asked.

"He says he'll meet you at the space station, in the private rotunda reserved for visiting dignitaries," Erland said. "Wylend and I intend to be there, with our own guards. Lissa will probably bring Gavin, Tony and the Falchani twins. Gardevik will likely be there as well. I don't think anything will get past them, including the Starr brothers and the reptanoids."

"They really turn to lion snake?" Norian wondered idly.

"Reah said they did," Lendill nodded. "She also said their speech wasn't perfect—that something happened when they were created. I wish she were here so we could ask questions."

"Lendill, we all wish for that," Norian grumbled. "And for Gavril to come home to Lissa. She hasn't been the same since his disappearance. If anything happens to that boy, she'll go crazy and Gavin with her."

~

"Little squirrel, don't do this if you're not ready." Lenden whispered to me after Astralan set us down inside a house on the outskirts of Kristl, a city on Roorthi. Teeg didn't own this one—he was borrowing it from a Roorthi businessman who'd been quite happy to allow us to use his summer home. It was late fall on Roorthi anyway, and the owner was embroiled in business deals in the capital city nearly two hundred clicks away.

"Lenden," I said.

"Call me Em-pah," he corrected gently.

"Em-pah, I have to do this." I did—Teeg had promised I'd see Gavril. I wanted that more than anything. I'd suffer through days of debilitation for just a hug from Chash.

"We'll do it tomorrow—we'll try to get her built up a little more today before we start," Jes said. He'd been fussing around me ever since I apologized for snapping at him. I didn't know what to do with his mindless devotion; it was starting to scare me, to be honest. Lenden wasn't sure what to think about it either, but he didn't say anything. He was only a bodyguard, after all, even if he had adopted me. Jusef was also protective, but not in the smothering manner that Jes displayed.

If I thought it might get me anywhere, I'd ask Teeg to send Jes back to Campiaa. There wasn't much chance of that—Jes was the only physician Teeg employed. Jes had already told me that. Farzi and Nenzi were also beginning to be wary around Jes, but knew not to say anything. They had no desire to upset Teeg. Neither did I, in case he withheld my visit with Gavril.

"How's the tummy?" Jusef asked. "Feel like a snack?"

"Jusef, someday I'll cook for you," I promised. He was very good at what he did—Lenden said that Jusef had been cooking for a long time. Jusef could work in any of Desh's restaurants and be comfortable there, I think. He never served anything that would sit heavily on my stomach, preparing lighter fare that was nourishing and very good at the same time. Plenty of fresh fruit and vegetables found their way into the menu, as did nutritious soups and stews. Now he pushed a plate of tiny sandwiches toward me as I settled at the kitchen island.

Farzi and Nenzi consented to share my snack, so Jusef made more for the others, who came to sit with us. Teeg's communicator buzzed while we ate.

"What is it, Dee?" He asked. I hadn't heard that name before.

"His assistant," Farzi said softly, grabbing another small sandwich from the tray.

"The assistant I wasn't allowed to meet," I whispered back, bumping my shoulder against Farzi's. He smiled at me and bit into his food. Now I had a name to go with the title.

"Teeg, that woman is causing trouble," the voice said. Teeg could see the image—I sat too far away to get any of it. All I could do was listen in.

"Ardalin? What's she doing?"

"Hired someone to hurl a few blastbombs at the palace," the voice said. "We have the culprits but we haven't located her yet."

"How much damage?" Teeg was cursing under his breath while his assistant spoke.

"Not much; the guards didn't let them get close enough to do anything more. Some burn marks on the western wall and the lawn is torn up."

"Keep looking for the bitch," Teeg growled. "And keep those bastards locked up. I may come and question them myself."

"Probably what she's hoping for," the voice replied.

"Well, she can keep on hoping. If I find her, well, we'll take care of that." Teeg ended the call. I could have told him Ardalin might cause trouble. Her eyes and expression said as much the day he sent her out the door. Teeg got up and walked through the house, heading for the door, raking a hand through his dark hair as he stalked away.

"Reah, not be upset," Nenzi whispered. I suppose my shocked expression had worried the reptanoids.

"Eat," Lenden said gently, tapping my plate. I went back to my food.

"Will this do?" Teeg, Lenden, Astralan and Jes had brought me to a small clearing about three clicks away from the house. Once again, I could feel the wrongness around me. I'd have to undress to turn again —I could only do this as Thifilatha.

"This will do, but I need to see the stars overhead," I told him, pulling off my light jacket. Lenden took it from me and waited while I handed him the rest of my clothing. It embarrassed me to have him and the others watch, but what else was I supposed to do? I might do a lot worse if it meant I'd get to see Gavril.

Lenden muttered an oath in a language I didn't recognize when I turned. Tory and his father, Gardevik Rath, had told me how unusual my skin color was while I was Thifilatha. It was gold; skin, scales, talons, even. My hair was still white and my eyes still green. Everything else was golden in color. Settling myself on the dry grass in the clearing, I lifted my head and selected the star from which I could *Pull* energy. Taking deep breaths to calm myself and prepare for what was to come, I coaxed the power away from the star.

"I felt it—the core's energy filling in and then getting sealed off," Astralan's voice held wonder, even as Lenden and Jes attempted to wake Reah. Still in Thifilatha, just as before, she lay sprawled across the dead grass in the clearing while Lenden called her name, begging her to wake.

"I hope it's easier for her to handle this time," Teeg muttered to the eldest of his warlocks.

"Same here; the longer we wait, the worse it gets," Astralan agreed. "Do we have everything set up for the meeting in twelve days?"

"Yes. And I have the writ from Karathia, releasing the criminal status for you and your brothers. You're free men, as of this moment. Of course, they say if you break the laws again, you'll be hunted, just as you were before."

"Won't be doing that unless you ask," Astralan said. "And it will only be if *you* ask."

"Let's hope it never comes to that," Teeg sighed. "Come on; let's go see if we have better luck than those two." Teeg walked toward Reah's Thifilatha.

"I wish there was some way to get you changed back without having to leave you out on that cold ground for such a long time," Jes grumbled as he examined me the following morning. They'd brought me home just before dawn—it had taken clicks to wake me and get me to turn. I'd been sick again, just as before, so they let me heave outside before bringing me home and cleaning me up.

Somebody washed me—I was asleep through all of it so I couldn't really say who. Jusef had prepared a jumble complete with the usual vitamins. My hand shook as I tried to suck some of it through the straw, so Nenzi was there, helping me hold the glass. Teeg had disappeared for a while—I hadn't seen him since I'd gotten back. I'd been unconscious most of that time, so he could have shared the bed and I wouldn't have known.

"Nenzi," I leaned my head on his shoulder and closed my eyes in weariness.

"Rest, Reah," he whispered. "This keep." He set the glass on the bedside table.

"We will watch, make sure she drinks," Farzi crawled onto the bed with me. Jes didn't want to argue with any of the reptanoids. Before I fell asleep, I heard him close the bedroom door behind him as he left.

"We will keep Reah," Farzi said softly. I let sleep take me.

"That's all I know," Yiri whimpered. "She said somebody else helped with the money." Teeg paced in front of Yiri inside a holding cell.

"Where is she?" Teeg demanded for the third time.

"If I knew, I'd tell you. She did this to us," Yiri was shivering under Teeg's unforgiving stare. "She only said she wanted to hurt you, because you hurt her. I don't know what the other one wanted."

"He doesn't know anything," Teeg growled in frustration. "Dee, see if he has any records anywhere. We'll punish to the fullest extent."

"Already done," Teeg's dark-haired assistant handed over the comp-vid he'd been holding.

"So, you and your brother are wanted for arson by the Alliance?" Teeg's smile spread slowly across his face.

"Don't send us there. Please."

"Well, you and your brother should have considered this before you accepted the job, don't you think?" Teeg's voice was almost pleasant. Almost.

"Should have had better sense than to attack Teeg San Gerxon," Astralan snapped. "Are you as brainless as I think you are?"

"Probably more so," Dee said cheerfully. "Shall we pack them up for your trip?"

"Sure. We'll take a cage full," Teeg said.

"We need to put the bloom back in your cheeks, pretty girl," Jes was back and fussing again. Why did he upset me so much? I couldn't really put a finger on it. Farzi and Nenzi helped me to the solarium and I was paging through a book on the comp-reader I'd been given. Nothing seemed to hold my interest and I felt listless at best. Jusef brought a jumble for me and set it down on the tiny table next to my chaise.

Teeg had been gone for two days without a word. More than anything, I wanted to skip away. Tory, Aurelius and Lendill would treat me so much better than this. The only thing that kept me from storming out of Teeg's apartment in a fit was the promise of the visit with Gavril.

"Jusef, you make wonderful jumbles, but I don't know if I can drink this," I rubbed my stomach as I gave him an imploring look.

"Just try—perhaps you'll feel better after a few sips," he coaxed, his bushy eyebrows wiggling. It made me think of Morwin for a moment and I smiled.

"There it is—the first smile in days," Jusef sounded happy.

"Is she feeling better?" Lenden came out to check.

"We're trying," Jusef said. Jes moved away and I released a breath I hadn't realized I was holding.

"Little squirrel, start drinking that thing for Em-pah. All right?" Lenden tapped the glass I held. He put an arm around me while I sipped.

"Do you think this is shielded enough?" Garde allowed a tiny bit of sarcasm to coat his words. Erland laughed. "I know it doesn't affect you in the least, but Wylend and I want to make sure this visit isn't a trap of some kind. Admit it—we'll have some very important people in this room."

"Important to us if no one else," Garde agreed.

"They won't get out of here unless we allow it," Erland added. "If Teeg brings the brothers Starr, well, they'd better mind their manners."

"Those reptanoids could cause some damage if they come," Garde reminded the warlock.

"Already thought of that. We have spells that will activate if they turn. They'll be trussed up in a black net. You don't get out of that until we let you out."

"Warlock, you frighten me at times."

"Not just a pretty face anymore, am I?"

"Haven't ever thought of you in those terms," Garde slapped Erland on the back, nearly knocking him over.

"Perhaps I should allow those Falchani to teach me bladework," Erland straightened with difficulty. "I might be able to match you physically in that way."

"Warlock, why are you worried about that? We are what we are. We each have our strengths."

"What about weaknesses?" Erland turned back to Gardevik Rath.

"Do we have any?" Garde laughed. Erland barely moved away in time to avoid a second slap to the back.

"You've tapped into the core. Did I not warn you against that? What are you intending to do, destroy everything?" Fardris glared at his oldest son, Nidris. "I allowed you to stay with us and this is how you repay our hospitality. By starting the drain on Tulgalan's core. We like it here. Now, this means we have to move in less than ten years."

"Zellar said it was all right to only tap a little here and there," Nidris whined.

"Have you been living in a cave the past fifty years? Nidris, he's killed countless worlds. All dead now—drained lifeless and entire populations killed off because he engaged in forbidden sorcery. Why do you think it's forbidden if it's harmless? If you want a case in point, go directly to Cloudsong. That world is wasted, now. Zellar did that. I should never have listened to that liar. He's the one who convinced me that Wylend and his handful of cronies didn't have enough power to stand against us when we took the throne away from Warlend. Only he was wrong. Yet you, against my wishes, went searching for him. If I'd known that's what you intended, I'd have killed you myself. I lost three children because of Zellar. Now, there's a price on all our heads." Fardris' chest was heaving, he was so angry. Tulgalan, his new home, was now doomed because of his own son.

Nidris stared at his father. He'd never seen Fardris Hazlan so upset before. Had Zellar lied to him and the others? He knew most of them were dead—Yebri, who remained on Xordthe, had told him. Yebri had sounded frightened when she'd passed the news on to him—only she and Nidris were still alive. Yebri had already curtailed the draining of the core on Xordthe—she'd said the same thing that Fardris was saying—that Zellar had lied to all of them. Now, Xordthe would die, as Tulgalan would die. Nidris shivered. He would murder if it gained him something, but countless millions and no gain—even he worried over that. Nidris was glad he'd sold Zellar to the Alliance and to the others hunting the old rogue. Nidris had thought to set himself up in Zellar's place. Now, he only wanted to remain hidden until he could feel safe again.

"Father, let us move from here, then," Nidris suggested.

"No. I have a place here and money coming in. We'll work for another five years and then leave. Tulgalan will certainly be feeling the effects by then and more money might be made. The Alliance will get as many off-world as possible, but there are always those who will not wish to come to the attention of the Alliance. We will transport them away and fill our coffers at the same time. Perhaps we can go outside the Alliance when we leave here—surely Teeg San Gerxon will have turned his attention elsewhere by that time."

"I'm thankful he can't reach us here," Nidris agreed. "The Alliance doesn't know to hunt us—we should be safe."

I wasn't about to tell Teeg how shaky I felt when we landed on Xordthe. A meeting with Gavril would be mine if I could get through this. I only hoped that I'd have enough strength to give Chash a hug when the meeting did come. I was desperate to feel better so I could, in Teeg's words, "heal the planet" the following day.

"Baby, if there was any other way," Teeg pulled me against him that night. He hadn't attempted to have sex—I was too drained and weary and he was too worried about something. Several mornings I'd wakened to his touch—he'd stroke my cheek as if he could coax color into it, somehow. The few times I'd bothered to look in a mirror, I'd appeared washed out and worn, so I stopped looking. I only dressed in the comfortable fleece outfits Teeg had purchased for me, wrapping up in an extra jacket or blanket whenever I could. I constantly felt cold, even in warm places.

"You said that before," I mumbled a response to Teeg's statement, closing my eyes. His arms were warm and tight around me as he kissed the spot behind my ear—the one that in better times would nearly send me into a climax.

"Reah, if things were different, you have no idea what I'd do," he whispered gently. I fell asleep with his breath tickling my ear.

"I think this is the place where the tapping occurred—Astralan and I want to see if it will be easier to do this at that precise location," Teeg said as he led me to another clearing. This one hadn't been cleared until recently—a house and surrounding courtyard had been destroyed so I could sit on the bare patch of ground and pull star energy to Xordthe. Piles of rock, lumber and most of a roof surrounded me as I began removing my clothing, barely listening to what Teeg had to say. Lenden took my clothes just as before, but Jes was hovering. Farzi and Nenzi were trying to keep him back while I undressed and turned.

"Reah," Teeg stood below me as I settled into a cross-legged position in full Thifilatha. I turned my attention to what he had to say. "Reah," he repeated, "please don't hurt yourself. Or—well. Just don't hurt yourself. All right?"

"Teeg, move away," I sighed. "Let's get this over with." I turned my head toward the night sky and selected a star.

"We should have thought of this before," Teeg raked a hand through his hair. Reah woke in half the time it had previously taken. She'd been ill again, true, but not nearly as long. A direct route to the tapped core had turned out to be the best solution. Reah slept now—Lenden, Jes and Jusef had managed to get something into her stomach after settling her in bed. Farzi and Nenzi had slid onto the bed on either side as lion snakes. They were worried about Reah too, they just weren't vocal about it. Lenden had been casting questioning looks at Teeg for several days now. He didn't like it any more than Teeg did.

"We have three days," Teeg said. "Three days to get Reah on her feet as well as we can. We'll be traveling after that. Jes, you'll go to Campiaa and work with Dee. The warlocks, Farzi, his brothers and Lenden and Jusef are coming with me."

"Where are you going?" Jes didn't like the idea that he wasn't included in the trip. "Who will take care of Reah?"

"Jes, you have to trust me. I have someone in mind where we're going who will watch over her until we can come back to Campiaa. All right? I don't know how long this trip will take, but I'll keep Dee informed. You can get updates from him. In the meantime, take some time off and relax a little. You've been working too hard."

Jes still didn't like it and he walked away muttering. "You need to watch him," Lenden said quietly.

"He's my physician and devoted to me and mine. Don't question me," Teeg snapped. Lenden turned away so Teeg wouldn't see the curl of smoke escaping his nostrils. It didn't happen often with Lenden—he could control it most of the time. It still escaped now and then, showing anyone who might know just what he was. Farzi was watching the entire exchange with a worried frown. He sided with Lenden on this, but there wasn't any way he could say that to Teeg.

"Baby, today's the day. We're traveling and you'll see Gavril when we get where we're going," Teeg threw open the curtains that faced our bed. I was blinking stupidly at him—he hadn't said a word the past two days about Gavril and I thought he'd lied to me about the whole thing. I'd been more depressed than usual as a result.

"Where?" I sat up, rubbing my eyes. I was still exhausted and only my will to get up and around had gotten me out of bed since I'd healed Xordthe.

"No, you know better than to ask that question, baby," Teeg was in a good mood for the first time in a long time. "Get up and I'll have Farzi and Nenzi help you in the shower." He knew I couldn't stand long enough to bathe myself.

The last two days I'd soaked in a tub while someone washed me. Farzi and Nenzi had done it the first day. Jes had elbowed everyone else aside the day before and done it. I hadn't appreciated the way his hands lingered here and there while he washed. Teeg had gone off on some errand with Astralan and hadn't gotten back until late the night before. Now, he was up early and getting me up as well.

"I don't want Jes' help," I muttered, causing Teeg to turn around quickly.

"I've already sent him to Campiaa. He saved your life after the explosion, so don't badmouth him to me, Reah. I know you don't feel good and you're grumpy because of it. Farzi and Nenzi will come and help you." He stalked out of the bedroom. I wanted to stick my tongue out at his retreating back, just like any angry six-year-old. Farzi and Nenzi came in moments later, helping me bathe and dress.

Teeg was dressed very nicely in an expensive suit, as were the warlocks—all four of them. Farzi, Nenzi and their six brothers were also dressed very well, only a bit more comfortably than Teeg and the others. Lenden wore what he usually wore—comfortable slacks and a nice shirt. Jusef wore the traditional garb any Amterean might wear—short trousers, boots with socks and a short tunic with a vest. I leaned down just a little to kiss Jusef's cheek. He smiled when I did it. Teeg had selected a high-waisted dress for me; Farzi and Nenzi had gotten me into the deep blue, long-sleeved thing and then slipped low-heeled shoes on my feet. My hair was combed out and left loose about my shoulders.

"Lenden, you stand behind Reah. Make sure she doesn't get too tired," Teeg nodded to the bodyguard as Astralan and Stellan made preparations to fold us and our luggage to some unnamed destination. I was hoping that Chash would be waiting for me when we arrived. I only wanted to fling my arms around him and cry happy tears.

"Ready?" Astralan nodded at Teeg.

Teeg straightened his cuffs and tie. "Ready," he nodded, a determined look in his eye. He looked as if he were going off to battle and I didn't understand that. Astralan folded all of us; Stellan brought the luggage. We landed in a sumptuous, round hall built of marble and expensive tiles. I gasped. I knew this place and knew it well. Had departed from it several times when Lendill didn't want anyone else to know I was leaving and he didn't want me to skip away. We stood in the rotunda reserved for visiting dignitaries on Le-Ath Veronis' space station.

Lissa and Tory were there, standing next to Ry and I cried out when I saw them. But that didn't prepare me for what came next. Nothing could have prepared me for that. Nothing. Lissa walked toward Teeg, a puzzled frown on her face. Gavin, Tony, Drake and Drew were right beside her. Her eyes widened after a moment and she shrieked one word. That word sent me into a tailspin and darkness gathered around me when I heard it the second time. "Gavril!" Lissa shouted, flinging herself into Teeg's arms. "Gavril!" Blackness came.

CHAPTER 8

"Tory, be careful," Teeg, once known as Gavril Montegue, cautioned his brother. "Reah's pregnant. It's probably yours." Tory jerked his head around at Teeg's words. He was having trouble reconciling what his mother had known immediately by scent alone. Teeg was Gavril. Only much older, now. And, like Kifirin had said, changed. Nobody had recognized him, although his hair and eye color were the same. Tory, Karzac and Lenden were kneeling next to Reah—Lenden had caught her before she could fall. Gardevik was standing nearby and blowing smoke—he knew Lenden, all right. Only by another name.

"We've exhausted her," Denevik muttered to Karzac as Karzac growled about Reah's condition. Lissa had finally stopped hugging and kissing her youngest child, who no longer looked to be the youngest. Lendill Schaff was also kneeling nearby; he just couldn't get any closer than he was already with the crowd around Reah. Norian, Erland and Wylend had gone straight to Gavril.

"How did this happen, son?" Gavin was attempting to deal with the changes in his child.

"Long story, Dad. Can we sit down somewhere after we make sure

Reah is all right? And just so you know, I won't be giving her up. She's the reason I'm where I am anyway." Eventually, when Karzac said that Reah could be moved, Tory lifted her and everyone was folded to Lissa's palace.

~

"I knew, when I was twelve," Gavril turned the cup in his hands. His four warlocks were just as surprised as the others, so they listened raptly to Gavril's tale. The reptanoids had gone with Reah and those taking care of her.

"What did you know?" Lissa asked.

"That I wanted Reah. It might have been puppy love at the time, but it was there. And it didn't go away over the next five years. When she got into that mess on Birimera, I asked Kifirin if I could help her. Told him I wanted her. Wanted to keep her safe, somehow. He looked at me with those damned stars in his eyes and told me there wasn't anything I could do for her at the moment, but the time would come and he would grant my request. He granted it, all right. Pulled me right off the transport and stuck me with a vampire to learn woodworking fifty years in the past. You see where I am, now. All his doing. He pointed me in this direction, told me it was in our best interest to do this and then left. I won't be asking him for anything again. Now, I don't know how Reah is going to take this when she wakes. I'm telling you again, though, that I'm not giving her up. We just need to take care of her."

"She's pregnant with a female High Demon. Karzac says so. Did you even take that into consideration?" Gardevik was trying to reel in his temper. They sat in Lissa's library, where tea and a light lunch had been served.

"I knew she was pregnant," Gavril muttered. "I kept telling myself that this wouldn't take long and I'd send her back so she'd get the care she needs."

"The fate of the High Demon race rests on any female born," Garde's voice was getting louder. "Even a quarter High Demon child.

Were you trying to kill Reah? Karzac says she's so weak it could take a while to get her back to normal."

"It couldn't be helped, Uncle Garde," Gavril said. "Do you know what she can do? Do you? Those fool rogues tapped the cores on Roorthi, Xordthe and Shillverr. Somehow, Reah pulled energy from the stars, replaced what was lost and sealed the leak. Those worlds will live, now. Reah can do that. It's like a miracle. And no, I'm not giving up the idea of the Campiaan Alliance. It's a good idea and almost within my grasp. Things are lining up. Mom, I'm going to do this. I'm sixty-seven now and this is my calling. I know it."

"Reah can heal the cores?" Wylend hadn't spoken until now, although his mind and his heart were with her in the suite she shared with Tory.

"Go and see for yourself," Astralan spoke for the first time. "Teeg—Gavril and I were shocked when she did it the first time."

"I can't believe she did that and risked the child," Garde muttered.

"She doesn't know. That she's pregnant," Gavril sighed. "She thinks that stupid implant the Alliance forces on its troops is still working. It's probably like everything else—wears off quicker due to her High Demon ancestry."

"You knew the baby belonged to Tory?" Lissa was trying to come to grips with being a grandmother.

"I was pretty sure, mom. I think he's ruined her for anybody else."

"I don't call that ruined," Garde began to rise in anger.

"Garde, settle down," Lissa hissed. "This will be our grandchild. Don't fuck it up."

"I want to talk to Denevik. Reah is his grandchild, after all," Garde didn't sit back down.

"I didn't know who he was. Kifirin just showed up out of nowhere and told me to hire him as a bodyguard. So I did. I'm glad he didn't remove my head over Reah." Gavril sipped his tea.

"I instructed him to keep you safe, as well as his grandchild," Kifirin appeared as if someone had called his name.

"We are going to have words later," Lissa handed him a hard stare.

"I saw the wisdom in the request; it just wasn't at his convenience," Kifirin defended himself.

"I'll show you wisdom," Lissa tried to go after him. Gavin held her back.

"I knew my mate would be justifiably angry," Kifirin stated. "Lissa, please try to see this from my perspective. This was an opportunity none of us could refuse. Imagine the Campiaan Alliance, run by your child."

"I'm still coming after your ass," Lissa muttered.

"Mom, we're trying to make this into a good thing. Give us credit for that much, at least," Gavril begged. "We're cleaning it up as quickly as we can."

"Reah? Reah, wake up for me, sweetheart." I knew that voice. Couldn't reconcile it with where I'd been for the past three moon-turns.

"Karzac?" I opened my mouth before opening my eyes. Didn't want the disappointment of not seeing my friend and healer when I did.

"I'm here, sweetheart. Open your eyes for me. Can you do that?" I blinked up at Karzac's face. "There she is. Little girl, you need to take better care of yourself and that baby. I think Garde's got her named already."

"Baby?" I was about to panic. Who said anything about a baby? Karzac had to be wrong. Had to be.

"Tory's daughter," Karzac said.

"Nooo," I moaned.

"Baby, it'll be all right. Your Em-pah will help take care of her," Lenden was there. "Little squirrel, I really am your Em-pah. I'm Denevik Lith, baby. If you don't believe me, ask Gardevik. He knows. Jayd and Glinda are on their way. I haven't seen Glinda in fifteen hundred years or more."

"Reah, do not faint again," Karzac muttered. "Do not place more on her right now. Do not," he snapped at the others. The healer had spoken and everybody else was backing off.

"Aurelius?" I was nearly in tears, now.

"They're trying to get him back—he's off on assignment. Jeral offered to take his place so he could come see you, baby," Tory put an arm beneath me and helped me sit up.

"I removed the birth control implant—it was completely drained," Karzac said, handing me a drink. Now I knew why they'd been shoving those things at me for weeks—they'd all known I was pregnant and neglected to tell me.

"Where are Farzi and Nenzi?" I demanded.

"Here, our Reah," Farzi and Nenzi came to stand behind Tory. "All here. We not leave."

"I don't suppose any of you would bite Teeg for me?" I wiped tears away. Of all the betrayals, that hurt the most. How had he done this? How could he be Gavril? I couldn't call him Chash. Would never call him that. Ever. How had he been in two places at once? It made my head hurt.

"No. He save us. Like Reah save us," Nenzi said softly.

"Karzac, when will I feel good again?" I covered my eyes with a hand.

"Not for a few days at the least," Karzac pulled my hand away. "Reah, don't let this bother you. Lissa has sent mindspeech; this involves Kifirin somehow. Do not blame Gavril overmuch. Wait and talk to him before you worry over this."

"Keep him away from me," I muttered.

"Kifirin?"

"Gavril."

~

"She's asleep," Tory spoke softly as Wylend and Lendill entered the bedroom. They'd put her in Tory's bed. It was his baby. He was trying to come to terms with the fact that he'd fathered a child.

"That's only natural, son," Gardevik followed Lendill inside. He'd read his son's mind easily.

"I need her up as quickly as possible—my father is demanding that

I marry her on the family grounds," Lendill sighed, sitting heavily on the side of the bed. "She looks so pale." He stroked Reah's hair carefully.

"Your father? I didn't know you had one," Wylend smiled at Lendill.

"Oh, I have one, all right. He makes his presence known upon occasion."

"Not wake Reah," Nenzi called from a corner of the room.

"Is that?" Lendill peered into Nenzi's corner. Nenzi and Farzi were still humanoid, the others that came forward with them were all lion snakes.

"They, uh, won't leave. Karzac said she needed to be watched over so they are her self-appointed guards."

"We guard Reah since before she marry Teeg." Farzi pointed out.

"We'll have to get used to that," Wylend sighed. "Who gave him that name anyway?"

"No idea. Ry's coming in—he and I want to wrestle with our little brother," Tory said.

"I wouldn't try too hard—I think Teeg San Gerxon might show all of you a thing or two," Garde pointed out.

"No try to harm Teeg. He will show you," Farzi said.

"Norian, I know you can fold," Gavril argued. "Mom did that for you when Ildevar Wyyld let her out of being Liaison ten years ago. We'll go, check to see whether the core has been tapped and come back." Lissa, Gavin, Tony, Norian and Lendill were all inside Lissa's study, with Astralan and Stellan. Galaxsan and Celestan were preparing Gavril's suite. The reptanoids had refused to budge from Reah's and Tory's suite. Denevik was talking with Jayd and Glinda over a late meal.

"You can tell that quickly? About the core?" Norian asked. He'd had to use sensitive scientific equipment that could take days to determine if the core was weakened.

"We know what to look for," Astralan replied. "It's a power leak and we can feel it."

"Then let's all go," Lissa stood. "I don't want my son out of my sight so soon, even if he does look older than he did before. I don't know how Tory and Ry failed to see this." She ran fingers through Gavril's hair.

"Mom, they weren't looking for this. I was safe at home the whole time they worked with me. Remember?"

"I'm still kicking Kifirin. I don't care how good his motives were," Lissa grumped.

"Mom, there's something else."

"What's that?" Lissa looked up at her son, who was now as tall and broad across the shoulder as his father.

"I had a chip implanted in Reah's collarbone. It keeps her from skipping and sending mindspeech. That's how I kept her with me the past three months. I don't want to remove it until she's comfortable with all this. I don't think we need to go hunting for her after she skips away because she's pissed at me. Not while she's pregnant, anyway."

"So, that's how you did it. Gavril, I'm not sure how I feel about that. Aurelius may pound you and I can't say that I'd blame him."

"Aurelius?" Stellan asked.

"Former vampire. Works with a different race, now," Gavril sighed. "You don't want to tangle with any one of those. They *can* beat your head in if you harm their mates."

"Not to mention that he's my sire," Gavin spoke for the first time. He'd been content to listen while he attempted to come to terms with his son being what he was.

"That's not complicated or anything," Astralan snorted.

"Oh, we haven't gotten to the complicated part," Lissa smiled. "Wylend will be asking the moment the ASD lets Reah go, and Lendill will be marrying her as quickly as possible."

"Vice-Director Schaff?" Astralan lifted an eyebrow.

"That would be the one."

"Has Reah consented to all this?" Gavril asked.

"No idea," Lissa said. "Maybe you'd like to ask her?"

"Mom, I think she wants to kill me, right now. And when she discovers I don't want the chip out, well, that'll make it worse."

"Glindarok, he didn't tell me what he planned," Denevik swore. "Tarevik said he wanted to make father see sense—that he or Brenevik could rule if he'd only find a mate for them. That was all I heard. Then Tare asked me to go to the Southern continent to check on our cane farms. That's when he put his plan into action. When I got back, all I could see was the devastation. I had to ask Bren what happened. When he told me, I called him and Tarevik fools. I was ready to kill them both, but they'd kill me first and I knew it. I skipped off the planet and I haven't been back since."

"Rorevik had those two put to death and it wasn't pretty," Garde joined the small group in Lissa's arboretum. "If Kifirin hadn't come to tell us that you weren't involved, I would have killed you the moment you showed up."

"I know." Denevik ran a finger down the glass of wine he'd been served. "I ask that you treat my granddaughter well. She doesn't know anything about any of this."

"Denevik, you are the last of my kin," Glinda placed her hand over his, surprising him into meeting her eyes. "You have no blame in this. Come to Kifirin with us—we will find you a place there."

"My place is with my granddaughter," Denevik sighed.

"She may be joining us—I don't like the idea of a High Demon female being born anywhere except on Kifirin," Jayd said.

"Is Norian Keef going to release her from the ASD? She still has two months' service owed," Glinda pointed out.

"No idea," Garde raked a hand through his wealth of dark-brown hair.

"Farzi, we won't get into trouble, I promise." I was hobbling through Lissa's palace on my way to the kitchen. I wanted something to eat and didn't intend to allow anyone to stop me. Farzi, Nenzi and all their brothers followed me. They'd taken their humanoid shapes again —we didn't want to frighten the guards.

"But Reah needs to rest," Farzi muttered. He didn't like doing this in a strange place. If we'd been on Campiaa, he wouldn't have said a word.

"Farzi, this is where I live," I pointed out. "They won't yell at you, they'll just gripe at me for getting out of bed." We turned the last corner, finding ourselves in Lissa's enormous kitchen. If I'd had more energy, I'd have made sweet rolls. Instead, I put crepes together, stuffing them with fresh fruit and sweet cream.

"This very good," Perzi was eating his portion happily, as were his brothers.

"What is this?" Drake and Drew walked in. I'm sure the palace guards had notified them somehow.

"Crepes—want some?"

"Lissa will kill us and Karzac will kill you," Drew said. "But before that happens, we'll take some." They were served quickly and I climbed back onto my barstool before Karzac came thundering into the room.

"Karzac, I was hungry," I said, trying to turn his wrath aside.

"You may be hungry and someone else may cook," he had his arms crossed angrily over his chest.

"But nobody makes these like this," Drake closed his eyes in pleasure after taking a bite of his dessert.

"There's three more," I lifted a plate in Karzac's direction.

Karzac, curmudgeonly physician that he was, found a place at the island and settled down to eat his crepe. Lissa and Gavin showed up shortly afterward, getting the last two.

"I know we should be upset, but I want to eat this first," Lissa sighed.

"Farzi glad she hungry," Farzi said. "Reah much sick, lately."

"Glinda was, too, when she was pregnant." Garde showed up. He helped Lissa eat her portion. "Every High Demon female I've ever known has had a hard time the first four months."

"It might have helped if somebody had bothered to tell me that's why I was sick all the time," I muttered. "I thought it was because I wasn't fully recovered after the bomb blast."

"I didn't realize we'd find a crowd." Teeg walked in, followed by all four warlocks.

"I'm going to bed," I slid off my stool.

"Reah, you can't ignore me," Teeg said. "We're married, remember?"

"Did you hear something?" I asked Farzi. "If I could only skip, I could get away from the noise." I hobbled toward the wide door that led into the kitchen. Farzi, poor soul, didn't know what to do. He looked from me to Teeg and then back again.

"Stay there, Farzi. I can find my own way." I waved Nenzi back to his seat as well. Teeg was Lissa's son and he had a place here. Tory was also Lissa's son and Teeg's brother. I wasn't about to call Teeg Gavril. He didn't deserve that name. My friend was gone forever, leaving a stranger in his place. As soon as Aurelius arrived, I was going to ask him to take me away from here. I no longer belonged.

"She has two months service left," Norian pointed out to Lendill.

"But she's pregnant. We've let others go early if that happened."

"It's not an official rule," Norian said. "I want them to build up her strength and then have her heal Tulgalan. As soon as that happens, I'll sign the discharge. Not before. Tulgalan is home to seven billion people. Reah can keep them safe."

"Are you prepared for what may happen when you demand this?" Lendill snapped. "Torevik may kill you."

"I'll give him some incentive not to snap me like a twig," Norian huffed.

"And what would that incentive be?"

"I can promise not to bring charges of any kind against his brother."

"I thought you already promised that when you agreed to the meeting. Besides, Lissa will have your head if you charge Gavril with anything."

"Well, maybe this needs a little work, but I still command Reah, pregnant or not. She's going to heal Tulgalan, one way or another."

"Norian, you're going to damage my relationship with her, aren't you?"

"As my Vice-Director, you're obligated to uphold my decisions."

"I haven't disagreed with you until now."

"You want Tulgalan to die?"

"No."

"Then Reah does what I tell her to do."

"Norian?"

"Lendill?"

"*I* may want to kill you."

∾

"Look she already despises me—this will be the last time she has to do anything for the Alliance," Norian snapped. His decision, presented to Lissa, Gavin and two others, hadn't been met with cheerful acceptance.

"It exhausts her," Lissa said. "That can't be good for the baby."

"Karzac said the baby was fine," Norian grumbled. "Besides, we're talking about billions of people here. What's a few days of exhaustion compared to that many lives?"

"Norian, I understand your stake in this, trust me," Lissa held up a hand. "But that poor girl hasn't made a decision for herself her whole life. Now, you're going to do this to her. There's no compensation for this, Norian."

"The ASD and the Alliance owns their conscripts, Lissa. They do as they're told and they go where we send them. It's as simple as that." Norian was frowning at his mate.

"That sounds like slavery and not conscription," Flavio said quietly. He and Aryn were the other two invited to the meeting. Norian had asked Lissa not to include Gardevik—he would see this as an attack upon a High Demon female and her female child—both rarities on Kifirin. Norian and Garde had certainly disagreed on Reah's service to the ASD. Garde had suggested repeatedly that Norian discharge Reah. Argued that Reah was related to royalty. Norian had flatly refused. "The rule is wife, consort or heir to the throne. Reah is none of those things," Norian pointed out bluntly. He and Lendill had gotten good service from Reah over the years. She could do things not many of the others could do. Norian found himself wishing he could convince her to reenlist. He realized that wasn't likely to happen—Lendill wanted to further his claim, as did Wylend Arden. Reah would be consort to the King of Karathia if Wylend had his way. And if Gavril managed to hammer out the Campiaan Alliance as he proposed, well, Reah figured into that as well.

~

"Reah, where are you going?" Tory stood in the doorway to our shared suite as I was about to leave. Getting dressed had nearly worn me out but I was determined to take Farzi, Nenzi and their brothers to Niff's for ice cream.

"I'm taking my friends to Niff's," I said stiffly, trying to get around Tory's wide body.

"Reah, all you have to do is ask—we'll bring you ice cream." Tory was frowning at me.

"Tory, I don't want it brought to me. I want to go to Niff's. Go play with your brother." Yes, I was angry. With all of them. I wanted to do something I wanted to do without having to ask for permission. Teeg had kept me confined—now I wanted my freedom back.

"Reah, you can't just," Tory raked a hand through his hair.

"Torevik Rath, don't tell me what I can or can't do. Teeg's done that enough for the past three months. Go away."

"His name is Gavril, Reah. He's your best friend. You've said that often enough."

"That is not my best friend. I don't know who that is. Go away." I pushed my way past Tory. I felt sorry for Farzi and his brothers—they'd had to stand there while Tory and I argued. They followed me out of the suite, though, while Tory watched us go.

"Always dark here?" Farzi looked around as we stood at the bus stop outside the palace wall.

"Yes," I sighed. "I'd take you to the light half of the planet but they'd come get us for sure."

"Bro, I'm still trying to get used to this," Tory gestured at Gavril's appearance. "But you did something to Reah. She won't call you anything but Teeg and it's usually with contempt in her voice." Tory had sent mindspeech to both his brothers to meet him in the arboretum.

"Look, she's just going to have to deal with this. It can't be helped." Gavril wasn't in the best of moods. Dee had contacted him earlier, telling him that Jes had disappeared and he couldn't locate the physician anywhere, although guards had been sent out to comb through Campiaa City.

"You could have let us know," Ry was still grumpy over the whole thing. Mostly he was angry with himself for not seeing Teeg San Gerxon as anyone but a stranger. But three months of suffering, wondering if Gavril and Reah were still alive rankled quite a bit.

"Back to Reah," Tory snapped. "She's not even supposed to be out of bed, yet she took those reptanoids into Casino City for ice cream."

"You're joking?" Gavril was on his feet in less than a blink.

"Not. She snapped at me and took off with all eight of them trailing along behind her."

"Come on, let's go make sure nobody tries to get close. I have no idea what Farzi or the others will do if they think Reah is being threatened." Gavril folded both his brothers to Niff's.

"Bro, maybe you should have warned us that you can do that," Tory was trying to get himself back in hand after Gavril set him down inside the sweet shop.

"It's not something I do often," Gavril muttered, searching the crowd inside Niff's for Reah and eight reptanoids. Spotting them in a corner at one of the larger tables, Gavril forced his way through the crowd with Ry and Tory right behind him.

~

"This very good, Reah," Nenzi loved his chocolate cookie sundae.

"I like it too," I smiled at Nenzi, although it took an effort to do so. The reptanoids were enjoying themselves, although we received several stares from tourists.

"Reah, what the hell are you doing here?" Teeg had managed to sneak up on me without my noticing. I'd been keeping an eye on the door but I'd missed him, somehow.

"I wanted to treat my friends to ice cream." I wanted to snap at him but I was too tired to make anything other than a weak protest.

"Someone would have taken you," Teeg snapped at me, "if you'd bothered to ask." Well, he wasn't having any weariness issues.

"Do I have to ask you for everything? Still?" I stood and flung out an arm. "Are you and Tory going to dictate every single thing I do from now on? Go away, Teeg. It's over." I stalked past him as best I could.

~

"Farzi, go with her," Gavril sighed as the reptanoids showed confusion over what they should do. "Make sure she gets home—she looks ready to drop."

Farzi and his brothers rose to follow Reah out of Niff's. "Now what?" Tory's gaze was following Reah as she wearily stepped around three customers blocking the door.

"She'll come around," Gavril muttered, heading for the counter and his first taste of Niff's ice cream in more than fifty years.

~

"Farzi, this is my home. I don't come here often and it isn't much," I pressed my thumb against the scanner so the door would open. The reptanoids followed me inside and I closed the door behind Perzi who was the last to troop into the house.

"Reah lives here?"

"I used to. I can again until Aurelius comes home. I'll ask him to take us to the light side so we can see the sun." Wearily I flopped onto a chair in the reception area. This couldn't compete with Lissa's palace or Teeg's home on Campiaa. I had most of my salary in a bank on Le-Ath Veronis—I could support myself and perhaps buy a small restaurant. People would come if the location was right and the food was good. I didn't need Teeg or Tory.

Lendill and Wylend had disappeared. Figuring it was because I was unexpectedly pregnant with Tory's child, I covered my eyes with a hand. "Farzi, you know where the bus stop is—why don't you go find Teeg. That's where you belong—with him. I need to sort out some things by myself." I dropped my hand so he could see that I meant what I'd said.

"Reah? You not feel good?" Nenzi was there, kneeling beside my chair.

"Nenzi, I haven't felt good for a while, sweet man. Leave me alone for a while—I have to think about what to do with my future. I get out of the ASD in two months. Maybe they'll let me go early since I'm pregnant."

"Reah not be with Teeg?" Nenzi sounded lost.

"Nenzi, I don't know how I can. Go on, now. Take the bus back to the palace. I need some time alone."

"I'm telling you, she can fix any core you damaged," Jes informed Yebri Hammal, the rogue Karathian witch. "I watched her heal the one on Xordthe. I got the idea that she pulls the energy from a star or something."

"Why are you coming to me with this information?" Yebri looked suspiciously at Teeg San Gerxon's hired physician.

"Because Teeg has something I want. And Teeg is what my new partner wants," Jes nodded toward the woman who stood next to him. Yebri almost laughed. She couldn't imagine many men wanting that one, especially one as wealthy and powerful as Teeg San Gerxon. She didn't say it, though. If Jes Wurfl was correct about the female High Demon, then Yebri couldn't pass up this opportunity. Nidris would be more than grateful for this information—he'd opened the core on Tulgalan before realizing exactly what damage he'd done. He'd contacted Yebri, telling her his family was quite upset over his mistake. If they could get their hands on the one Jes spoke of, they could repair the damage and no one would be the wiser. Plus, if they kept the female, they could dip into the power of any planet, arranging for their captive to correct it afterward. The prospect was almost too good to be believed.

"Name your price," Yebri said. "I must confer with my partner, but we might come to some sort of arrangement."

"I want the woman after two repairs," Jes said right away.

"And I want Teeg San Gerxon. I want him given to me, as a willing husband. Can you do that for me?" Ardalin Nathil smiled at Yebri.

"I can't believe they came back without her," Tory was about to go Thifilathi. All eight reptanoids had gotten back to the palace after Gavril, Tory and Ry had returned. Minus Reah. Farzi told Gavril that Reah wanted to be alone at her home. Gavril and his brothers had gone straight there, only to learn that Reah had left again.

"Where do you think she is?" Ry was trying to calm Tory, making him think of other things instead of letting his emotions get the better of him and allowing his Thifilathi free rein.

"She might have gone to the light side—Nenzi said she mentioned that," Gavril's anger was rising. He had other things on his mind and didn't need to be chasing after Reah.

"Bro, if you hadn't deactivated her mindspeech," Ry whispered.

She's with me, came mindspeech from Aurelius. *And Gavril, if you ever worry us like that again, we will have words.*

Not to worry, grandfather, Gavril blew out a mental and physical sigh.

"So, Norian, are you just going to drop this bomb on her now?" Lissa glared at the Director of the ASD.

"We only have two months of service left. We have to move quickly on this."

"Don't you think you ought to go hunting the asshole who drained the core? He may still be there and if so, he could tap right back into it after Reah does the repairs." Lissa seldom got information regarding ASD business anymore, though she was mated to Norian.

"We're already on that, Lissa. Do you think I'm stupid?"

"Not stupid. Just blind, sometimes." Lissa turned away from him and stared at the painting behind her desk, not really seeing the beautiful landscape painted by Corot. Merrill had given it to her not long after she'd become Queen of Le-Ath Veronis. *To make up for past mistakes*, he'd said. Both knew it was a peace offering between them. Lissa had accepted.

"Reah, Norian Keef is on his way," Aurelius said gently. I'd fallen asleep, leaning against his shoulder as we sat on the balcony of his home on the light side. Overlooking the Western Ocean, the location was peaceful most of the time, with waves washing ashore instead of pounding it as the Eastern Ocean did at times.

"What does he want?" I rubbed my eyes to wake up. Had Teeg deactivated the implant, I might have received the mindspeech myself. Now, that wasn't an option as long as he held the control.

"To talk to you," Aurelius helped me off the wide, comfortable swing. He'd installed it himself, just so we could sit quietly and watch the ocean when we were together.

"I hope he'll tell me I'm getting discharged early," I grumped. Thankfully, Aurelius didn't have a problem with my unplanned pregnancy and he'd sat beside me, rubbing my slightly protruding belly gently until I'd fallen asleep next to him.

"I hope that too, for your sake and the baby's," Aurelius agreed. "Reah, have you made any plans with Tory? Where will you stay when the baby comes? I think she will need some sunlight, don't you?"

"Auri, is that an invitation?" I smiled up at him. The one mate I had who seemed glad to see me. I couldn't explain any of it.

"If you want it to be." He leaned down to kiss me gently, just as Norian and Lendill folded in. Well, Lendill wasn't high on my current list. I wanted to tell him to go away. Except I couldn't—he was still my boss, just as Norian was.

"Reah, we want to speak with you about your remaining service time," Norian said. "Is there somewhere we can sit?"

CHAPTER 9

"You want her to do what?" Aurelius was up and shouting at Norian Keef. Lendill had remained silent the whole time Norian informed me that he wanted me to heal Tulgalan's core. Too stunned to argue, I sat staring at the Director and Vice-Director while Aurelius yelled. In the end, it did no good whatsoever. Norian said that in two weeks I would be taken to Tulgalan where I would do *whatever it is you do*, he'd snapped, to heal up the weakening core.

Aurelius seemed to be my only champion in this cause and he was waging a hopeless war. I'd learned over the years that when Norian or Lendill made up their minds, you weren't going to change them. Perhaps it made them good at their jobs, but on a personal level, those attitudes could be devastating for their individual agents. The Alliance still owned me—Norian hadn't softened that reality for me.

Lendill still hadn't said anything and now he wouldn't even meet my eyes when he and Norian folded away. What was I going to do? Norian was going to wring every remaining tick from me until my six years were up. Right then, I think I truly hated him and Lendill both.

"Auri, I wish I were anywhere but here right now." I moved to his side, bumping my forehead against his shoulder.

"I know, love. Is there somewhere else you want to go? I'll take you."

"There isn't any place out there that really appeals to me. Nowhere I can go to get away from them. Did they want to make me miserable? Is that what they want?" I felt like crying. Aurelius knew it.

"Love, perhaps I should ask for the healer to come," he said softly, tucking my hair behind an ear. Aurelius must have sent out mindspeech; Karzac was there and cursing under his breath in moments.

"Reah, the baby is fine at the moment—it is still tiny and difficult to harm," Karzac informed me after settling me on Aurelius' wide bed. "Still, I have the urge to bash in the Director's head—he should not be doing this to you. Surely one of the other High Demons has this ability."

"Kifirin says they don't," Lissa folded in. "Norian just wants to flex his ASD muscle." Lissa didn't like this any more than Karzac or I did. "While I realize that billions of lives are at stake on Tulgalan, surely it could have waited another six months."

"I would be out of the ASD by that time," I grumbled.

"Yeah." Lissa nodded as Karzac healed up little aches and pains for me.

"Keep eating good meals," Karzac said. "Don't skip any. Is the nausea subsiding?"

"I think so; I haven't felt queasy in the past few days."

"Good. Let's hope that's a thing of the past," he smiled. "If you feel up to it, I'll allow sex."

"Karzac, stop embarrassing her," Lissa took his arm and folded him away.

"How do you feel?" Aurelius pulled me against him. "Karzac says no biting while you're pregnant, by the way."

"I'm okay," I said, using one of Lissa's slang terms. Aurelius smiled, lifted me up and settled me on his bed.

∾

"Dee, what have you found?" Gavril paced inside his suite while talking with his assistant via communicator.

"Nothing, Teeg. Word has it that Ardalin managed to get off-planet too, before we could stop her. I'm still trying to work out how she managed that."

Gavril cursed at the news. "Any idea where she was headed? We can have someone go after her."

"None. Sorry, Teeg. She was more slippery than we thought she could be."

"What about that female rogue—Yebri? Anything new there?"

"Nothing. It's as if she vanished without a trace. We're still looking, though. Any chance you might send one or two of the warlocks back?"

"I'll send Galaxsan and Celestan," Gavril said. "Maybe they can pick up the trail on Ardalin and Yebri. We're about to leave for Tulgalan—that idiot Nidris has tapped into the core there. I'm hoping he hasn't left yet—that would make my life a bit simpler. Keep looking for Jes—he was upset when I wouldn't bring him with me. Perhaps he's in a snit and just decided to go away for a while without saying anything. Keep trying to reach him on his communicator."

"Will do, boss." Dee terminated the call from his end.

"Fuck," Gavril muttered. "If it isn't one thing, it's another."

"Tory, why are you here? Reah probably needs reassurance from you right now." Garde gave his son a concerned look.

"She's with Aurelius," Tory grumbled. "She didn't even tell me he'd come back—we were afraid she'd disappeared on us until Auri sent mindspeech."

"Well, she doesn't have mindspeech at the moment—have you thought about that?"

"Ry pointed it out to Gav, but he didn't say anything. He doesn't want to remove the chip just because he's afraid she'll run. We might not find her if she does."

"I don't like this even a little," Garde said, holding his anger in check. "Reah doesn't have any way to call for help or to defend herself in that way."

"But Dad, we're here—we can do that for her."

"You're here. Reah isn't," Garde pointed out the obvious. "Jayd wouldn't leave Glinda's side unless she was well-guarded by High Demons. That's a High Demon female child, son. What are you doing to keep her safe?"

"Ah, I was hoping to find you here," Norian folded in. "I just wanted to let you know that Reah will be healing the core on Tulgalan in two weeks."

"No!" Tory and Garde said at the same time. "Tell Reah this is foolish. We can't risk the child," Gardevik was blowing smoke.

"It isn't Reah's decision to make," Norian snapped. "She's still ASD property. I told her she had to. She likes it less than you, I think."

"You're forcing her?" Garde lunged at Norian. Norian defended himself by folding away.

"At least he had the balls to come tell you himself," Lissa attempted to calm Garde and Tory down. They'd folded straight to her study after Norian had gotten away from them. "Have you talked to Reah?"

"We haven't," Tory grumbled. "We've been too pissed off."

"Where is Gavril? Has he been told yet?"

"Don't have the answer to that either. He's up to his chin in Campiaan Alliance shit," Tory was blowing smoke again.

"I don't know what to think about all this," Lissa said. "My son, fifty years older than he was when he left three months ago. Kifirin hasn't shown up again, the coward."

"Father, it couldn't be helped," Lendill was whining to Kaldill Schaff and he knew it. His father had said to bring Reah the moment she returned and he would perform the marriage ceremony. Now, Reah would slam the door in Lendill's face if he proposed such an idea. Why couldn't Norian have let her go so this could be done? His father would never have asked if it weren't important.

"Child, this makes everything worse, if not impossible, now. You will see." Kaldill slapped the comp-vid, terminating the communication.

"Fuck," Lendill muttered angrily before going back to his research —he was trying to determine where Nidris and his family might be upon Tulgalan.

~

"Call me Em-pah, baby girl." Lenden—well, Denevik—had come with Glinda and Jayd. Glinda was uncomfortable—I could tell. At least she'd set aside her aversion to seeing me and come with her husband. I was glad, too, that I'd put a seafood stew together for Aurelius and me. We shared out our meal of stew and freshly-baked bread with our visitors. Denevik hugged me when they'd arrived and I'd called him Lenden.

"Did you take that name to honor our father?" Glinda paused, her soup spoon halfway to her lips. Glinda is more than beautiful and Jayd always looks at her as if the sun rises in her eyes.

"I did. Baby, your great-grandfather's name was Lendevik Lith," my grandfather smiled at me. "And there wasn't anyone who treated his children better. All of us were bathed by our father at night when we were small. And he played with us and smiled when he put us to bed. Your great-grandmother, Belarok, dealt with us during the day while father worried over Kifirin. I think he looked forward to his time with us every day."

I wanted to ask my grandfather why his oldest brother felt compelled to kill his father, then, if his father had been so kind to all of them. Denevik took the thought from my mind. "The Ra'Ak, child. They promised something and twisted Tarevik's mind. Made him believe he was entitled to something not given to him. I'm sure father never saw the attack coming, he loved his children so much."

"Are you saying that children shouldn't be loved?" I rubbed my belly at the thought. I was determined that my daughter would have love—as much as I could give to her.

"No, granddaughter. I know why you say this," he added. "There is a middle ground. We will give her love and firm guidance without harming her."

"We will make sure she thrives," Aurelius added. Lissa always said he was a better parent to Gavin than his biological parents had been. It made me wonder if Gavin had been mistreated when he was small. That was something I'm sure he would never say and now that I had pushed his child away, well, I wouldn't get that answer unless Aurelius knew it.

"This is wonderful," Glinda liked her stew and bread.

"It was a simple meal I prepared for the kitchen staff when I was at Desh's," I said. "Edan would go home the moment the doors were locked, leaving the rest of us to clean up and prepare for the next day's menu. We didn't usually get to eat during the course of the evening meal—we were always too busy. I'd throw this together and we'd eat. Of course, my brothers Wald and Ilvan still didn't speak to me so the rest of the staff followed suit. It didn't keep them from emptying the stew pot and finishing off the bread."

"What made you prepare this instead of something else?" Jayd asked.

"I took all the seafood that would go bad in the next day or two and used that. It kept us from having to throw it out. I tried not to be wasteful and the staff's contracts said that they were entitled to a meal if they worked through the dinner hour."

"How old were you when you started making this?" My grandfather rubbed my shoulders. What was I to do with this affection from a family member? I would have to get used to it, I think.

"Twelve," I said. "I found a recipe on Edan's comp-vid and added to it to use up the shrimp that was about to turn. It was good the first time—better each time after that until I got it just the way I wanted it. Eventually, Edan found out about it so we served it in the restaurant two days per moon-turn. Guests showed up on those days, just to get the fish stew. And Edan beat me when he discovered I'd used his comp-vid," I added.

"He'll get out of prison in only a few weeks," Aurelius grumbled.

"I wish there was some way to make it so he'd never father another child," I grumbled. "I think he would be a terrible father."

"Already has been," Aurelius sighed. "But Marzi still has another seven years on her sentence since she masterminded the murder. The physician disappeared after giving testimony," Aurelius tore off another piece of bread to dip in his stew. "Nobody knows where he is."

"As long as he doesn't have a license, he shouldn't be allowed to practice medicine in the Alliance," Jayd said.

"Should I find him," Denevik opened and closed his right fist.

"Denny, don't. He isn't worth it," Glinda patted her brother's arm. "Reah, are you going to be able to do what Director Keef wants—repairing Tulgalan's core?" She changed the subject, steering us toward safer ground.

I heaved a sigh at my aunt's question. "I hope so," I told her. "It drains me physically and even when it's under ideal conditions, I'm unconscious for clicks afterward. And then I'm exhausted for days. It was better this time, since Karzac helped me."

"Reah, someone will be there with you," Aurelius stroked my hair. I'd left it loose—he liked it that way. I didn't point out that someone had been with me all three times I'd repaired cores and still I'd experienced unconsciousness followed by exhaustion.

"Why didn't somebody tell me there was food?" Tory appeared between Jayd and Glinda, giving Glinda a kiss on the cheek.

"Tory, I didn't invite you," I muttered.

"Baby, you can't mean that," he said, picking up a bowl and helping himself to the stew. "Pass the bread, please." Jayd scooted the plate of bread in Tory's direction as Tory took an empty seat on Jayd's other side. Unwilling to get into an argument with him while the others were here, I stared at my half-eaten bowl of fish chowder.

"Reah, finish your lunch, love," Aurelius coaxed.

"Not hungry," I said.

"Karzac won't be happy if you don't eat. I won't be happy if you don't eat. Come on, finish that for Em-pah." Denevik was tapping the edge of my bowl.

"Reah, this is Torevik's child," Jayd said softly. "Allow him to be a father."

Jayd's words made me snort. I hadn't seen much in the father department yet—all I'd seen was him going off with his brothers and taking Teeg's part in all this.

"Why weren't we invited?" Ry showed up with Teeg. Well, that was it for me. My appetite was gone and now I felt nauseous. Slipping off my stool, I headed toward the small bathroom right off Aurelius' kitchen.

~

"Shit, she's losing her lunch," Tory was up in a blink and walking toward the bathroom with Gavril, Aurelius and Denevik right behind him. They found Reah crouched in the floor, dry heaving. She'd already lost everything she'd eaten earlier. "Get a wet cloth," Gavril ordered. Someone complied and Tory was kneeling in the floor next to Reah, pulling her against him and washing her face with the cool cloth.

~

"Tory, leave me alone," I sputtered weakly when he began washing my face with the wet cloth. "Go away. Go build the Campiaan Alliance with your brother."

"Reah, stop talking like that," Tory sighed. "You have other mates. Aurelius doesn't get a monopoly."

"Aurelius is the only one who cares about me." I bent over the toilet to heave again.

"Shit," Tory muttered. "Baby, that's not true. You know it's not true. Now straighten up and come talk with Gavril and me."

"Is that all you have to say?" I wiped my mouth on my sleeve and stared at him. "Straighten up and come talk to you? If I could skip away, I would, you poor excuse for a weed hen. Get away from me. Now!"

"Reah, can you stand up, love?" Aurelius lifted me off the floor. Tory grabbed my arm. I tried to jerk it from his grasp. I was pounding on his chest as soon as he lifted me off the floor and carried me away from the bathroom. Teeg was right behind him; Aurelius followed, a puzzled frown on his face.

Sitting with my arms crossed angrily over my breasts, I refused to look at Tory or Teeg as they did their best to explain to me that they had other things to tend to and couldn't—in Tory's words—ride herd on me every minute. I hadn't asked for them to do anything of the sort. In fact, Teeg needed to stay as far away from me as he could possibly get. "You don't need to be going off to Casino City on your own and you don't need to be sending your bodyguards away," Teeg decided to get in on this.

"I'm not listening to you," I muttered.

"Reah, you will listen. Farzi and the others are upset now that you just up and left them behind."

"They're welcome here. You're not."

"Reah, you are going to be the death of me," Teeg snapped.

"I have three words for you, Teeg San Gerxon," I snapped right back. "Remove the chip."

"Not likely," he almost shouted. "Forget that right now. I don't need to be combing the universe for a missing mate while I have other things on my mind."

"Gee, how inconvenient for you. I'm not your mate. Don't want to be your mate. Take the damn chip out. You don't own me, Teeg."

"I worked fifty fucking years for you. I'm not about to throw all that away because you think you don't belong with me!"

"Don't I have anything to say about this?" I shouted. "The next time you and Kifirin cook something up together that involves me, I'd appreciate it if you'd let me know!" I was crying and shaking now, my breaths becoming heaving sobs with the effort it had taken to yell at Teeg.

"Enough of this," Aurelius was up and snarling. "We're not going to sort this out today and Reah is still recovering."

"Fine." Teeg disappeared. Tory looked from me to the spot Teeg had previously held. He disappeared right behind his brother.

"Are you sure that nephew of yours is High Demon?" Denevik looked at Jayd. They'd witnessed the entire argument and now I felt embarrassed—not only that they'd seen it all but that I was still sobbing in front of them.

"He's half," Jayd muttered, as if that should explain something.

"Reah, let's get you to bed—you're tired and out of sorts," Aurelius led me away.

Gavril was growling and stalking through his suite like a wounded lion. Tory and Ry watched him, unsure what to do. Gavril's communicator beeped. Pulling it out of his pocket, Gavril looked at the sender tag and answered the call. "Jes, where the fuck have you been? We've been looking everywhere for you. Dee is about to have a stroke."

"I just wanted to be alone for a while," Jes' voice came through clearly on the comp-vid. "How is Reah? Is she all right?"

"She's as well as can be expected," Gavril was still growling. "Where are you? Have you checked in with Dee?"

"Yes—I'm at the palace on Campiaa now. I didn't mean for everybody to get so upset because I took a few days off."

"Next time, check your messages," Gavril snapped. "And I may need you in a few days to help with Reah. I'll keep you informed." Gavril ended the call. "Fuck," he rubbed his forehead. "How upset do you think Reah is?" He turned to his brothers.

"Things are falling into place," Jes informed Ardalin later. "Teeg wants me to go help with Reah in a few days. That means we'll have both of them together to make this easy. Are you sure Nidris is ready to help?"

"Yebri says yes," Ardalin's image nodded at Jes. "They're working on the spell that will make Teeg care only for me. I'm looking forward to getting what I want," she laughed. Jes didn't like the sound of her laughter but didn't say anything—he wanted what he wanted, after all.

～

"She's asleep—I had to call for Karzac when she wouldn't stop crying," Aurelius was as polite as he could be under the circumstances when Lendill dropped by.

"Just tell her I came to visit," Lendill felt uncomfortable under Aurelius' stare.

"I'll tell her if it won't make her cry again," Aurelius said, nearly shutting the door in Lendill's face. Lendill nodded and walked away. It had been a wasted trip. Lendill hunched his shoulders and walked toward the hovercar he'd borrowed from the ASD transport pool.

～

"I think I have information on Nidris and his family," Norian informed Gavril, Tory and Ry. "Lendill and I could use your help, I think."

"I can bring Astralan and Stellan," Gavril offered. "They have no love for any of those. Nidris' family killed their father, Skye."

"Then bring them. We can use the firepower, I think," Norian agreed. "We're targeting an area in the garden district near the equator —most of the fruit and vegetables Tulgalan produces comes from there and it's the least populated in this particular portion—the oceans where the tourists visit are hundreds of clicks away. The only ones living in that part are the plantation owners and their employees. We think the Hazlan clan have bought an old tomato farm and are producing just enough to keep them away from suspicion."

"How did you find them?" Ry asked.

"We looked for purchases of homes or land parcels in the right time period and coupled that with unusual events reported for the same time period. You know there's nobody with any sort of wizard or warlock abilities native to Tulgalan. We dug up report after report of the neighbors' dogs coming home unable to bark or not coming home at all."

"Stupid," Gavril muttered.

"And we're glad of it," Lendill said. "We might have taken longer to find anything on them," he added.

"You think this is where the tapping originated?" Gavril asked.

"Yes," Norian replied. "We'll take Reah there as soon as we clean out the nest. We have everything under surveillance and should be able to provide images soon of anyone coming or going. Who can identify them?"

"My warlocks can easily identify them," Gavril offered.

"Good. We'll get the images to you as quickly as possible. Now, since you're still bent on setting up the Campiaan Alliance, what are your plans for creating a unit to mirror the ASD?" Norian settled into the chair behind his desk and put the tips of his fingers together, waiting on the one who called himself Teeg San Gerxon to outline his plans.

"It's just a precaution—stop whining about it," Nidris cast the spell to make his brother Derdris look exactly like him. "Father says it's for the best."

"Then why isn't Father casting the spell?" Derdris was still whining.

"Because I have the resources to do this quickly," Nidris snapped. He'd tapped the core gently again, he just hadn't told his father about it. What was one more small tap? The core was already leaking power. "Just a little longer," Nidris spoke mostly to himself. "There. We're twins now." He lifted the mirror so Derdris could see his image.

"I don't like this," Derdris muttered.

"They won't know which one to shoot if it comes to that," Nidris smiled nastily at his brother. "It could keep us alive if we're found. Besides, I have plans to get us all out of here. Just be patient—we'll live like kings in no time."

Derdris glowered at his brother. He'd heard that phrase before—on the night prior to a coup that left them in charge of Karathia for less than three days. Then, Wylend Arden, Erland Morphis and a stable of warlocks they hadn't even guessed at or calculated their power swept in and destroyed everything. They'd been hunted for so long afterward that now all Derdris wanted was to live his life in peace. He enjoyed farming—it was quiet. He could touch the earth and make it fertile. He'd found ways to keep the insects away from the crops and he it was who took the boxes of tomatoes to market, selling to upscale restaurants across Tulgalan. Desh's was one of his best customers.

"You'll either save us or kill us both, brother," Derdris grumbled and used his power to fold away from Nidris.

"Aurelius, I don't want to do this." I looked at him as I dressed to go to Tulgalan. Norian wanted to get there early. Seven days early, to be exact. I was hoping to spend my time with Aurelius on Le-Ath Veronis. Norian still held my leash so I had to go.

"Love, I hope to be here when you return but I may be sent out again," Aurelius closed the bag I'd packed.

"No," I whispered, going to him and wrapping my arms around his waist.

"My love, it cannot be helped," he kissed my forehead. "Come, I am receiving mindspeech from Tory. They are waiting for us at the palace."

"All right." I moved away from Aurelius. Ry, Astralan and Stellan were going to fold us to a plantation on Tulgalan temporarily housing ASD operatives. Norian wasn't taking any chances on letting Nidris and his family escape. The plantation was far enough away from the farm the Hazlan family supposedly ran that Nidris, as a power-seeker, wouldn't detect any of the warlocks with us. As soon as we had the Hazlans in custody, I would be sent out to heal the core.

Aurelius folded me to Norian's office inside Lissa's palace. Lendill was there, as were Teeg, Ry, Tory, all eight reptanoids and Astralan and Stellan.

"We will take our Reah's bag," Nenzi stepped up right away, so Aurelius handed it over.

"Nenzi," I hugged him tightly. I'd issued an invitation for him and the others to stay with me and Aurelius but they hadn't come. I blamed Teeg for that.

"Our Reah well?" Farzi got the next hug.

"I'm all right," I assured Farzi as the others came forward to get hugs as well.

"Reah, I'll see you soon," Aurelius leaned down to give me a kiss before disappearing. Without him, I felt I was in enemy territory. Only Farzi, Nenzi and their brothers would be any comfort at all. If I were truthful, I felt cold and abandoned. I had no desire to heal Tulgalan and wished I could wait until after my daughter's birth. Just the thought of it made me rub my belly.

"Reah well?" Farzi repeated his question.

"I'll be fine," I lied to reassure Farzi.

"We're ready," Norian nodded to Ry, Astralan and Stellan. We were folded away quickly.

"Tory and I will be trading nights," Teeg said the moment I was shown to my bedroom. Both of them, in addition to the reptanoids, had followed me. Nenzi still carried my bag.

"No," I turned and glared at both of them.

"Reah, this is the way it's going to be," Teeg snapped. "One of us will be with you at night and Farzi and the others will be in the bedrooms on either side. Get used to it!" I was just about to tell Teeg what I thought he could do with his high-handedness when Lendill walked in.

"I'd like a night, too," he said.

"No. Absolutely not," I almost shouted. I only held back a little—he was still my superior, after all. In fact, he shouldn't be trying to push himself on me. He and Norian would be lucky if they ever saw me again the moment my time as a conscript ran out.

"If either of them get to trade nights, then I demand time as well." Lendill had his arms crossed angrily over his chest. All three stood there in identical poses, almost, all glaring and snarling. I wanted to tell them to get out but there wasn't any chance they'd listen. They never listened. Every time, it was what they wanted. They got their way, too, every single time. Suddenly, I was too tired to fight with any of them.

"Nenzi, will you help me unpack?" I turned to my friend.

"Nenzi help," he nodded eagerly. He and the others had my bag on the bed and unpacked in very little time.

"Reah, baby, Norian wants one of those fruit and rum drinks," Tory poked his head inside the door. I just stared helplessly at him, all the fight gone out of me. Forces outside my control had decided my fate and I had no more strength to do battle against it. I walked wearily out of the bedroom, brushing past Tory and heading toward the kitchen to put drinks together.

"Reah, that was wonderful as usual," Astralan complimented me on the meal. I said nothing, gathering plates from the table instead. The reptanoids had helped me as much as they could with dinner. Now they would help me clean up. I hadn't been included in Norian's meeting with the others while they planned their assault against the Hazlan family in a few days. I was there to cook and do cleanup afterward.

"Reah not feel good," Farzi was rubbing my back as I huddled on a barstool at the island later. We'd cleaned the dishes and the kitchen, leaving me worn out afterward. Perhaps I was depressed. That might explain the feeling I had of a terrible inevitability stretching before me.

"Aren't you done yet?" Teeg stalked into the room, drawing to a halt a few feet away. "What's wrong with her?" He demanded. My head was buried in my arms at the island and I hadn't sat up when he walked in.

"We not knowing," Farzi was still stroking my back.

"Sweetheart, I can get Jes here in no time," Teeg had come closer.

"No. Keep him away from me," I muttered, still not lifting my head.

"Reah, if you don't sit up and come to bed with me, I will have Galaxsan bring him immediately." I sat up. "See," he said, holding his arms out. "Problem solved." If I'd had any energy, I'd have punched him in the gut for his arrogance.

"Come on, you don't have to do anything. Just let me love you," Teeg was nuzzling and kissing. He'd insisted that I not wear pajamas to bed. I wanted to push him away. I didn't have the strength. At least he was gentle. I think I wept while he loved me; I couldn't hold back the tears.

"What's wrong with her?" Wylend demanded the moment he'd folded in with Erland. Tory didn't want to argue with his grandfather; Since Tory was High Demon, Wylend couldn't hurt him but that wouldn't matter—Wylend was family and an older member at that. Tory didn't have to argue with Wylend—Gavril decided to answer.

"She'll be fine after we get this over with," Gavril unfolded his arms and picked up a small sculpture that adorned the desk inside the plantation's study. "She doesn't like that Norian's forcing her to do this. Karzac says the baby is fine—I don't know why she's balking like this."

"Right now, you're all riding over her—as if what she wants doesn't matter." Wylend didn't like it either—he understood Reah's position better than the others might think—he was in the early years of a female cycle. With Karathians, the cycles ran around a hundred years. Erland's was currently in a male cycle—Wylend's and Erland's tended to be opposites.

"Don't say that—we'll make this up to her when this mess is over," Gavril set the sculpture down again. It was a stone carving of a tiny Skycatcher.

"So, you don't care that she's miserable right now. Is that it?"

"You make us sound like unfeeling louts," Tory muttered.

"Well, aren't you?" Wylend glared at Tory now. "If I understand correctly, that little girl she's carrying may help revive the High Demon race. I think your father is none too happy with where Reah is at the moment."

"Yeah, don't remind me," Tory sighed.

"And since we're taking turns—you never should have told Rylend, by the way," Wylend was still glaring at Tory, "then I demand a night too. I wish to take Reah to dinner while she's here."

"Fine. Take her out tonight. See if you can get her into a better mood." Gavril was giving permission without consulting Tory. Tory turned a stunned look on his brother.

"When did you get to be in charge?" He snapped before skipping away.

"I was wondering the same thing," Wylend said. "You've only been around for a little while, Gavril. I don't care what you've gone through the past fifty-odd years. Being a King or in charge of anything means that you need to stop and listen to your people occasionally. If you want to be successful at ruling, that is." Wylend nodded to Erland and both of them folded away.

"Fuck," Gavril rubbed his forehead with shaking fingers.

"Reah, my love, I heard you weren't feeling well. Does this mean you can't come out to dinner with me tonight?"

I'd fallen asleep with Farzi and Nenzi watching over me. Wylend had come in to wake me with a careful kiss.

"Wylend?" I wanted to fling myself into his arms and sob out my misery.

"Reah, pretty Reah, don't do that, you'll make me weep as well," Wylend sat on the edge of my bed and pulled me against him. Wrapping my arms around his neck, I sniffled for a moment before getting myself back in hand. Being pregnant was certainly playing with my emotions.

"Where did you want to go?" I wiped my face with the heel of a hand and pulled away from Wylend to search his face.

"It'll be a surprise—I made reservations already—they know the King of Karathia is coming with his intended." Wylend held out a hand, palm up. Light formed around it and suddenly there was a beautiful ring lying there. "This is yours, Reah. You know I want to marry you. You have led me to believe that you will when your service to the ASD is over. It is not too early for us to make the commitment, Reah. I know you cannot wear Aurelius' ring while you work, but you can wear this tonight when we go out. I expect those people at the restaurant to fawn over us and give us only the best of what they have," Wylend smiled and offered the ring. When I nodded, he placed it on my finger. "See," he said, "it fits perfectly."

It did. I wanted to sniffle again—I'd never gotten a ring from Tory and now wondered why that was. It was his baby after all, but then he hadn't shown much interest in her, either.

"Come with me, love. I will take you to dinner. These louts can fend for themselves for one night." Wylend had brought a dress with him—it was turquoise and nearly matched my eyes. It also had a high waist so my early pregnancy would not show at all.

"You look beautiful," Erland offered his arm to me when I came out of the bathroom later. Erland, Ry and two of Wylend's personal guards were there to protect us as Wylend folded us to a restaurant.

"Wylend, no," I moaned when we appeared at the private entrance to Desh's in Targis. Doormen were already falling over themselves to greet the King of Karathia and his entourage.

"Reah, I want your fool of a grandfather to know he can never touch you again," Wylend whispered softly as he led me inside.

We were handed over to the master of tables, who bowed respectfully to a visiting monarch and his intended—that's how Wylend had made the reservations. The man had never seen me and had no idea who he was ushering into his restaurant. If Addah learned I was there, he would seethe but he wouldn't say anything to Wylend —he'd know that the King of Karathia could ruin him in more ways than one.

"Sorry I'm late," Lendill rushed in, joining our party invited or not. Wylend lifted an eyebrow but didn't say anything. Erland cleared his throat a little and Ry scooted over a bit to give Lendill room.

"Are we expecting other guests?" The master of tables asked pleasantly. His job consisted of making the guests welcome, no matter the difficulty.

"I believe we are all present," Erland said just as Teeg and Tory came rushing in. I wanted to curse but settled for moving closer to Wylend. This was supposed to be our time together. Teeg and Tory were going to ruin it. "Now. Now we are all present," Erland almost snapped at Tory and Teeg.

"Very well—please follow me, Lord King." The two guards went ahead of us, Ry and Erland came behind and Teeg, Tory and Lendill had to follow. Just as well, I didn't want to talk to any of them anyway.

We had the best private room in Desh's. I remembered it from years ago. Addah had updated things over the years but the room was spacious and richly dressed. Water and wineglasses sparkled atop snowy tablecloths. The silver was polished until it shone in the muted light. The wine steward came forward immediately and offered up a selection of Desh's finest even as one of the best waiters poured our water and asked if there was anything else he might get for us.

"Reah, what would you like to drink?" Wylend turned to me first after the wine had been offered to him.

"A pineapple and orange ice," I said.

"Bring that for my intended and we will have the Ifthis Redburn," Wylend made the wine selection. He'd asked for the wine I might have taken if I could drink it at the moment.

"Very well, Lord King," the wine steward removed the cork and poured for everyone except me.

Someone would come to take our order next, only I hadn't expected Addah to come himself. He stood at our table looking quite shocked when he saw me sitting there. I knew he wanted to have a fit —I could see the muscle working in his jaw—it always did that when he was about to shout at someone. Even Edan had been frightened by that small gesture.

"I see you remember Reah," Wylend said casually, sipping his wine. "And should you become curious, she had no idea I was bringing her here this evening. Reah and I will be wed before the year is out, Master Desh. And as I understand it, your son will be getting out of prison before long. Should he ever threaten my intended, I can assure you that Karathia will most certainly protect its own."

"And my father will see to it that Reah is protected, once she marries into my family," Lendill added. I turned sharply in his direction—I had no idea what he was talking about.

"I have seen you before, Vice-Director Schaff," Addah wanted to sneer but held it back.

"But you have not met my father, Master Desh," Lendill pointed out.

"Please stop," I wanted to shout it but my voice was barely above a whisper.

"Master Desh, perhaps we should dine elsewhere," Wylend lifted my hand and kissed it gently. "I see you have no love for your granddaughter. I should have expected as much."

"No, please, we will serve you our very best," Addah inclined his head respectfully. He wanted to add Wylend's name to his list of royalty and visiting dignitaries that Desh's had served over the years.

"Wylend," I said.

"What love?" Wylend turned toward me.

"He only wants to add your name to the list," I said.

"I know. I just wanted to come tonight and see if he had any love or respect for you, my darling. He does not. We will not come here again. Master Desh has no idea how precious his girl child is."

I could almost hear Addah's mental derision. A girl had never mattered to him. Ever. "How is Ilvan?" I asked. Ilvan had never challenged Edan when he'd mistreated me but he also hadn't joined in or taunted me like the others had.

"Ilvan has been gone these past six years," Addah snapped, angry that I'd thought to address him directly.

"You think to treat my future wife in this way?" Wylend was toying with his knife. It grew in his hand until a long, sharp dagger formed. Wylend casually stabbed it into the table. I wasn't sure how he'd done that—I was sitting next to him and no threatening spell was supposed to work at such close range.

"Wylend, don't waste your time with him," I put my hand over Wylend's. "Addah Desh never knew how to be a parent. All he knew how to do was fuck his wives. I'd like to leave now." I rose from the table, scooting my chair back and stepping away.

"I will be leaving as well," Wylend stood, too. Erland, Ry and the two guards also rose from their seats.

"You think to insult me?" Addah almost shouted, allowing his temper get away from him.

"Addah," I turned to him, already weary, "none of your children call you father. Perhaps it's time you asked yourself why that is." I walked out of Desh's best private room and everyone there trailed after me except for Addah Desh.

CHAPTER 10

"*I* made the second reservation just in case," Wylend smiled as we were led to a large table inside the *Star Gazer,* Targis' second-best restaurant. Erland had dumped a credit chip on the table when we left Desh's. I'm sure it was for more than enough to cover the expense of our brief stay there. Teeg and Tory both watched me but they hadn't said anything before or after leaving Desh's. They hadn't been invited, so I did my best to ignore them.

The fish was good—not as good as what I might do but good nonetheless. I complimented the cook when I finished my meal—the management was more than delighted to get Wylend's business and Wylend happily posed for vid images. I had a feeling those images would go into an advertisement soon. Lendill kept me out of the photographs—he didn't want anyone to know I was on Tulgalan until after the take-down.

"Reah, stand over here," Lendill pulled me aside while Wylend was photographed with the owner and then signed a hard copy of the image afterward. I thought about asking Lendill what he meant about his father but I was still angry with him. My thoughts and my words I kept to myself.

"Come, love," Wylend took my hand after the brief session was over, leading me out of the restaurant.

~

Wylend helped me out of my gown later. "Reah, do you know about the Karathian cycles?" He asked, pulling me down on the small sofa inside my sitting room. I'd dressed in my pajamas after putting the dress away.

"Cycles?" I didn't know what he meant.

"Every hundred years we go through cycles after reaching adulthood," Wylend said, pulling me against him. "It doesn't affect our true mates—we will always be attracted to them no matter what cycle we are in," he said. "Every hundred years we swing from attraction to females to attraction to males. I am in the eighteenth year of a female cycle, love. That means that males are more attractive to me than females. But as you are my true mate, I want you, no matter what."

I blinked up at Wylend, unsure what to make of the information. It stunned me, certainly—I hadn't expected this.

"You'd rather have a male now?" I asked, my voice quavering.

"No, Reah. If you are in my arms, nothing else matters."

"But you will be going to males during this cycle?"

"Yes. It is the way we were made."

"Will they—will they—try to destroy this?" I twisted Wylend's ring on my finger.

"If they try, I will destroy them," Wylend muttered. "You will be my mate. Anyone I take to my bed must understand that first."

"And Ry—is this how things will be for him?" I think I felt numb, suddenly.

"More than likely. He is currently in a male cycle—his father and I both know this. But when he reaches his first century, we will know for sure. He has already been instructed in the ways of his race—although he is half what Lissa is. Reah, this will never affect my love for you. Please understand that. The Karathians were made this way—our planet rides the line between the dark and the light realms. I think this is why the cycles happen and why some of us tend to go so far into good or evil—it is either darkness or light with us, my darling."

Worrying my lower lip, I pondered what Wylend was trying to tell me. "How often?" I asked, not looking at him.

"How often will I invite someone else to my bed?"

"Yes."

"Perhaps once per moon-turn. It is a desire for strong arms around me, Reah. And reassurances from a male while I am in a female cycle. I hope you can understand that."

"I think I do," I nodded. "Do you keep the same partners?"

"Yes—I have three that I depend upon and trust."

"Will I meet them?"

"Erland you have met already."

"But," I couldn't finish that statement.

"Lissa understands now, although at first she didn't," Wylend said softly. "Erland and I have complete trust between us. And our cycles are opposites, as are the other two. When they are in their female cycles, I provide the strong arms and male assurances for them."

"I feel cold," I whispered, trying to hug myself.

"Reah, no," Wylend wrapped his arms around me. "I know this is difficult for you and perhaps harder still to comprehend while you are pregnant. You deserve to know this now. All I want to do is take you to my bed and remove that lost look from your face. I love you and that will not change."

"The three—they will not belittle me? Think me a weak female? Teeg and Tory do." Tears were threatening and I was doing my best to keep them from falling.

"Reah, every emotion you feel they have felt—it is unique to us, I think," Wylend murmured, kissing my shoulder and breathing on bare skin—my top only had the thinnest of straps.

"You mean they know what it's like to be pregnant and thinking the father doesn't give a damn about his child?" I broke away from Wylend and walked away to stand across the room. I could see the guards Norian and Lendill had stationed outside the house through the window of my sitting room.

"Reah, tell me this isn't from your childhood—this fear that the father will abandon or mistreat his daughter."

I whirled to face Wylend. "Of course that fear is with me," I snapped. "And every male is the same, are they not? They think they know better and the female is to be humored or ignored. I think I want to spend the night alone, Wylend."

"Reah, do not do this to us, I beg you. I will not ask for sex if you do not wish it."

"Then you'd be the first one," I said.

"You told her." Erland didn't make it a question—he saw the look on Wylend's face.

"Yes. Her pregnancy is a factor, my dear. That poor girl is terrified that her child will be treated as she was treated. I'm not sure she truly trusts any male right now. She worried that you and the others would belittle her because she is female."

"Corolan would treat her so gently she could not help but trust him," Erland snorted. "His children have a loving father. And Garek—he would think the sun had landed in his lap if Reah smiled at him."

"And what would you think, Erland?"

"That our tiny Reah needs attention and reassurance. Even Ry has remarked on Tory's reluctance to spend time with her."

"Is it merely new father jitters or something else?" Wylend hadn't realized that Reah's fears were founded in anything other than imagination.

"I think that plays a part, but I also believe that Tory was unprepared for this role. He loves her but this has overwhelmed him, I think."

"If we go to him and express our concern, it may serve to drive him farther away."

"True," Erland nodded at Wylend's assessment.

"Then how are we to comfort Reah? She thinks we discount everything she says and ignore her desires because she is female."

"I do not know—and all of us saw how Addah Desh treated her earlier—he became outraged because she addressed him directly, the pompous ass." Erland shook his head. "If a daughter had been born to me, I would have been equally as happy as with my son."

I thought about going to Farzi and Nenzi and asking them to come to bed with me. I felt chilled and couldn't explain it. Why had Wylend chosen tonight to tell me what he did? And that after the confrontation with Addah. Addah had never noticed me. Never thought to speak directly to me—it had been through a nanny or through Edan. Now, others controlled my life. Truly, I'd been surprised that Wylend had honored my request to go to bed alone. I knew I needed someone with me—it just couldn't be him. Not this night. Perhaps I could find a way to deal with this soon—I hoped so— I didn't want to give up our relationship. Instead, I curled into a small lump and sniffled miserably throughout the night.

"I want Karzac," I muttered the following morning when Teeg announced that I needed something to get out of my mood and offered to send for Jes. I didn't expect him to listen, but Karzac was there in moments, checking me over. Exhaustion was the verdict after Karzac finished his examination. I think every male in the house grumbled when they learned they weren't getting any meals cooked by me for two days. It only served to make me feel guilty about it. Karzac put a stop to that by placing a healing sleep for six hours, after making sure I'd eaten something first.

"Stop pushing her," Karzac growled at the room filled with males. "I fail to understand the logic employed to expose her to that miscreant who was once her grandfather. Nothing good would come of that, no matter when it happened. I have spoken to Erland—Reah is frightened that her child will be treated as she was treated." Karzac glared at Tory, who refused to meet the healer's eyes. "Perhaps you thought only for yourselves, is that it?" Karzac was so angry he folded away rather than allow his temper to run away with him.

"I should have brought Jes anyway," Gavril muttered.

"Take these—they are locating beacons," Yebri passed the small chips to Jes and Ardalin. "These are not spelled—they will work unless someone with power realizes that you have them and deactivates them. Keep them hidden so we may find you when the time is right," Yebri held up the small receiver in her hands. Jes had asked for something—he knew the time was close when he would be taken to Teeg. He'd informed Yebri and Nidris that it was likely that one of the warlocks would be transporting him, so they would have to wait and strike when a message was received from Jes. Jes already had a communicator for that purpose.

"This is going to be easier than I thought," Ardalin gloated. Yebri schooled her face—she disliked the obsessed female more and more as time went on. In fact, Yebri was only waiting until this was over—she intended to get away from Nidris and hide somewhere so she couldn't be found by any of them.

A storm of activity surrounded the plantation—nobody was saying anything but it would have been clear to even the uneducated; they were gearing up to take the Hazlan family. I felt better after my two-day rest, although I guided Nenzi through the making of dinner on the second night. I had to if I expected to get much in the way of a meal. Nenzi did very well with help from his brothers Perzi and Darzi. They would make excellent assistants in any kitchen.

"I'm surprised you're not asking us about the preparations," Astralan accepted the plate I handed to him—breakfast was a casual affair and people wandered in when they had time.

"I think I know what's going on," I said, offering him a cup of tea and juice. He accepted both. "All I ask is that you get them all."

"We intend to, though Nidris is our main target. Wylend may even come and do some questioning with Erland and two others."

"Astralan?" I looked at him—he was a warlock, after all—from Karathia.

"What is it, Reah?"

"I learned about the cycles the other night."

"Ah. And you want to know about my brothers and me."

"Yes." I ducked my head—I'd never been so forward with Teeg's warlocks before.

"Stellan and I are currently in male cycles. Galaxsan and Celestan are in female cycles. It isn't always easy on us, pretty girl. We've gone through this for several thousand years."

"I can see that it might be difficult," I nodded.

"He won't love you any less, Reah." Astralan reached over and tilted my chin up with a finger. "My father loved my mother until the day he died. They were together for twenty-seven thousand years. We also knew the males and the females who were our parents' lovers. All of them were like an extended family to us. My brothers and I were devastated when Nidris and his cronies attacked Warlend Arden's court—both our parents died in that coup. They held the throne for three days before Wylend, Erland and a handful of others came and wrested it away. My brothers and I were angry and blamed Warlend and his son for allowing this to happen. We left Karathia and signed up with anybody who'd hire us. Some good, some bad. Until the Hardlows hired us. We were paid beyond anyone's imaginings and none of it settled well with us. Teeg came along and pulled us out of that hole."

"Then I'm glad for you," I sighed. Astralan removed his hand—he'd been gentle when he'd touched me.

"Reah, you have other mates and Wylend doesn't mind that. Offer him the same trust, Reah. Show him how much you care."

"I trust him. I was worried about the others who share his life."

"Understandable. Ask for a meeting, little girl. Wylend will arrange it."

"I'll try." I went back to my breakfast preparation as Tory and Teeg walked into the kitchen. I'd barely spoken to either of them and after Karzac's reprimand, none of them had bothered me in bed, choosing to sleep elsewhere. I was and wasn't happy about that, but Farzi and Nenzi had been spending the nights with me instead. They were warm and supportive. That's what I needed most at the moment.

∾

"We're going," Tory came to my bedroom later as I was putting laundry away. There wasn't any staff to do it for us, so I'd done as much as I could with help from the reptanoids.

"Try to keep everybody alive," I gazed steadily at him. When had we become estranged? I felt like blaming Teeg for this—I thought I knew Tory until Teeg had dumped me on Le-Ath Veronis and we'd all learned he was Gavril. I couldn't even use his name anymore. My friend was gone forever, leaving a cynical autocrat in his place. And now, he'd managed to take my High Demon mate away. My child might be fatherless before it was over.

"Reah, I don't have time for this," Tory almost exploded. He must have seen the emotions crossing my face.

"Then go. Do whatever it is you're going to do, Tory." I turned my back to him, stuffing clothing into a drawer. I wasn't paying attention to what was going into the drawer or whether it even belonged there.

∾

"Of course I'm sure, you idiot!" Jes was shouting into the communicator. "Teeg just contacted me—said he'd have someone transport me to him tomorrow. That means the take-down is today! Get the fuck away from there!"

Nidris stood rooted to the floor for precious seconds after Jes ended the call. If he took time to gather his family and warn them, it could be too late. The ASD and Teeg San Gerxon had allied in order to capture him. His family was of little consequence if Nidris escaped. Nidris was more than thankful that Derdris now wore his face—it would buy him time. Nidris had a safe place set up on Tulgalan and tomorrow he might tap the core well enough to achieve what needed to be done to fulfill his agreement with Jes and get his hands on the female High Demon. Jes would placate the little female until Nidris could force her to his will. Then Jes would become superfluous and could be dealt with easily. Nidris felt a pang of regret for his family, but it only lasted for a moment before he shook himself and folded to the safe place he'd prepared for an emergency.

Derdris was frightened out of his mind when at least twenty ASD agents surrounded him, all with ranos rifles pointed in his direction. He might have thought about folding away but two powerful warlocks were there, placing a shield around him. The only thing Derdris could do was raise his hands in surrender when one of the warlocks snarled a hate-filled "That's Nidris," to his companions.

"I'll allow Wylend to question him tomorrow, after Reah heals the core," Norian said. "So far, we haven't been able to get anything from him or the others, and we're still missing Derdris, the youngest son."

"Have you told Reah that you're doing this tomorrow?" Lendill wasn't sure how he felt about all of it. Reah still thought she had three days in which to prepare.

"No—I don't want to upset her any more than she is already. She's not talking to anyone, Lendill. But I'm sure you realize that as well as anyone."

"Yes, Director. I have met with that silence coupled with the wounded look in her eyes. How do you respond to that, Norian? How?"

"I'll let her go after she does this, Lendill. I promise," Norian wasn't able to look his oldest friend in the eye.

"It may be moot—I think the only people she might want to be with are Aurelius and Wylend."

"Then ask Wylend to plead your case for you," Norian sighed. "Why don't you let her go home with him? Let her be pampered by the servants in Wylend's court while she recovers from this."

"I was going to ask for time off so I could pamper her. My father still wants me to bring her if I can. I just have to convince her that I want only the best for her. That every time I've sent her into harm's way over the past few years it has squeezed my heart to do it."

"Lendill, she was the best thing to send out when we did send her. You and I both know that."

"I know that if she wasn't pregnant, that you'd be working on her to renew."

"Yes. I would," Norian acknowledged. "I was going to offer you something else as an incentive so you could be with her."

"And what would you offer me?" Lendill crossed arms over his chest.

"Head of Security for the Eastern Sector. That includes Wyyld and Le-Ath Veronis."

"You'd offer me that job? That's more than a hundred planets."

"And pays better than what you earn now, in addition to giving you complete control over everyday security and law enforcement. The RAA in that sector would be yours to command. Ildevar says that he could move you into that slot easily."

"Well, Reah isn't going to come back to the ASD. That's a given," Lendill said. "And as much as I might enjoy getting my hands on a quarter of the Regular Alliance Army, I like what I'm doing."

"Think about it for a few days. The offer will be open anyway."

"I will."

"Are you ready?" Galaxsan looked up at Jes, who'd dropped a single bag in the floor of the kitchen at San Gerxon palace. "I'm surprised you're not packed for a siege."

"Teeg didn't say how long I'd be staying and I can always ask for more to be brought in."

"True," Galaxsan rose from his seat at the island. "Teeg says he doesn't want Reah to know you're there until after she heals the core—something about a surprise or some such."

"I'm a surprise for her? Good." Jes grinned. Galaxsan folded the physician away.

"Stay here—I'll have your dinner brought in," Teeg settled Jes into a guest bungalow within a quarter click's walk of the main building on the plantation. "I don't want her to know you're here until she needs your help tomorrow."

"Not a problem, boss." Jes smiled.

"Do you have everything you need?" Teeg asked.

"Sure do." Jes patted his bag.

"Good. I'll bring your meals out and come get you tomorrow."

"Thanks."

Teeg nodded at his employee and left the guest bungalow behind.

"Reah, eat a good breakfast, beloved," Lendill was trying to settle me on the barstool instead of taking it for himself—I'd prepared ham and eggs for his meal.

"But I made that for you," I argued. Why was he doing this? After days of non-communication, now he wanted to talk?

"Reah, just eat, for the stars' sake," Teeg walked in snapping at me. Any energy I might have had was sapped away immediately. How did he do this to me? How? I never had any energy to fight with him nowadays. Even Tory didn't drain me this badly.

"Gavril, please." Lendill's voice held a warning.

"Are you going to let her eat and then tell her so she'll heave it up again?" Teeg wasn't mincing words. I watched both of them bristle at each other.

"Tell me what?" I asked, puzzled.

"Since we hauled in the Hazlans yesterday, Norian wants you to heal the core today. He wants off this planet, Reah. As soon as he can get off it."

Teeg was right about one thing—they wanted me to heal the core and just the thought of it was making me queasy. Were all of them on the outs with one another? Everything had felt that way to me from the moment we'd landed here. Was it that the core had been tapped and now Tulgalan felt its life draining away? I hadn't noticed it that much on the other worlds and they'd been leaking energy for a longer period.

"Then I'll ask this now," I said. "I'll promise to heal the core after the baby comes if you'll let me wait."

"No!" Norian almost shouted as he walked into the kitchen. "You'll do this now because I tell you to do it now."

"Director, I'm sorry to say that I lost my respect for you long ago. I don't feel like eating." I pushed the plate of food toward Lendill and walked out of the kitchen.

"Boss, is it your primary goal to fuck up the rest of my life?" Lendill never snapped at Norian, but he did so now.

"Lendill, I didn't mean that the way it came out," Norian half-apologized.

"We'll baby her after she finishes this," Gavril pulled the plate of food over and cut into the ham.

"I don't want it—I'll just get sick." I held a hand against my stomach—there wasn't much keeping me from heaving right then. Somebody had folded us to the site of the core tapping while Tory was attempting to hand one of the fruit and protein jumbles to me.

"Let's just get this over with—you can feed her later," Norian had arrived and was cracking the proverbial whip. I had less than a full moon-turn left with him and his ASD. I couldn't get away from either one fast enough.

"Turn, Reah. We'll make sure you're cared for afterward." Teeg was handing out a bit of autocracy of his own. Maybe this had turned into a contest of genital length between Norian, Teeg and the others. How could I know? Sighing, I began to remove my clothing, stopping for a moment to rub my slightly swelling belly before sitting on the grass and turning to full Thifilatha.

Gavril watched Reah as she stroked her belly, perhaps reassuring her child. He felt a sudden qualm and thought to stop her from repairing the core. He didn't, watching instead as Reah settled on the grass and turned to her alter ego; a full fifteen feet of golden Thifilatha.

Nidris knew his family had been arrested. He ignored the pang of guilt over his brother Derdris—Derdris might face the penalties for Nidris' crimes. Instead, Nidris settled himself on the ground twenty-six clicks from where he'd originally tapped the core of Tulgalan, preparing to tap the planet for the last time in preparation for his next task—that of taking the little High Demon for himself. His fingers itched in anticipation of his future, where anything he desired might be had with the use of unlimited power—all obtained by tapping cores and then forcing his little captive to repair them afterward. He might have gloated more than he had if the tiny bit of guilt over his family weren't nagging at him. Resolving to put it out of his mind, he turned to his current task.

~

This was my first repair during daylight; Norian had ordered me to pull the energy from Tulgalan's sun. It was the only star I could see during the day. I'd hugged myself, shivering as he'd snapped out the order. Director Keef was used to being obeyed without question. He would likely be as glad to see the back of me as I would the last of him. And my child, when she became an adult, would not be brought anywhere near ASD Director Norian Keef. Turning my head upward to the noon sun riding high overhead, I prepared to pull energy from it.

~

Nidris lowered his head, closing his eyes and preparing to tap into the core. Zellar had taught them to reach through the planet itself, carefully moving their power along until it met with that at the planet's very center. Then all it took was a small jolt of his warlock strength to breach the core and pull energy away, adding it to his strength and talent until he felt as if he could control the universe with what he'd stolen. Then he would disengage, but the tapped core could not be resealed. Not by him. He had no idea how the High Demon female could accomplish what even the strongest warlock could not. He resolved not to think on it; Her talent could be exploited without delving into the why of it. Carefully, Nidris felt his way through the crust and mantle, seeking the outer and then the inner core of Tulgalan.

~

Jes fretted. He should have heard from Nidris by now. He'd contacted the warlock as soon as everyone left the plantation, taking Reah with them. Teeg had promised to return for him when Reah needed help. They'd been gone for nearly a click and Jes knew it would take less than two for Reah to make her repairs and fall unconscious. His medkit ready, Jes waited.

The moment Reah was moved to a bedroom somewhere—after bringing her back to humanoid form, of course—Nidris and Yebri would fold in with Ardalin, snatch Reah and Teeg and then disappear again, taking Jes with them. The prearranged site was prepared and waiting—Jes had everything he needed to tend to Reah there. He would treat her while handing out soft words and promises. Her child he would accept as his, and they would spend their days together, after Reah healed one more core for Nidris. Jes considered contacting Nidris again but thought better of it. The warlock wasn't someone to offend lightly. Jes experienced a slight tug of guilt for making a deal with an enemy—Nidris hadn't drained Jes' home planet but Zellar, who'd taught Nidris, certainly had. No matter—Jes could claim Reah from this bargain and he had to be satisfied with that.

Tulgalan's sun was much easier to connect with—faster, too. The gathering of power was almost immediate when I reached out for it. It came willingly, too, as if it knew its child suffered and needed help. I pulled even more of its energy toward me, shunting it into the ground beneath my body, sending it on its way toward the wounded core.

"The path of the energy Reah sends to the core is simple to track, we just can't touch any part of it," Astralan explained to Lendill. He and Norian were witnessing this for the first time. Reah was glowing golden in the bright sunlight, surprising the Director and Vice-Director. "You should see this at night," Astralan went on. "If you aren't spiritual in any way, you might become so afterward. Her wings shine and unfold when she seals up the breach," he breathed, recalling the wonder of it.

"Then she falls over in a dead faint," Stellan added. "And we spend clicks sometimes, trying to convince her to wake and turn back."

"Are you still monitoring this? I'd like a full report on the process," Norian said, keeping an eye on Reah. Gavril and Tory stood close to Reah, watching her as she glowed with power.

"Of course we're monitoring it," Astralan almost snapped at the Director of the ASD. And if the fool would stop asking questions, he might be able to monitor more closely. Astralan was keeping track of the energy flow through Reah; Stellan was monitoring the core itself. "Everything should be fine and finished within a quarter," Astralan didn't finish his sentence—Stellan shouted in dismay as Reah screamed in agony and convulsed, falling over and beating her wings against the ground, forcing Gavril and Tory to scramble out of her way.

"She's having a seizure!" Lendill shouted, attempting to get to her, but Reah was too large for almost anyone to help her through this.

"She's suffering!" Stellan shouted. "Someone tapped into the core and now they're pulling energy from her!"

"What?" Norian shouted. "Stop it! Somebody stop it!" Reah shrieked again, her body convulsing on the ground as if she'd been shocked with high doses of electricity. Gavril and Tory were still attempting to reach her but it was impossible—neither of them could get close. Tory finally did what he should have done in the beginning, going full Thifilathi and lifting Reah off the ground, breaking the link with whoever had connected with her. Reah was still now and lifeless in Tory's arms as his Thifilathi blew clouds of smoke from his nostrils. Then, when the bloody discharge showed between her thighs, his Thifilathi threw back its head and keened to the skies.

"I'll kill you!" Lendill shouted at Derdris, who cowered in his cell. "I'll kill you for not telling us!" Lendill was nearly in tears as he shouted at the warlock. They hadn't thought to perform a power scan on him, depending upon sight alone to identify him as Nidris. Now, Nidris was still out there and had tapped the core at the same moment Reah had attempted to repair it, shocking her and breaking the connection she had with Tulgalan's sun. Instead, Nidris had followed the energy, tapping into Reah's power and draining her and the tiny child nestled in her womb. The child was dead and Reah nearly so.

"What the fuck did you think you were doing?" Karzac shouted at Norian, Gavril and Tory. Karzac had called for Larentii right away—Lenigar and Renegar had come—they were the two strongest healers who worked with the Saa Thalarr. As Aurelius' mate, Reah was entitled to their care.

"What's going on?" Jes had taken a chance and walked into the mansion.

"What the fuck are you doing here?" Norian went for Jes' throat as chaos erupted around them.

Farzi, Nenzi and their brothers stood quietly against the wall in Reah's room, weeping as the Larentii worked diligently to save Reah's life. Her tiny child was dead already—Teeg had tried to tell them what had happened but broke down in the middle of it.

Nenzi didn't understand any of it—someone had attacked their Reah with power, killing her baby and attempting to kill her too? And then, when the two women and the man appeared inside Reah's room, blasting the walls away, the Larentii sealed the fate of one of the female attackers, reducing her to particles as Nenzi turned to lion snake and sunk his fangs into the arm of the other. He recognized her immediately, as had his brothers.

Ardalin screamed as she stabbed Nenzi with a knife before dropping to the floor, dying from his poison. Nidris tried, using the power he'd gained, to reach the small woman lying on the bed. He hadn't counted on finding Larentii there, ready to separate his particles. Those he'd never have the power to overcome. Nidris cut his losses and folded away, leaving Ardalin dead on the floor, a lion snake bleeding out next to her, Yebri's atoms scattered somewhere and Jes held in a chokehold by Norian Keef.

"Don't let him die, it will kill Reah," Gavril shouted, struggling to get to Nenzi. Renegar, seeing the wisdom in Gavril's shouted command, knelt next to the bleeding snake and placed his hand over the wound.

CHAPTER 11

"You hired this as your personal physician?" Norian shouted in disbelief at Gavril. Jes sat in a chair, his wrists and ankles enclosed in zapcuffs. Jes couldn't escape—if he tried, Norian could send a killing jolt through the cuffs and Jes would die in mid-step.

"You seem to know him, why don't you tell me who he is," Gavril snapped

"Does the name Gergi Jarveston mean anything to you?" Norian paced in front of Jes' chair.

"The one who helped Marzi and Edan Desh kill Reah's mother?" Gavril's statement had Jes jerking his head up. He'd never heard the name of the child that had been born—he'd only seen her as a tiny baby when he'd handed the drug to Marzi—the drug that could cause hemorrhaging in a new mother. No names had been given—the money offered had precluded the need for information.

"That's the one," Norian snapped. Norian was in the foulest of moods and he had a headache. Not that he thought anyone would take pity on him and heal it—he it was, responsible for the death of Reah's daughter. Gardevik and the High Demon King hadn't been informed as yet and Norian didn't want to be anywhere near them when they learned of it. Reah's daughter was hope to them. Now, with Reah and Tory practically estranged, they might not get another child from that union and it could very likely be a boy if they did. Lissa and the others weren't going to forgive this. As it was, the Larentii were still working on Reah, pouring energy into her. According to Karzac, she'd been so close to death when Tory broke contact with Nidris' draining that only a blink later she would have died.

Tory had been placed in a healing sleep—Pheligar had forced him to return to his humanoid form and Karzac had been ready to place the sleep. Tory's Thifilathi had known, even if Tory hadn't—the baby was dead the moment he'd lifted her off the ground. Now, Jes was listening intently—Reah had been harmed? How had that happened? He ventured to ask the question.

"How-how is she?" He stuttered getting the words out.

"You don't know? I'm surprised—didn't you and Ardalin mastermind this?" Gavril shouted. He'd seen Ardalin's body—carried out of the room and tossed in the hall outside Reah's suite. Nenzi had killed her, as she'd stabbed the reptanoid. If Renegar hadn't saved him, Nenzi would also be dead.

"Ardalin wanted you," Jes snarled, lowering his gaze. "I only wanted Reah. Nidris promised to deliver if I could get him close enough. What happened to Yebri?"

"She thought to attack a Larentii," Gavril snapped. "It was the last thing she thought to do." Jes jerked back in fear; he'd never seen Teeg so angry. In fact, Teeg's eyes were red and were those—Jes huddled against the back of his chair.

"Didn't expect this, did you," Gavril hissed in Jes' face. "I was born vampire, you piece of shit. And if I'd listened to Reah, I'd have gotten rid of you long ago. Something wasn't right with you and she knew it. I just wasn't paying attention. And not only am I vampire, I'm a *King* Vampire. Do you know what that means?" Gavril's face was so close to Jes' now that Jes had wet himself; he was so frightened.

"N-no," Jes whispered.

"It means I can tell you to kill yourself—and you'd do it. I can tell you to kill yourself in the worst possible way and smile while you do it. Shall I do that, *Jes*?"

"Gavril, should I leave the room?" Norian asked.

"I say no—my son needs to get himself back in hand." Gavin Montegue stood inside the doorway, watching as his son threatened Gergi Jarveston, known to those in the Campiaan Alliance as Jes Wurfl, physician to Teeg San Gerxon.

"Dad, don't interfere," Gavril muttered.

"Son, the one thing that kept what little humanity I had left from slipping away is that I never toyed with my kills. If you're going to kill him, then do it swiftly and mercifully. I have a suggestion, however."

"What's that?" Gavril turned to look at his father.

"You may need additional information from him. Keep him alive— at least for a while. That's what the Council on old Earth used to do— hold onto them while the members considered and questioned. Then a sentence was passed. I don't think Norian will mind if we haul him to Le-Ath Veronis and let him sit in the dungeon for a while."

"I don't care what you do with the scum. He's managed to ruin any relationship I have left with Lissa. She won't be speaking to me after this and Garde will come for my head." Norian's future—from his perspective, anyway—looked extremely bleak.

"The Larentii are done and Karzac's hooking up an IV and feeding tube," Ry poked his head inside the door. "Bro, I was afraid I'd see that one's intestines draped around the room," Ry jerked his head toward Jes.

"You almost did," Gavril muttered angrily. "Dad talked me out of it."

"Thanks, Dad," Ry nodded to Gavin. Gavin and Aurelius had treated all three boys as their own during their childhood. All of them looked up to both former vampires.

"Has Wylend been informed?" Gavin asked Ry.

"He's here now, with Dad," Ry said. "They're watching Karzac work."

"Who's Karzac?" Jes spoke out of turn again.

"A healer's healer," Gavin answered Jes' question. "You aren't worthy to wipe his boots." Gavril, Ry and Gavin walked out of the room, leaving Norian to glare at Jes.

～

"When he woke after Renegar healed his stab wound, he almost went crazy until we allowed him into the bed with her," Karzac mumbled, slipping the IV into Reah's hand. Nenzi slept peacefully next to Reah's unconscious body. "He lost some blood, so we did a quick transfusion after the healing. Jeff came for that," Karzac added.

"Farzi see this," Farzi nodded. He and six other reptanoids still stood against the wall, watching everything that went on with Reah. Farzi and two of his brothers had donated the blood used in the transfusion.

"How are we going to tell her?" Ry asked. "Aurelius said she wanted to give the baby everything she didn't have as a child. How are we going to tell her it's dead now?"

"There isn't an easy way," Wylend stepped out of the shadows on the other side of Reah's bed. "And I think she'll know, the moment we allow her to wake."

"This is my fault," Gavril sighed. "Karzac, can you remove the chip without hurting her?"

"I already have. You were so afraid she'd get away from you. Now, I think it doesn't matter anymore, does it, young one?" Karzac held the tiny chip out to Gavril, who took it and crushed it in his fingers. "If she'd gotten away from you, her child might still live."

"Karzac, don't bludgeon me with facts I already know," Gavril sighed.

"Knowing and understanding may be very different. Did not Master Morwin teach you that? I will return in an hour or so to check on Reah. And as I understand it, Director Keef still does not have Tulgalan's core repaired." Karzac brushed angrily past Gavril on his way out the door.

"It's still leaking power," Astralan walked in with Stellan and Galaxsan.

"When will they wake Tory?" Gavin asked.

"No idea. If he goes Thifilathi again, who's going to stop him? If we call Garde, he'll turn, too. And if Jayd comes along, I don't want to see what will happen with three rampaging Thifilathi." Erland came to stand next to Wylend, placing an arm around Wylend's shoulders.

~

"Lissa, do you think I haven't called myself every kind of fool?" Norian's face was haggard. He'd sent mindspeech to Lissa, asking for the Falchani to come and haul the prisoners to Le-Ath Veronis' dungeon. She'd come with them, staying behind after they'd left with Jes and the Hazlan family. Norian had agents looking for Nidris, but they couldn't find any traces of him. More than likely, he'd already abandoned the planet.

"This will kill Garde. And we haven't even taken Denevik into consideration."

"Bloody, fucking hell," Norian muttered. "She asked me to wait until the baby came, right at the last. I yelled and told her to get on with it."

"Norian, tell me you've never had innocent blood on your hands." Lissa watched him closely.

"Not like this," Norian raked a hand through his hair. "Not ever like this."

~

"Kifirin, you need to be there when I tell them that Reah's baby died when she tried to repair Tulgalan's core." Lissa hugged herself as she paced in front of the one who'd created the Dark Realm. She'd sent mindspeech and he'd finally answered. Lissa was shocked by the keening that came from Kifirin as he slumped on the sofa inside her study.

~

"As near as I can tell, he tapped into the core while Reah was transferring the power from Tulgalan's sun. He must have startled her when she felt him siphoning away the power she was feeding in—she lost the contact and he was siphoning her energy instead. It killed the baby quickly and then took almost everything she had before Tory pulled her away."

"How are we to tell them?" Lissa knew what Glinda was asking. Garde and Jayd had already begun their search through the lists of male High Demons, seeking potential mates for Reah's child. Now, there would be no tiny female for a High Demon to cherish. No promise that the High Demon race might flourish again.

"Karzac says that if all goes well, Reah can become pregnant again in the future." Lissa was offering what solace she could.

"Lissa, I've tried so many times to become pregnant again. And I keep trying. As have my daughters. Nothing is happening. We needed the child now, to give the race hope. Now, that is destroyed. I don't know how Jayd and Garde will react. Denevik—he has already purchased a crib."

"Oh, Lord." Lissa rubbed her forehead with shaking fingers. "And Aurelius is out again—he won't know until he gets back."

"And what about Reah—has she wakened?"

"Karzac is keeping her in a healing sleep—he doesn't think she's ready, yet."

"What's going on—I tried to get to our son and I'm told he's in a healing sleep?" Garde appeared and was already breathing smoke.

"Garde, something terrible has happened," Lissa stood to give him the news.

"Half the palace in Veshtul is in ruins, now." Cheedas handed a cup of tea to Drake. Drew was busily sipping his tea already.

"I heard Garde went crazy." Drake nodded his thanks to the vampire who'd once been chief cook in Lissa's kitchen.

"Jayd, too. Glinda couldn't get him calmed down. Lissa called for

Kifirin, but he went into mourning and disappeared after hearing the news. Denevik—I hear he was seen walking the edge of Baetrah."

"Oh, no. Reah doesn't need to hear that her grandfather killed himself on top of everything else." Drew set his cup on the island.

"He didn't. He's back at the palace, looking at the ruin that Jayd and Garde made of the place."

"Cheedas, have they wakened Tory yet?"

"That I can't tell you. I only know what I do because Lissa came and talked to me. I babied her a little. She needed it."

"What is Reah going to need? She didn't want to do this until after the baby came. That's what I heard. And I think Norian is going into hiding. If he wants to live, that is." Drew shook his head over the whole mess.

∾

Gardevik Rath stood in what was left of his suite inside the High Demon palace as a cold rain beat against his skin. He was naked—hadn't bothered to dress after his Thifilathi had spent its anger. Veshtul seemed dull and gray in the early spring rain upon Kifirin. Garde sat on the chilled marble floor and watched while the rain pounded the city below. Jayd, also naked, walked up and sat beside his brother.

∾

"Gavril, we're just as guilty. We did this, just as much as Norian did. We pushed her. Belittled her when she wouldn't do what we thought she ought to." Tory didn't say it, but the unspoken matter of the implanted chip was between them. Tory had wakened to find his father sitting on the side of his bed. Tory had wept in his father's arms. His Thifilathi had known, even when Tory hadn't—just what the baby meant. Now, Garde listened while the brothers talked. Ry had also come, but he listened with Garde. Erland had asked him to bring information to Wylend, who worried about Reah and how the others might treat her as a result of the tragedy.

"What do we do now? She'll push both of us away." Gavril stood, rubbing his forehead. He had the worst headache.

"Young one, I gave you what you wanted. And now, all may be lost." Kifirin appeared in a brief flash of light.

"It wasn't supposed to be this way," Gavril cursed under his breath. "She was supposed to be mine—I was supposed to help her."

Kifirin turned his dark eyes upon Gavril. "Everything you requested was granted. However, there was something in the granting that I did not consider. I will ponder this." Kifirin disappeared swiftly.

"Speaking in riddles," Garde muttered.

"Have Farzi and the others had anything to eat? They won't leave Reah's suite. Thank the stars the Larentii put it together again before they left." Ry said.

"Let's get them something for dinner," Gavril stood. "Maybe it'll take my mind off the guilt."

"Little girl, as much as I'd like to keep you sleeping peacefully for a while longer, you must wake and talk with us." Karzac's words were the first I heard upon waking after. After the world had fallen upon me, that is. My daughter was dead—I'd known exactly when the cruel viper tapping into the core had drained her life away and then attempted to take mine as well. I had no recollection of how the link had been broken but it must have been—I was still here and my child wasn't. I felt empty, cold and abandoned as I opened my eyes, trying to bring Karzac's face into focus.

"You know already." Karzac's statement was flat.

"I know." I nodded, my voice and my throat as dry as dust.

"Here—only a little," Karzac held a cup to my lips. "We still have the IV in your hand and the feeding tube is still there," he added as I slurped ice water. It may have been the best water I'd ever had, mostly because it was the most welcome.

"There are several who wish to come and grovel," Karzac said gently, taking the cup away.

"I don't want to see them," I muttered, picking at the blanket that covered my narrow bed. I'd been transferred to one built for medical patients, I discovered.

"Who would you like to see?"

"Farzi and Nenzi. And their brothers. Wylend maybe. Aurelius, if he's in." I wanted to weep in Aurelius' arms, if I were honest. He would soothe me with foreign words I didn't understand and that was perfectly fine right then. I wiped a tear off my face. Karzac burst that bubble immediately.

"Aurelius is out, little girl. I will bring the brothers in and see if Wylend is available." He patted my hand and smiled gently. "Tomorrow, I will see about removing all these things." The lines and tubes hooked up to me were checked carefully. Mindspeech must have been sent—Farzi, Nenzi and the others crept into my room. I held my arms out and I was hugged quickly by all of them. Karzac stole away while I wept on Nenzi's shoulder.

"She said she didn't want to see any of you—the shapeshifters are consoling her," Karzac wasn't accepting arguments from Gavril, Tory or Lendill. "And I have sent for Wylend—she asked for him as well."

"If she worked for him, she wouldn't want to see him either," Lendill's voice held bitterness. "And what are we to do about Tulgalan? Power still drains from it." Lendill cursed in a language Karzac hadn't heard before. He had to *Look* to understand it.

"Reah may surprise you, Vice-Director." Karzac folded away.

I was napping later—just the brief waking had worn me out—when Wylend and Erland appeared. Two others were with them.

"Reah, darling, this is Corolan," Wylend introduced me to the tall man with wide shoulders, blond hair and an easy smile. Seating himself on the edge of my bed, Wylend motioned for Corolan to approach. "He is one of my trusted loves," Wylend went on as Corolan nodded to me.

"May I touch?" He held out a hand. Wylend nodded encouragingly, so I did as well. I thought he'd take my hand. Corolan leaned down and brushed his lips against my temple. "We will care for you," he whispered. "There is no need to fear."

"And this is Garek," Wylend introduced the darker haired man. Shorter and stockier than Corolan, Garek also leaned in to kiss my forehead. He stroked my cheek with a careful finger before stepping away. I blinked up at both of them, unsure what to do.

"You don't have to do anything, Reah. We know you are struggling now. I just wanted to reassure you," Wylend took my hand in his. "It is my hope that when you are well enough you will consent to come to Karathia and stay with me for a while. You will be cared for, I promise."

"I'll think about it," I sighed, closing my eyes. Already, I was weary again. I'd asked Karzac what they'd done with my daughter. He'd explained gently that there was only clots and a bloody discharge—Nidris' attack had destroyed her. There would be no body to bury or to mourn. The Larentii had cleaned out what remained inside my body afterward. It made me want to weep that my daughter hadn't been substantial enough—she'd been as ephemeral as a dream.

"She's sleeping," Wylend sighed as he was handed a cup of tea by one of the reptanoids. Gavril wanted to growl at the two warlocks who'd come with Wylend and Erland. He kept his feelings to himself with difficulty. These were Wylend's other lovers—Gavril was very aware of the Karathian cycles. He looked suspiciously at anyone who might serve to replace him in Reah's heart and life.

"Reah?" I had to work to come back to consciousness.

"Chash?" I was dreaming. Chash was gone. Someone had taken him. He wouldn't ever come back to me. I don't know what made me say his name, unless it was a longing that might never be satisfied.

"I'm here, baby. I'll always be here."

"No." I opened my eyes to find Teeg sitting on the edge of my bed, his hand stroking my forehead. "Chash died. Like my daughter. Go away, Teeg."

"Reah, can't you see past this now? I can't do anything about the baby. I wish I could. But I'm still here. Your Chash is here." He looked upset. That wasn't the Teeg knew. But then I hadn't known him all along.

"The Gavril I knew would have asked me what I thought. He would never have ordered me to do anything. We always talked and he listened. You don't listen, Teeg. Except to yourself. Maybe something happened to make you as hard as you are. I don't know. I lost the friend I had and now, all I have is somebody who only wants to go to bed with me, even when I don't want that." I turned my head away from him; couldn't look at his face any longer. What would my daughter have looked like? I had to stay away from thoughts like that —they only made me weep.

"They took you too young, baby. The Alliance, the ASD, Arvil—all of us. And you weren't strong emotionally on top of that. I know we exploited everything you had, just to get what we wanted. I don't know how to take it all back, Reah. All Tory can do is hold his head in his hands and moan. Norian—he's like a ghost. And Lendill, I think he's empty, now. He looks like the man who's lost everything."

"Like any of you care," I huffed, brushing a tear away and curling into a ball. "I don't even know why Wylend is trying so hard. I don't have anything left to give. Empty? You don't know empty. None of you do."

"Reah, I'm sorry. About the baby, about pushing you, forcing you to help me—all of it. But we got rid of some nasty people together. I realize that's of little comfort now, but I wouldn't have been able to do it without you."

"Where is Nidris now?" I know it was spiteful to mention Nidris, but he'd killed my child. They thought they'd gotten him—Farzi had explained it as best he could earlier. They didn't realize that Nidris' brother had been changed to resemble Nidris until it was too late. Now, Nidris could be tapping cores across the universe, with none the wiser until it was too late.

"We don't know." Teeg sighed and slid off the bed. He walked to the other side and sat on a chair, watching me. Pleading silently with his eyes. I thought about turning my head away again. "He could be tapping cores from here to the end of the universe and back." Teeg voiced my own thoughts and fears. "What are we going to do, Reah, if he kills everything?"

"What do you mean, *we*?" I asked spitefully. He couldn't do a damn thing about it and he knew it.

"Norian's letting you go—I saw the paperwork this afternoon. He's eaten up with guilt, baby. And Karzac removed the chip. I asked him to, but he'd already done it."

"Then I wish he'd done it sooner." I rubbed my forehead—I was getting a headache. "Why are you bothering to tell me?" I asked.

"I can take care of the small stuff—if you'll let me," Teeg offered. It reminded me of what he'd done when he and Jes had restrained me after my injuries in the bomb blast on Kareed.

"Why did you take that name—Teeg?" I asked instead, brushing his offer aside.

"It was given to me. By Dormas. He's an old vampire, Reah. He taught me carpentry first, and then taught me how to be a contractor. Everything I know about running the business I learned from him. He sent me to school and paid for my architecture and engineering degrees. Then got me involved in politics. I served as Vice-Governor on Malindor, did you know that? Twenty-five years ago. Decided not to run again, even though somebody offered to make me Governor of the Realm. All of that was done under an assumed name, of course. Vampires are still adept at creating identities and backgrounds."

"And where is your mentor now? Did you shove him aside when Arvil crooked his finger?"

"No. Dee is still with me. He's working as my assistant, now."

That made me snort. "Did you squash him, too?"

"Reah, don't." Teeg raked fingers through his wealth of dark hair. "Dee knew long ago that I was a King Vampire. He recognized it in me when I placed compulsion on another, older vampire—one who was trying to destroy Dee. When I ordered him to stop, he did. Just like that. Dee turned him over to the Vampire Council on Malindor. They sentenced him to death. Dee is important to that world."

"And now to the Campiaan Alliance." I closed my eyes—the headache was getting worse.

"Yes—Dee is very important. He's my personal advisor, Reah. He knows how to build this thing from the ground up. We've had to be ruthless, Reah—this Alliance is in its infancy and some of the worlds we are trying to shape aren't the most law abiding, as you know. The San Gerxon clan and the Hardlows were in charge for too long. Now, we have to wrestle those worlds away from the criminals who have a stranglehold on them. Their people want something else, they're just afraid to stand up and say it."

"So what is your current project, Teeg?"

"We're entertaining delegations from all the worlds that want to be a part of the Campiaan Alliance. That's next week. I'll be asking Wylend to attend."

"I see." Wylend would be too busy with politics to have time for me. It didn't matter—I hadn't expected anything else. "And what will you do about Nidris in the meantime? What does Norian intend to do?" I was massaging my forehead, attempting to get the headache to subside. It wasn't helping.

"Norian is gathering people and they'll probably have a conference on Wyyld or Le-Ath Veronis. Nidris will be desperate, now. None of the worlds Zellar destroyed had the population Tulgalan does. That doesn't make Zellar more humane in my eyes, but Nidris—he sold out his own family. This one will do anything, Reah. I don't think he cares who or what he destroys as long as he gets what he wants. Come on, baby. Let me take care of that for you." Teeg moved my hand aside and brought blessed relief to my aching head. Darkness descended immediately.

~

"How quickly can I get up?" I asked Karzac—he'd removed both the feeding tube and the IV line, healing up both wounds.

"You may sit up for a while—perhaps for dinner tonight. But no solid food until tomorrow, if everything stays down today." He hooked a strand of hair behind my ear. "I think your reptanoids want to help you in the shower."

"Karzac, please let me get clean," I begged.

"I'll allow it, but you should sit while they bathe you."

"How long until I'm back to normal?" I was almost afraid to ask. Almost. Karzac wasn't stupid.

"Reah, you shouldn't worry about that right now, don't you think? I'll let you know in a few days."

"All right." At the moment, I was glad he'd consented to allow me to bathe. Farzi and Nenzi walked in while Karzac was finishing up. I had a reptanoid on either side as they helped me wobble into the bathroom. A plastic stool was already inside the shower, waiting for me.

"I heard you took Ardalin out and she stabbed you." I pulled Nenzi's head down for a hug as he and Farzi prepared to give me a bath.

"Nenzi would do it again," he declared, giving me a smile.

"I love you both," I said. "As well as your brothers. I don't know what I'd do without you."

"We feel same," Farzi nodded. He got a hug too. The bath exhausted me, so Nenzi carried me to the bed and Farzi pulled back the sheet and blankets—someone had come to put fresh linens down. Both of them climbed into bed as lion snakes and I snuggled between them, drifting off to sleep.

~

"Their skin is smooth and their patterns are beautiful," I explained to Ry, who'd come in to tell me that dinner was waiting. He was surprised to find Farzi and Nenzi in my bed—both had lifted up and spread their hoods when he suddenly appeared inside the room. I stroked Farzi's and Nenzi's scales, trying to calm them down.

"We've set up a chair for you at the table," Ry said, eyeing both snakes. The reptanoids changed and helped me off the bed before dressing and coming with me.

"Couldn't someone at least add a little seasoning to the broth?" I complained at the bland taste of my dinner.

"But you have delicious gelatin for dessert," Lendill attempted to get me interested in a decidedly uninteresting dessert. All were present at the table except Wylend and Aurelius. The gelatin was supposed to be a redberry flavor. I would have preferred the redberry fruit instead of that.

"Eat it, baby," Tory coaxed. I wanted to snap at him. I didn't.

"Reah need her strength," Farzi tapped my bowl. I was sitting between him and Nenzi. Nenzi was smiling encouragingly. I sipped more of the broth.

"Please tell me we can leave this place behind soon," I mumbled, forcing myself to dip another spoonful of broth.

"Karzac says we can move you tomorrow. Mom already has a room set up for you at the palace," Teeg said. He was calling Lissa what Gavril had always called her. Perhaps she recognized him as her son—I didn't.

"Reah, I have to return to Campiaa tomorrow. I'll leave Farzi and Nenzi with you if they want to stay. I need the rest of them to come with me," Teeg said.

"We stay with Reah," Farzi said. Nenzi nodded. I rubbed Nenzi's back gratefully.

"Reah, I'm only going to carry you to bed," Tory looked hurt when I jerked away from him after dinner was over. Somebody had cooked for us—an Alliance recruit or ASD operative—I didn't ask. She was silent throughout the meal and nobody thought to introduce her. I'm sure she was just another nameless, faceless entity to Director Keef—somebody he'd use and cast aside as it suited him.

"Farzi and Nenzi can get me back," I huffed. Truthfully, I was running out of energy, but I didn't want Tory to know that.

"Reah, I'd get on my knees and beg if it would do any good." Tory looked ready to drop to his knees right then. I didn't argue further when he lifted me and carried me to bed.

"Baby—I'm really sorry," Tory was covering me with a blanket while Farzi and Nenzi watched. "Please don't shut me out. I promise I'll be better next time—the Thifilathi knocked some sense into me—when it was too late. We'll try again, baby, if you'll allow it." I wanted to jerk away from him again. I didn't. I just didn't answer him. Some other, stronger woman might have forgiven him. I couldn't. Not right then. "Do you need something to help you sleep, baby?" Tory asked. "I can get somebody here if you do."

"No. I'll be fine." I turned over in the bed so I wouldn't have to look at him. He waited for several minutes before walking out and closing the door.

"Beloved—we'll take you to Le-Ath Veronis if you'll wake now." Lendill touched my face. "Breakfast is waiting just as soon as you're ready."

A frown was all Lendill got from me—Farzi and Nenzi helped me dress. I was ready to get away from Tulgalan. For now. Surprisingly, Renegar had come to transport all of us. He put his hands carefully on me, checking to see how I was healing.

"Ren, I'm all right," I muttered.

"Little one, your body is healing." He didn't say anything else but his eyes held concern. If anyone would know how things truly were, the Larentii probably would. He didn't comment further than that and I was grateful.

Farzi and Nenzi had packed our things—Teeg was coming with us but only for a short while—he was expected on Campiaa before the day was out to make preparations for the upcoming meeting. I had no desire for the Campiaa Alliance to fail—quite the opposite, actually. As long as a standard set of laws were set up and adhered to, I didn't think it a bad thing. Teeg, though, would have his hands full as the founder. He neither needed nor had time for a mate. Just as well—I didn't know how I felt about him, anyway. Perhaps he'd been Gavril once. He would never be that again. Not for me.

Renegar folded all of us to the palace, where Lissa and Gavin waited. Lissa hugged Teeg and Tory. I slipped my arm through Nenzi's and he and Farzi helped me down the hall to my room—it had once belonged to Aurelius when he'd stayed there.

CHAPTER 12

"Son, she barely speaks to anyone." Garde was attempting to get Tory out of his depression over Reah.

"Dad, she won't talk about the baby. At all. She just turns her back on me and waits for me to leave."

"Torevik, this has been traumatic for her. And for all of us. Give it time." Garde was worried about his son and Reah. He was also angry that Kifirin had chosen to leave as quickly as he'd gotten the news. Perhaps the god was abandoning all of them, now. A tendril of smoke curled from Garde's nostrils. He was thankful Tory had his head down and didn't see it.

"Reah, come with me to meet my father. Please." Lendill had said the same thing for the past six days. Begging me to go with him somewhere—he never said where—to meet his father. I ignored him as best I could. I was mixing cake batter in Lissa's kitchen—Karzac had said I could get up and around if I didn't tire myself. Therefore, I decided to make a cake. Lendill was interrupting. Farzi and Nenzi sat at the huge island, watching me cook and listening to yet another exchange between Lendill and me.

"No, Lendill. What do you think that will accomplish?" I blinked at him helplessly, stopping in mid-stir, the large bowl held in the crook of one arm and the wooden spoon held in my other hand. Wylend had indeed gone to the meetings that Teeg was holding, although he'd offered to take me to Karathia and allow his servants and staff to care for me. I'd declined. He hadn't pushed it. Now that I'd officially been discharged by the ASD, Lendill had become relentless. I wasn't having any of it. What did he think we might have after he'd repeatedly forced me to do his and Director Keef's bidding, though it had harmed me and ultimately killed my daughter?

"Reah, breah-mul, don't do this to us. I beg you."

"I'm not your breath. Only your breath is your breath," I muttered.

"I will ask you again tomorrow. I promise." Lendill stalked out of the kitchen. Did he think to wear me down? Tory thought the same thing. Had tried to put his hands and his lips on the claiming marks on my neck. I'd walked away from him. Every time. Sighing, I pulled the cake pan over and poured the batter in.

"Reah, the cake is exceptional," Drake said. I'd still not gotten to travel to Falchan, I remembered as I studied him. He and his brother Drew sat together at the long table during dinner. The staff was serving my cake as dessert, as I'd intended. A trip to Falchan might never happen now. Not if things went as I planned. Later, inside my bedroom, Farzi and Nenzi wore worried expressions as I tossed clothing into a small traveling bag. I hefted a knife into my bag—I'd used it as a backup. It wasn't the black-bladed one Glinda had given me—Teeg still had that one. This was standard ASD issue. It would have to do. A small, sealed box filled with non-identifying credit chips was tossed into the bag next. Farzi and Nenzi already had their bags packed. I offered to send them to Campiaa but they'd refused, telling me instead that they'd inform everyone else of my plans if I didn't take them with me. Therefore, they were coming with me. I was zipping the small bag closed when Kifirin appeared in my bedroom.

"Get out," I snapped at him. He'd brought me to this. Taken Gavril away and made him a monster. Told him to form the Campiaa Alliance and Teeg had done his best for this one; all else be damned. Right then, I didn't care that he was the god. If he wanted to reduce me to cinders with a look, then he was welcome to do so. I was weary of the constant emotional pain of losing the baby. Tired of the others thinking that everything would be just fine and we could have another baby somewhere down the road. Right then, I didn't think I wanted any of them.

"I have something to say first," Kifirin said, his voice echoing through the room.

"Then say it and get out." I jerked my bag off the bed. I was ready to go. Farzi and Nenzi stared at Kifirin—he had stars in his eyes.

"I owe you," Kifirin said. "Tell me what you want and if it is within my power, it shall be given to you."

"I don't want anything from you," I almost shouted, remembering at the last that Lissa's palace was packed with vampires, who could hear an eyelash drop from one end to the other.

"When I granted Gavril's request, I failed to consider your part in this. You were forced into it, having made no request of your own. And it led to disaster, as should not have been. I did not see this. You were promised to me long ago, by the one who formed the darkness in me. I was once light, like the others. I accepted the darkness to create the balance."

"How nice for you," I muttered. I had no idea why he was telling me this. He'd said before that I'd been foretold but it hadn't meant anything to me.

"A daughter of your heart will come, he told me," Kifirin went on, ignoring my rudeness. "A demoness, clad in gold. The High Demons will be reborn through her. Your daughter was to be the first," Kifirin sounded sad, and that couldn't be. He'd coldheartedly ripped Chash away from me, replacing him with Teeg. Things would never be the same. Tory hadn't been prepared for fatherhood, either. I knew that now. It made me weep for my child.

"When I grant a request and it interferes beyond expectations with the life of another who made no request," Kifirin repeated, "I must make amends or offer compensation of some kind."

"You can't undo this," I said. "I don't want anything from you. Good-bye, Kifirin." I was ready to skip away.

"You are the daughter of my heart," Kifirin said. His beautiful face looked as if it were filled with pain. That had to be a lie.

"And I'm supposed to call you father? I don't have a father."

"I could give you gifts for this alone," he ignored what I was saying to him.

"No, thank you," I said as firmly as I could.

"I will choose if you will not."

"Don't bother."

"It is already done." Kifirin disappeared in front of me.

"Come on," I said to Farzi and Nenzi. They gripped their bags tightly, worry on both faces as I skipped us to Tulgalan.

"Reah, no. We not knowing how to wake you or change you back," Farzi was fretting as I dropped the basket of food next to the tent I'd erected for us. I was going to heal the core, asking the two reptanoids to care for me afterward until I gained my strength back. Then, we'd find the other worlds Nidris was likely tapping indiscriminately as he fled from the ASD. My ultimate goal, however, was to find Nidris myself. Hand him his death in retribution for my child.

"Farzi, here is a communicator—it has Lendill's and Tory's numbers programmed. If there is a problem or if you decide you don't want to stay, then call them. Just know that I won't be going with you. I mean to finish this, one way or the other. I want to kill Nidris before this is over."

"But he almost kill you before," Nenzi was nearly hopping in frustration.

"I didn't know he was out there before," I said. "Now I do. I'll be watching for him." I spread out the sleeping bag I'd purchased, after putting up the tent—It was big enough for all of us. Barely.

"When you do this?" Farzi wanted to argue with me but wisely decided to back off for the moment.

"We'll do it tonight—when the stars are out. If you can't wake me, then pull me into the tent and let me sleep. I'll wake tomorrow."

"I know she's gone, Dee." Dormas brought the communication from Lendill. "You taught me to manipulate people. I practically sent her after the bastard myself—I certainly pointed her in that direction." Teeg sighed. "What if this kills her, Dee? I told her—when she was vulnerable—that Nidris could destroy everything. She was thinking about going after him the moment those words left my mouth."

"Child, why did you do it, then?" Dormas had been Dee to Gavril almost as long as Dormas had called him Teeg—a nickname Dormas had given one of his human sons long ago, before he became vampire. Gavril had reminded him so much of his own child that it wasn't difficult to see him as one of his vampire children as well. Dormas had few turns to his credit over his long life and of all of them, Gavril was the most dear, though he'd come to Dormas already vampire.

Born that way, Kifirin had said. If the god hadn't said it himself, Dormas would never have believed. Then, when Gavril had offered his blood to Dormas, telling him it would enable him to walk in daylight and eat normal food, Dormas had been skeptical. Teeg's words had proven true, however, and now Dormas—nicknamed Dee by the son of his heart, walked in daylight and ate whatever he pleased.

"Dee, I can't answer that. Every time I think about her healing a core with only Farzi and Nenzi with her, my heart seizes up. And finding Nidris may be like searching for a toothpick in a hayfield. She has an impossible task, Dee. Anything could happen to her."

"Yet you sent her in that direction."

"She's the only one who can do this."

"As you are the one for this task—with my help, of course. Come, child. Let us check our security, one last time."

"Bring something of hers to me." It was an order, and Kaldill seldom issued orders to his youngest son. Lendill almost jerked back as his father made the demand via comp-vid.

"Father, you're not thinking of leaving Gaelar n'Seith, are you?" Lendill was nearly trembling.

"Child it will only be for a moment. I have not and will not perform the Alim'alu with any of your brothers—I am not ready for that!" Kaldill huffed at the thought of it.

"Good," Lendill breathed a relieved sigh. Lendill refused to believe that any of them would take care of the Elvish lands as well as his father did. "What do you want me to bring?"

"It matters not—clothing or jewelry that she wears often."

"I will find something. Who will come to get me?"

"I will send your brother, Faldill."

"Good. As long as it isn't Naldill. Or Reldill."

"Those are your remaining brothers. Do you have something to say to me about them?" Kaldill lifted a pointed eyebrow.

"No, father." Lendill hung his head, feeling as if he were too young again and at the mercy of his older brothers' incessant teasing and bullying because he had no power. Faldill had been the easiest to deal with, although he still teased at times, as did the others. At least he was less cruel about it.

"Be ready in half a click." Kaldill ended the communication.

"What is this?" Kaldill accepted the ring from Lendill.

"The ring Aurelius gave her. Reah wears it whenever she isn't on assignment. No agent is allowed jewelry such as this when they're working. It could give the enemy information they should not know."

"Then why isn't it with her now? You told me she was no longer ASD property." Kaldill pushed long, wheat-colored hair behind his left ear, revealing the pointed tip. Lendill had been born with the rounded ears of his humanoid mother. Another thing to be teased about, as it turned out. He and Reah had that in common—High Demons also had pointed ears. Tory's were only slightly pointed, but pointed nonetheless. He generally wore his hair over them so humanoids wouldn't guess his heritage, although many races had pointed ears. Reah had ears just as rounded as Lendill's.

"I don't know, father. If I see her again, I'll be sure to ask."

"Leave this with me. The working will take a while," Kaldill had his mind on it already, shutting everything else out, including his sons. Lendill looked down at

Faldill. Lendill's height was the only advantage he'd ever have over his brothers, although Naldill had threatened once to use his ability to make Lendill shorter. Lendill figured that the only reason he wasn't shorter than his brothers was that Kaldill would have noticed.

Lendill had left Gaelar n'Seith behind when he went off to school —his mother had asked it of Kaldill and Kaldill had relented. Lendill had met Norian during his studies and the two had been friends ever since. Lendill had only gone back to visit—never to stay. And when his mother died after a long life, the visits had become less and less frequent.

Faldill shrugged at his younger brother. Kaldill could be at a working for days. Someone would have to remind him to eat. "I'll take you home," Faldill muttered and folded Lendill away.

~

Farzi, Nenzi and I set up the tent as comfortably as we could. The sleeping bag was ready and we'd bought enough food to get us through several days if it were needed. All of it was suitable for camping trips and such—packaged against insects and ready to eat when opened. It wasn't fine food but it would do. Taking my seat on the ground after removing my clothing, Farzi and Nenzi stood back so I could turn to my full Thifilatha. Once that was accomplished, I focused on a star twinkling overhead and reached out for its energy.

~

"Destination?" The standard question was asked of all released prisoners. Edan Desh stared at the Alliance employee tapping the information into a comp-vid. None of his family had come to meet him. He hadn't expected them. All of them were selfish and wrapped up in their own lives.

"Targis," Edan almost snapped at the man. "Desh's restaurant on White Heron street."

"You're not free yet—I can have you locked away for another moon-turn." The employee didn't bother to look at Edan who stood before him, flanked by two guards.

"I know. My apologies." Edan nodded respectfully to the man. He'd noticed that in the past few eight-days, everyone had been on edge for some inexplicable reason. The prisoners, many of them, had been sequestered—they'd wanted to fight the others.

"All right, everything seems to be in order. Escort him to the gate," the employee jerked his head at the two guards. Edan Desh was accompanied down a narrow hall painted prison gray and smelling faintly of antiseptic soap. He was then escorted through a door held shut with an electronic lock, followed by three more hallways until they walked away from the prison. The heavy gate in the wall rolled back while Edan's meager belongings plus a small credit chip were handed to him. He was thankful to get that—he had no transport otherwise; a hoverbus stop just outside the walls brought visitors twice each week.

Edan hadn't received visitors the entire time he'd been incarcerated. Turning to look behind him after walking through the gate, he watched as the heavy steel and titanium door closed behind him. Few there would remark on his absence. Edan pulled up memories of Marzi Desh. He realized after five years of imprisonment that he hadn't missed his mother. Hadn't missed her whining and ordering him about.

She'd been more than willing for him to take complete blame for Raedah's rape and death. Now, Edan felt differently. Was he seeing Marzi as she truly was? Edan shook his head to get the images out of his head. Memories were there, but they were hazy. He walked down the concrete path toward the bus stop, the only passenger waiting for the next transport to come along.

Tulgalan's core was difficult to repair since it had been tapped from two locations. It bled energy as a body might bleed from multiple stab wounds. Nidris had wounded the planet in a similar manner—I could feel it while connected to it in this way. Energy poured through me, replenishing what had been lost. With two tapping sites, the energy was draining out twice as fast. Plugging up the largest leak first, I turned my attention to the smaller one, forcing the energy back inside that I'd just placed there. The power was threatening to bleed out again. "There," I sighed, once that feat was accomplished.

Blinking my eyes open, I found Farzi and Nenzi staring up at me in complete mystification. I hadn't fainted and merely felt tired, not completely exhausted as I had the times before. How could this be? I forced the turn back to myself and Nenzi ran to get clothing for me— the night had gone cool and moist around us.

"What happened?" Nenzi and Farzi both wanted to know.

"It's done—the core is healed," I said, slipping into trousers and a shirt that Nenzi held out for me. Socks and boots came next, even as I tried to discover what had been different. "Kifirin," I finally sighed.

"Kifirin? He do this?" Farzi blinked at me quizzically.

"He must have," I muttered. "This would have caused me to faint, otherwise."

"What he do?" Nenzi asked as I walked toward our tent. I was thirsty and hungry, but that was all.

"I don't know, sweet man," I hugged Nenzi to me. Never one to pass up an opportunity, he hugged me back—hard. He and Farzi had been worried to death over this. Now, they were both showing signs of intense relief. "Come on, let's eat," I said, flopping down next to the food basket and digging through it for the least offensive of available meals.

～

Edan was stepping off the bus when it felt as if a heavy load had been lifted from his shoulders. Others behind him were feeling the same, he saw. Sighs came from several and some even laughed or giggled for no reason. *Something had happened,* Eden thought. Something momentous, but none of them were ever likely to find what it might be. Edan pulled the strap of his small bag up and squared his shoulders, walking toward Desh's number one and a meeting with his father.

～

"You'll start at the bottom," Addah snapped. "With appropriate pay. And I've already filed the writ of detachment—your mother won't be coming here again. You've both embarrassed the family, but she's the worst. Do you know what your daughter has done? Do you?"

"The last I heard, she was wanted for drakus seed crimes." Edan shifted uncomfortably in his seat as he watched his father's face go pink.

"Faugh. That was just a cover-up. She was transferred to the ASD, you idiot. Reah was working undercover for them at the time. And that isn't what I meant."

"Then what did you mean?"

"She's intended to the King of Karathia," Addah's face almost went purple. "He brought her here and I blew up. Now, the *Star Gazer* is running ads showing Wylend Arden thanking that fool Worden for cooking a fine meal for him and his intended."

"That's not like you, Addah, to hurt the business in that way," Edan said quietly.

"I know." Addah looked at Edan as if he were seeing him for the first time. From where had that insight come? Addah had never seen it before.

"Did Reah look well? How did the Karathian King treat her?"

"Like royalty," Addah muttered angrily. "Why would you care anyway? You beat her. Broke her bones. I was forced to look at those reports by that ill-mannered Vice-Director of the ASD."

"Things have changed somewhat, father."

Addah snorted his derision. "You change? Not likely."

"I can't explain this in any way you'll understand, father. When would you like for me to start work? I warn you, I'll be rusty at first. I'm glad you're starting me at the bottom so I can relearn all of it. Perhaps I'll be better, this time. And if you hear anything at all from Reah, I'd appreciate it if you'd pass that information along."

"Don't go after her—that Vice-Director will be watching you like a lion watches a gazelle unless I miss my guess. One step out of line and you'll be living inside prison walls again."

"Trust me; I have no wish to harm her."

"Reah, when you make cookies again?" Nenzi lay back on the sleeping bag, staring up at the roof of our small tent. Thankfully, it was waterproof. The three of us watched as raindrops pattered on the synthetic cloth, dripping down the sides and into the trench I'd dug as a precaution. I'd had training through the ASD on how to live in the wild if it became necessary. Farzi and Nenzi, as lion snakes, could do it by instinct.

"Nenzi, if I can find a kitchen sometime soon, I'll cook. All right?" I turned my head to look at him. We ended up rubbing noses. Nenzi loves that. Farzi, too, so I turned to him and did the same.

"Where we go after this?" Farzi asked, smiling at me.

"I don't know, honey snake," I lay on my back and stared at the ceiling again. "We have to follow Nidris, but who knows where he's going or how much damage he's done already? We may have to guess, Farzi."

"Reah sleep here," Farzi pulled my head onto his shoulder. I tucked in against him, content to do as he asked.

~

Nidris had contacts. Good contacts. He'd worked for several, under Zellar. Now, he was going to offer his services again, if they had any need for him. They hadn't been thrilled with the idea of the Campiaan Alliance—in fact, they'd hired three warlocks already, all trained by Zellar, in an attempt to kill Teeg San Gerxon and the Alliance at the same time. Somehow, the Hardlows' warlocks had managed to thwart the assassination attempt. Now, Nidris could show them that he still lived. They'd hire him; he knew they would. Perhaps Nidris could do what the others couldn't, bringing that portion of the universe back to lawlessness and rule by the powerful. It would guarantee his safety, working with the ones who sought to take over.

~

"Aren't you suspicious that they're playing along?" Dee looked up at Gavril.

"Of course—but we need to keep them where we can watch them. See if Wylend will lend us a few of his," Gavril sighed. "Lersen Strand and his cousins will destroy the Alliance before it ever becomes official if they have their way."

"It will require your death to be successful," Dee pointed out.

"They're welcome to try."

"You can't ignore that possibility, Teeg. You're powerful in your own right, but they have plenty of support."

"Paid support."

"But support, nonetheless. Don't disregard that threat. I beg you."

"I'm not disregarding it, Papa Dee."

Dormas sighed as he closed the application on his comp-vid—he'd been going over the attendees for the meeting. "Too bad we don't have Reah; I think she could force all of them into submission with food alone. I miss those meals." Teeg had sneaked food to Dee on many occasions—food that Reah had prepared. Dee had gotten quite addicted to it.

"Dee, I think she might have loved you if I'd thought it safe to make introductions. Now, we may never get that chance."

"You have yet to introduce me to your parents." Dee didn't meet Teeg's eyes.

"I know; I don't want to upset any of you over this. I think of you as a father, too, but I don't want to upset Dad. He didn't have a hand in any of this and doesn't deserve anything less than my love and respect."

"I don't want to replace him."

"Dee, there's room for both of you. You did for me what Dad couldn't at the time. There's no need for you to be anything except my second father."

"Some have two fathers, others have no father at all," Dormas sighed, thinking of Reah.

"There's nothing we can do about that."

"Child, what will you do if she doesn't come back?"

"I don't know, Dee. I just don't know."

The rain had stopped by morning, so the three of us scrounged for our breakfast before packing everything up. I knew where we had to go—it had come to me in a dream. Another gift from Kifirin, if you could call what he'd done a gift. "Where we go, Reah?" Nenzi asked. I stood on tiptoe and kissed him, making him smile.

"To Reliff. Have you ever been there?" I smiled back at him.

"No. Not remember that one," Nenzi shook his head.

"Then let's go. And after we're done with that one, we'll make a trip to Cloudsong."

"No, Reah, that one long dead," Farzi was trying to steer me away from it. Cloudsong was one of the first worlds drained by Zellar. Nothing lived or grew on it, now. I'd do that one during the day—I still remembered the daystar's reaction to the healing on Tulgalan, before Nidris had interrupted. He had much to pay for, my daughter's life not the least of that.

～

"Edan, what makes you think I want to hear from you?" Ilvan hadn't been difficult to locate—he worked for the government on Tulgalan, inspecting restaurants and eateries in Targis and three other cities. He'd known going in what was expected, since he'd worked in a restaurant before.

"Ilvan, I just wanted to apologize. For past mistakes. I know you left the business and the family because of what I did. Now, I just want to take responsibility. For everything. I think Addah would welcome you back if you wanted to return—he grumbles about the pastry Aldah prepares."

The mention of Aldah's name made Ilvan mutter. Aldah, Addah's third son, was Fes' full brother and thick with Fes on everything. Fes covered for Aldah's lack of skill much of the time. Farla's two sons stood to inherit much of what Addah had built. "Reah could put both Fes and Aldah in the dirt," Ilvan said angrily. Addah never noticed Ilvan. It had always been Fes and Edan. Until Edan was convicted and sent to prison. Now, Fes and Aldah were the ones Addah spoke with. Ilvan never said it, but he was grateful that Marzi had only birthed Edan.

"I know."

"Is that why you called? To see if I knew where Reah is? I don't. I think she probably wouldn't want to see any one of us. I saw the advertisement for the Star Gazer. I heard from someone I know there that Reah is intended to the King of Karathia."

"That isn't why I called. I wouldn't mind seeing Reah, just to say

I'm sorry, but she likely won't accept my apology any more than you will."

"Edan, if you're trying to wriggle into Wylend Arden's good graces, don't. I don't believe he's held his throne by being weak as a warlock."

"Also not the reason I called. Ilvan, I don't need anything from you or father or the King of Karathia. What I truly want is forgiveness. From you and from Reah. I'm a different man, Ilvan. I hope you come to believe that, someday."

"I'll tell you what—if Reah ever forgives you, then I will, Edan. And you likely know that will never happen." Ilvan ended communication with his brother.

"This Reliff?" Farzi asked after I'd landed us in a park outside the capital city of Beedaris.

"This is Reliff," I nodded, pulling two credit chip bracelets from my bag and handing them to Farzi and Nenzi. "Just in case," I said. Both nodded their understanding. I wasn't familiar with Reliff and wasn't willing to pull out my comp-vid to do research. My comp-vid was ASD issue and likely had a beacon chip embedded. I wasn't going to turn it on, just in case. "Come on, let's see if we can find a room for the night." We walked through the park, eventually finding the nearest hoverbus port.

"I can disrupt the meeting," Nidris smiled at Lersen Strand. His cousins, Darsen, Ansen and Morsen were there, nodding at Nidris.

"And what if we want more than disruption?" Morsen smiled.

"Whatever you want," Nidris replied. He'd never tapped the core on Campiaa.

"We want Campiaa for ourselves," Lersen interrupted Nidris' thoughts. "The Casinos—all of it. Give us Campiaa and the rest will follow. I think we can promise you anything you want, after that."

Nidris agreed. What did it matter that Campiaa would die within a decade or two? Other worlds waited, and Nidris had no desire to work for the Strands more than a handful of years. He wanted to hunt the female High Demon. Still desired to have her under his command. Unlimited power awaited if she were his.

"Corolan, Garek, I want you to search for Reah. Bring her back to me," Wylend read through political requests for audience day. He'd finish with those before traveling to Campiaa. It would assist Gavril in building the Campiaan Alliance if Karathia was a strong ally. Wylend had made up his mind. The Reth Alliance might frown upon some of Wylend's methods for tracking and dealing with prisoners. Gavril's Alliance made allowances for those things.

"Who will protect you while you are upon Campiaa?" Corolan didn't mind searching for Reah, he merely wanted to keep Wylend safe at the same time.

"Erland, Rylend and Wyatt are coming with me," Wylend signed the request for a hearing after reading it. "Plus my personal guards."

"All right," Corolan sighed. With the Starr warlocks employed by Gavril, that should be sufficient to guard both Wylend and the founder of the Campiaan Alliance. "Are you sure Wyatt is a good choice? Having you both in the same place?"

"He needs the experience," Wylend muttered. "His head has been elsewhere, lately. Ry is more than dependable. Perhaps some of his focus will attach itself to my heir."

"As you say," Corolan nodded. "We'll work on this from our end before striking out blind."

"I expect nothing less," Wylend agreed.

"It may interest you to know that Tulgalan's core is now healed." Lendill stood in the doorway to Norian's office.

"And how do you know this?" Norian grumbled. "Does Torevik know? Reah hasn't been gone that long, she still might be there."

"My father told me," Lendill replied. "And I informed Tory first. He has already gone looking for her. I don't believe he'll find anything. I sent someone out myself. All they found was an abandoned camping site."

"How did you find it so quickly?" Norian was very curious. He had agents scattering to find Reah. It was the least he could do—he was worried she might harm herself or do something dangerous and come to harm in that way. He was worn down with the responsibility of the baby's death. None of Lissa's other mates were speaking to him. He'd been too afraid to approach Ildevar with the news.

"We knew the two tapping locations—I sent someone there. Reah went to the first one. It makes sense—I didn't think she'd want to return to the place where her child died, do you?"

"It does make sense," Norian scrubbed his jaw. Since Lissa had given him blood, making him immortal, he no longer needed to shave. The habit of a beard was still with him, however. "Does your father know where Reah might go next?"

"Not at the moment," Lendill hedged. Norian lifted an eyebrow at his friend's words.

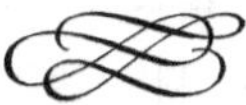

CHAPTER 13

"Why you order this, Reah?" Farzi watched as I cut into my roast fowl.

"Because this is something I can walk away from if it's cooked badly," I sipped my glass of wine. The fowl was a little dry but edible. Farzi and Nenzi both ordered steak. They preferred it rare, but tonight it came to the table slightly overcooked. We'd chosen the hotel restaurant for our meal; it was convenient. Our bags were stowed in an upstairs room, our packed tent and basket of camping rations there as well. I hoped the staff wasn't curious—there weren't any camping spots or tourist attractions nearby that would warrant the equipment and supplies.

"When you do this?" Nenzi asked, frowning as he cut into his steak. The cut wasn't as tender as it might have been.

"Tomorrow, sweet man. We'll leave right after."

"I do not like Cloudsong decision," Farzi reminded me.

"I know, honey snake. If it looks too hard, I won't try, all right?"

"That will do," Farzi nodded. "I like this name you call me."

"You do?" I smiled at him.

"Me, too," Nenzi was enthusiastic.

"Good. Let's finish this up and go to bed—I'm really tired," I yawned.

"We see that Reah sleeps," Nenzi nodded.

~

"My son, wake now," Kaldill stood over Lendill's bed. In any other situation, Lendill would have a ranos pistol drawn and threatening anyone standing over his bed. His father had taken away that fear. Lendill knew that only his father might accomplish that.

"Father, what is it?" Lendill sat up quickly.

"I have located her—it was quite easy, actually. I merely had to search for the nearest tapped core. She is on Reliff. You must come with me now."

"But," Lendill thought to protest. He should have saved his breath.

~

The lights were on and Farzi, Nenzi and I were blinking at Lendill and another man who stood behind him. Shocked that Farzi and Nenzi weren't lion snake and threatening, I stared at Lendill.

"How did you get in here," I snapped at him. I'd been sound asleep when something had wakened me and the reptanoids.

"My, uh, father," Lendill coughed in embarrassment.

"This is your father?" I stared at the man with Lendill. Lendill didn't look anything like him. He had long, golden hair, pointed ears, piercing green eyes and a feeling of power about him. He also appeared young—as young as Lendill. I didn't know how that could be.

"Kaldill Schaff," the man held out a hand. Not wanting to be rude, I took it. "King of the Elves," Kaldill Schaff added. "The ring, son. Quickly." Lendill handed a ring to the one who'd just identified himself as King of the Elves. Elves weren't real. Those were tales from children's books. I stared openmouthed at Lendill's father while he placed the ring on one of my fingers. I thought to take my hand away, but Kaldill Schaff was stronger than he looked. He muttered words that I failed to understand, then Lendill muttered more in the same language.

"Now, young woman, say yes," Kaldill nodded to me.

"What?"

"Wrong word. Say yes." Kaldill was staring at me.

"Yes?" I didn't know what he wanted.

"Good. Very good." Kaldill relaxed visibly, sighing and releasing my hand. "You are now married to my youngest child. Therefore, I can offer a gift. The Elven race is obligated to protect you in the next few days. Would that you had come before the child was lost. I could have offered the same gift, then."

"You couldn't have done anything about that," I grumbled, wanting to cry. "And I'm not married to Lendill."

"Yes. According to Elvish law and tradition, you are most certainly married to him. And if you'd married him before, I would have come for you and refused to allow you to leave our lands until the child was born. Without the marriage bond, I am not allowed to interfere."

"Fuck," Lendill almost shouted.

"What are you saying?" I was crying now and Farzi and Nenzi were upset on my behalf. Somehow, they knew not to threaten Kaldill Schaff.

"Reah, daughter, do not weep," Kaldill sat on the side of my bed. "All things turn in a circle, did you know? What we lose, we gain. What we hate, we love. It is the way of the universes." He reached out and cupped the back of my neck, bringing my head forward to touch against his. "So much is yours, pretty one. So much more will be yours. I cannot mitigate the harm. That is not mine to give. My child loves you. I beg that you remember it." Kaldill Schaff disappeared, breaking whatever spell he'd placed on all of us.

"You can't be an Elf," I wiped tears away, deliberately not looking at Lendill.

"I'm half," he said. "And I didn't always look like this. A Larentii changed my facial features nearly thirty years ago after I was attacked. An enemy had surgery done to make his face like mine. This was the way to distinguish me from him. I kept the disguise because it was more handsome."

"Your father was very handsome," I sniffled.

"I didn't resemble my father. I resembled my humanoid mother. She was my father's third mate. I have three brothers—all fully Elven. They tease—sometimes cruelly—because I was born an immortal without power among the Elvish race."

"We're not married," I repeated.

"Reah, my father says we are. In his eyes, that's binding. He will protect us both if necessary."

"He couldn't save my daughter. Nobody could." I refuted Kaldill's words.

"Reah, I've learned not to question my father's words. I've learned to eat my own too many times." Lendill took the spot on my bed previously occupied by his father. Nenzi scooted over to give him room.

"You need to leave." I turned my face away from him.

"Reah, I know the core needs healing here. Father told me. I'll stay and help Farzi and Nenzi guard you. I can smooth your way, *Deah-mul*. Those words are Elvish in origin, did you know?"

"I don't want your help." I hugged myself, feeling chilled.

"*Cheah-mul*, I do not—I cannot—live without you. Your tenure with the ASD is done. You may say anything you want to me and still I will love you with everything I am. You are not obligated to love me in return. I am broken, Reah. You hold my heart and soul within yours. I cannot live without you. It is the way of my race. It broke my father's heart when my mother—his third wife, died. He still mourns her, and that was more than two hundred years ago. He loves my brothers' mothers, but he misses mine."

"Lendill, don't do this. I just lost my daughter. There's nothing to take away that pain and emptiness."

"I know," Lendill whispered, gathering me against him. Farzi and Nenzi, now lion snakes, slipped off the bed, crawling across the carpet toward our camping gear.

Lendill didn't ask for anything. Soft words were spoken that I didn't understand and I fell asleep with his arms around me.

"Reah not faint now," Farzi explained to Lendill as I sat on the small patch of grass. Lendill didn't say anything, he settled for watching me with concern instead. Nidris hadn't tapped the core that long ago—it was an easy fix.

"That's it?" Lendill sounded skeptical. I didn't know how to explain what Kifirin had done. I wasn't sure myself. Shrugging, I slipped into my clothing with Farzi's and Nenzi's help. "Now what?" Lendill asked.

"I was going to Cloudsong," I said. "To see if I could do anything about that."

"Reah, no," Lendill shook his head in disbelief. "That sounds like a fool's errand."

"Most likely it is," I agreed. "But I want to try. Unless you have information on Nidris' whereabouts. I want to kill him."

"So do I," Lendill's hands clenched. That surprised me. Where was the Vice-Director of the ASD, who wanted to capture and question? "But we don't know where he is right now," Lendill added. "Why don't you allow me to buy a meal for all of us?" Lendill motioned for Farzi and Nenzi to join us. Much taller than both reptanoids, Lendill put an arm around both their shoulders and smiled at them.

"This isn't bad," Lendill smiled over his dinner.

"No, not bad," Nenzi grinned at him. We'd found a small diner on the outskirts of the capital city and slid into a booth. The cook worked in full view of the diner's patrons. Lissa would have said he was slinging hash. I never determined just what the phrase meant.

"It's decent." I took a bite from my sandwich. The meat wasn't dry and the lettuce and tomato fresh enough.

"Coming from you, that's a four-star review," Lendill smiled at me.

"I'm still trying to determine why your appearance was changed so dramatically," I said to him.

"I used to look like my mother's family, with light-brown hair and such. Lissa initially made me look like Flavio's twin. Reemagar modified that to what I am, now. I decided to keep it."

"Yes, you do look a bit like Flavio," I examined his features. Lendill sat next to me, Farzi and Nenzi sat opposite us. "But Flavio's sire is not the King of the Elves. I thought Elves were myth."

"No, just hidden. For a very long time," Lendill went back to eating. Perhaps he didn't want to talk about it. I was wrong—as soon as he swallowed, he said, "Ask my father all the questions you like next time. Some he may not answer, but most he will. You're part of the family, now."

"Lendill," I muttered.

"Reah, please don't. Don't deny me or us. I'm sorry we've treated you as we have, but others were treated in a similar manner during the same period of time. We've been ruthless over the years—I admit it—just to keep the Alliance going. You've seen it yourself—the Drakus seed and the crime families and assassinations—we use our best agents mercilessly. Reah, your discharge papers recognize your service. You have the awards to show for it—you know those aren't handed out until the agent leaves, just like the military. And you got the bonus that all agents receive for exemplary service. When you're ready to see all that, let me know. In the meantime, they're in my office."

"At least you're not making me go to Norian to get them," I snapped.

"Reah, someday we'll talk about the Director. Not now. He cannot harm you again. Not as he did. I know that once was more harm than anyone could expect from their service. Let's leave it for now, all right?"

"I didn't bring it up." I wasn't hungry anymore.

"Deah-mul, eat. You need your strength. You repaired the core this afternoon. Surely you must be tired and hungry. At the very least. Let us be gentle with you now. To make up for the past."

"Does the phrase *too late* mean anything to you?" I drank from my glass of milk.

"Reah," Lendill sighed. "I can't take away the pain. It's still fresh. That wound too new. All I can do is love you as much as I can. Come back to the hotel room with me. Let me take care of you for a bit."

I relented. As it turns out, it was a very good thing. Hotel security and the local constabulary were waiting outside my room, wanting to question me about the camping equipment inside.

"Official business," Lendill flipped out his ID. I wanted to laugh at the facial expressions, but didn't.

"But why?" The hotel security chief should have left things alone.

"Tracking a rogue warlock," Lendill snapped. "We came prepared for any emergency. Unfortunately, our quarry has escaped. We will leave immediately."

We did leave—packing up while security watched. Farzi and Nenzi hauled our equipment out while Lendill and I took charge of the bags. I overheard one of the locals cursing as we walked angrily toward the lift. "I told you we should have asked questions downstairs," he hissed. "Now I'll never be considered for a position with the ASD. That was the fucking Assistant Director!"

"You're right," Lendill nodded to them as the elevator doors closed on us.

"We can hop a ship or you can get us out of here," Lendill pulled me against him outside the hotel.

"I'll do it, where do you want to go?"

"I'd like to go home. To Wyyld."

"You live on Wyyld?"

"I have rooms at the palace. Ildevar saw to it when he gave a wing to Norian long ago. Norian is on Le-Ath Veronis, so there's little chance of meeting up with him. Besides, my father's lands aren't far from Ildevar's palace grounds. They're hidden, though. Most people navigate around them without realizing they're doing it."

"You're joking?"

"Not. Can you get us to Wyyld?"

"I can get you to Wyyld." And I did.

"This nice," Farzi looked around him at the vaulted ceilings, marble floors, rich tapestries, rugs and fine sculpture that lined the hall we walked through.

"Deonus Wyyld's assistant knows we're here," Lendill smiled down at me. I'd never met Ildevar Wyyld, the Founding Member of the Reth Alliance. Or his assistant. "Hello, I'm Wegg, Deonus Wyyld's private assistant," Wegg introduced himself as we walked into his office. Wegg was Wyyldan and completely humanoid, Lendill sent mindspeech explaining that to me.

Just in case you thought he might be part Elf, Lendill added.

"Should I bow or kneel?" I asked, suddenly worried.

"No," Wegg laughed. It was a good laugh, with no contempt mixed in it for those of lesser importance. "If Ildevar were here, he would make a proclamation that Reah Nilvas Schaff should never bow to anyone."

"But why?" I wasn't sure what was going on. Lendill had a warm and comforting arm about me, refusing to say anything.

"Anyone who brings worlds back to life by repairing the core—something that only a Larentii might do otherwise, should never bow or kneel. I don't care how important the other person thinks they are." Wegg was grinning widely. He was handsome in his own right, with brown, wavy hair trimmed to his shoulders and deep blue eyes brimming with good humor. I couldn't help but smile back at him.

"I was going to Cloudsong before Lendill found me." I hung my head. I'd allowed his words to distract me for a time.

"Come, I'll walk with you to Lendill's suite. I've prepared rooms for our lion snakes as well." Wegg included Farzi and Nenzi in his smile.

"I brought clothing for you, when Lendill informed me that you were coming with him," Wegg led me to a closet inside Lendill's suite. Lendill kissed the top of my head as I found an entire side of his closet was now filled with clothing in my size.

"But, I can't," I said, wanting to cry. Nobody did things like this for me.

"Shh," Lendill said softly, his lips next to my ear.

"Reah, Ildevar signed off on all your awards. This is the least we can do for you. Come. Look." Wegg led us toward a spacious sitting room, and then into a study. Behind the desk were all sorts of gold certificates with Lendill's name on them. On an adjacent wall were others.

"All these are yours, I put them up this morning," Wegg informed me, pointing to the adjacent wall. "This one is for single-handedly bringing down the drakus seed trade. This is for handing some of the most wanted criminals in the Alliance to ASD officials. This is for the arrest of six assassins. Need I go on, Reah? There isn't one important enough for saving entire planets. Ildevar is working on that problem now."

"You don't need to—tell him to stop," I sighed. "This is nice, but I'm glad to be out of the ASD."

"I know. I grieve for your loss," Wegg said. Somehow, he knew about the baby.

"As do I." I was wiping tears away and very close to sobbing my heart out.

"Was it that bad? Truly?" Ildevar Wyyld appeared next to his assistant. "Were your years in the ASD so horrible?" His voice was gentle, and he expected some sort of answer. I gave him the truth as I saw it, as painful as it was.

"Every one of them," I sobbed and skipped away from the Founding Member of the Reth Alliance.

"We tend to push the ones with special talents and abilities." Norian admitted over dinner. Farzi and Nenzi, left behind by Reah when she'd left so abruptly, were sitting with Lendill on one side of the table while Norian Keef sat on the other. Ildevar Wyyld sat at the head; Wegg sat at the opposite end.

"Do we not provide any sort of treatment for those agents in need of it?" Wegg asked. "For emotional problems? Don't you test them before accepting them into the ASD?"

"Not in Reah's case," Lendill shot a glance at Norian.

"When she, ah, fell into our laps after her stint on Mandil, there wasn't time to do it before sending her out on the drakus seed thing. And then, when that turned out as well as it did, we, ah, didn't." Norian busied himself with his plate of food. "Corners are cut in the interests of the Alliance," he added. "Sometimes."

"Child, perhaps you should rethink your policy improvisation from now on," Ildevar said quietly. "Do we know where she might be? I had no intention of upsetting her so badly."

"Deonus, she lost her child. What can you expect?" Wegg offered Ildevar a glance across the table.

"When did this happen? Did someone forget to tell me?" Ildevar was shocked.

"I, uh," Norian mumbled.

"You didn't tell him?" Even Lendill sounded upset.

"You treat her bad," Nenzi stood, pointing a finger at Norian. "She ask you to wait for the baby to come. You force her. I want to leave." Nenzi stalked away from the table.

"I'll get him—we probably should take him to Gavril," Lendill stood and slapped his napkin into his seat. Farzi rose right behind Lendill and followed.

"Child, what have you done?" Ildevar stared at Norian.

"Reah lost Torevik's High Demon daughter," Wegg stated. "I hear things, Deonus. I was waiting for Norian to report this to you."

"I can't take it back. I wish I could." Norian rose from his seat.

"Norian, don't let this mistake take you down," Wegg said, rising as well. "Ildevar is correct—review your practices. Don't let this happen again. Be strong, Norian. Everybody needs you to be strong."

"Why didn't you hand that pep talk to Reah, Wegg? Why?" Norian folded away.

"Wegg, I know not what to do," Ildevar gazed sadly at his assistant.

"Deonus, at times, things remain outside our control. We know this. A higher hand stirs the waters and we are left to deal with the ripples."

"Spoken as a true Seer, Wegg," Ildevar agreed.

~

"It will take a connection to six stars to pull enough energy without damaging any of them." A Larentii came to sit beside me. I was already in full Thifilatha and towered over him, although he was at least eight-and-a-half feet tall in Earth measurements.

I'd been thinking of Aurelius and using his archaic methods to gauge heights seemed appropriate. Evening had fallen on that area of Cloudsong and the stars were beginning to appear overhead. I'd originally planned to do this during the day, but events had prevented it. At least something was going right, since Renegar said it would take energy from six stars to make repairs.

"Renegar?" I smiled—I couldn't help it—he'd come to Cloudsong. "You haven't come to talk me out of this, have you?" The others had. I expected nothing else, although I might listen to Ren before I listened to anyone else. According to Lissa, Ren had fathered a Larentii Wise One, and was grandfather to another. I wouldn't discount anything Ren said.

"I am here to monitor your efforts," he smiled up at my full Thifilatha. "I knew I would find you here. Shall we begin?"

"Are you helping?" I asked, a bit surprised.

"I will only tell you when you have pulled enough energy from each star, so you may switch at the proper time," he said. "I cannot help by pulling the energy, but there is nothing to prevent me from passing on information."

"Oh." I nodded at his words and turned back to the stars, selecting my first target. Altogether, it took the better part of six clicks, one click per star. Renegar did as he'd promised, giving me the proper time to change. I was exhausted afterward and wishing I had my tent and basket of food. Both would have been welcome.

"That is also why I came," Ren watched as I changed back to myself and reached tiredly for my clothing. He helped me dress. "I will take you to Beliphar; Graegar asked me to do this. There is a place on that deserted world where you might stay, unless you wish to go to one of your mates, tonight. Or to more than one of them."

"They don't need me and I don't think I want them," I sighed.

"Little one, your first statement is not true. I only hope that eventually the second will not be true as well. Meanwhile, Beliphar awaits." He folded me to the abandoned world.

"Everything here is in stasis—you may use it as your own," Ren informed me as I wandered through the huge kitchen. The cold keepers hummed—the solar collectors still operated. Food was in the keepers and cabinets that I could prepare if I wanted, or I could nibble on fresh fruits and vegetables if I were too exhausted to cook.

"Do you know if Farzi and Nenzi are all right?" I asked. I'd worried over them as soon as I'd skipped away from Wyyld.

"They are well—Lendill contacted Gavril Montegue and they have been taken to Campiaa."

"Good." I heaved another weary breath. "Thank you for your help," I nodded to him.

"It was the least I could do, little demon." He inclined his head briefly and folded away.

I truly felt too tired to cook, but forced myself to do it anyway. I had a broiled steak, seasoned just right, with a salad and two glasses of wine. The dishes could wait until I woke—I found a bed not far away from the kitchen and huddled into it, too tired to cry, even, over the turns my life had taken.

"Will you be able to conceal them?" Lersen Strand waved a hand to encompass the army of Giffelithi mercenaries. Giffel was a sister planet to Liffel, and they were still angry that Liffel had been destroyed by the Reth Alliance. They had no love for any part of it, and looked to profit from anything that might bring about its downfall.

Lersen and his cousins had paid top credit for this army, and then spent another fortune equipping it. Few had ranos pistols or rifles—those were extremely difficult to come by since Teeg San Gerxon had taken over. That was about to change. Giffel didn't want to be under San Gerxon's thumb any more than the Strands, but they wouldn't refuse the money the Strands offered.

"I can easily conceal all of them," Nidris smiled at Lerson's question. Once he tapped into Campiaa's core, anything might be accomplished. He looked over the assembled army of Giffelithi dwarves. Nidris had no idea how the Strands managed to put funding together to hire five hundred mercenaries, and cared even less.

He'd do his job, the Strands would have Campiaa, wealth would be his and he'd find another crime family to hire him. No sense in staying around for the Strands to connect him to Campiaa's tapped core. He recognized the three warlocks Lersen Strand had hired—Zellar had trained them but hadn't taught them how to tap cores. That he'd reserved for the power finders. None of the three held that talent.

"Good," Lersen Strand smiled at Nidris' reply. He, his three cousins and Nidris stood on the catwalk overlooking the floor of the warehouse. The other three warlocks would transport the army; Nidris would conceal it when they landed on Campiaa. Then, when all the visiting dignitaries were in one spot, signing up for membership in the Campiaan Alliance, Lersen and his army would strike. Nidris chuckled.

"Why do you laugh?" Lersen frowned at his newest warlock.

"I would like very much to see the look on San Gerxon's face when he dies."

"I will describe it to you. In detail," Lersen promised.

～

"Fes, he's working on the pastry," Aldah muttered.

"And he's doing a good job. Why do you care, brother—you hate making pastry." Fes stared at his younger brother. "You like making desserts better—handle that."

"You don't see it, do you," Aldah accused. "He'll try to take this away from us."

"Relax, he'll not get away with anything. Father has already cut him out of the will. Didn't I tell you?"

"You said that, but what if Addah changes his mind?"

"He won't. You worry over nothing. Use Edan as much as you like. He's the lowest-paid cook we have at the moment. Revel in that, brother. Desh's number one is on top and will not lose that spot. Ever. We will make sure of this. Go back to work—we are booked up tonight. Make that chocolate crème cake you are so fond of."

"All right, but do not forget that I warned you," Aldah walked away in a huff.

"Paranoid," Fes sniffed and went back to his accounts.

Spring brought rains to the High Demons' world, named after Kifirin the god. Veshtul was awash in small rivers, the water flowing down cobblestone streets paved with multicolored stones. Gardevik Rath walked through those streets accompanied by Denevik Lith. They'd destroyed half the palace, now they sought an architect who might help rebuild that part of it. Garde had thought of approaching Adam Chessman, but the Saa Thalarr were quite busy with Ra'Ak spawn cropping up in too many places.

The Ra'Ak were hiding for some reason, reluctant to do more than send their young turns out in an attempt to make others such as themselves. Garde shook his head. Denevik worried about his granddaughter. He'd gone looking for her, too, on several occasions. Had even been on his way to Wyyld when he'd heard she was there, only to learn she'd skipped away at an ill-placed word from Ildevar Wyyld.

"I forgot about the rains," Denevik lifted the collar of his jacket. Jusef had offered to come. Denevik had told his dwarf companion that there wasn't any need for both of them to get soaked. Garde seemed determined to punish himself in whatever way possible. Denevik felt numb on the best of days. Still, the cold spring rain wasn't helping his mood any.

"Every year," Garde grumbled. "This architect better be worth his weight in Tiralian Crystal."

"She was on Reliff for a short time. Healed the core there—we found the residual power," Corolan gave the news to Wylend. Wylend stood, half-dressed, inside the suite Gavril had given him in San Gerxon palace. "Lendill Schaff pulled her to Wyyld, but she was only there for a brief time—less than a click—when she became upset and skipped away. Now, we hear through channels that Cloudsong's core has also been repaired. I have no idea what kind of energy she had to pull to accomplish that." Corolan was shaking his head. Garek still had trouble believing what he'd seen when they'd landed on Cloudsong. Somehow, a rain had come and he and Corolan both felt the rumbling of growth across the dead world.

"Do you think she'll go to Thiskil?" Wylend sat wearily on a chair in his sitting room.

"No idea. That fool Gergi Jarveston is from Thiskil. Do you think she knows that?"

"That I cannot say." Wylend raked a hand through his thick, light-brown hair. "Place a surge detection on it, just in case."

"I'll do it," Garek offered. "Wylend, my dear, stop worrying. We'll get her back."

"Thank you," Wylend nodded gratefully.

"If they hit us, it'll come tomorrow," Dee sighed. The meeting hall was ready. Astralan and Stellan had placed wards around the meeting hall inside The San Gerxon, the largest casino on Campiaa.

"I know," Gavril agreed. "I've sent Farzi and Nenzi out as lion snakes—they'll keep an eye on the Strands' suite. If anything goes on that raises suspicions, I'll know."

"They're coming in tonight?"

"Yes. They're scheduled to arrive at the space station before eight bells. Hirzi and Bekzi will drive them in after they reach the shuttle port. I've got the rest of them scattered around, ready to spy on the Strands at a moment's notice." Gavril shook his head.

"Child, I hope we live to celebrate tomorrow evening."

"So do I, Dee. So do I."

"Who's there?" Jes had been sitting on his bunk when the noise came—a shuffling, as if someone were walking toward his cell. He stood. The light was dim outside his cell and he had difficulty seeing past the illumination inside his cage.

"Why, Jes?" He knew my voice and it made him shiver.

"Reah, I swear I didn't plan it that way. I swear it. He was only supposed to take you out of there. You have to believe me. He never said he was going to tap the core."

"You were going to let him take me. Why?" I stepped closer to Jes' cell, enabling him to see me.

"Reah, get me out of here. I promise I'll take care of you. You look exhausted."

"Like you took care of my mother?"

"Reah, they offered me money. A lot of money. I was hoping to get my family off Thiskil. Only it was already too late. I didn't even hear the name, pretty girl. Didn't want to know the one I'd killed. I figured they were going to kill the baby, too. They just didn't." Jes hung his head.

"Do you know what I just did, Jes?" I stopped an arm's length outside his cell. He couldn't reach me, even if he tried.

"What, Reah?" He still wasn't meeting my eyes.

"I healed the core on Cloudsong. Now, I might consider doing the same for Thiskil. It won't bring your family back, but it will allow all the Thiskilhin expatriates to return, once it rejuvenates."

"You'd do that?" Now he was looking at me.

"In exchange for information." I said.

"What information?" Jes demanded.

"Nidris. Where did you find him? Where might he go? Is he running as far as he can to get away, or is he planning some other devilry?"

"You want to kill him."

"He killed my daughter. Almost killed me. What do you think?"

"Good. I want him dead, too."

"Then tell me what you know."

"All right." Jes began to talk.

"My son, I believe you should be on Campiaa tomorrow," Kaldill said. "And just so you know, I've known about your mindspeech since you gained it. I have not used it out of respect for your privacy." Lendill examined his father's face in the comp-vid. He wasn't surprised that his father knew. He was used to such things by now. "If you cannot find someone to take you, I will send Faldill."

"I think I can find someone to take me, father."

"Good. If things go badly, send mindspeech. Promise me this."

"Of course, father. I promise." Lendill was tired, out of sorts and ready for bed. He'd had Reah with him; had nearly convinced her to stay. Then things had been said, sending Reah flying away from him. Now, he'd have to search for her again.

"Child, this is important. Do not forget."

"I will remember, father."

"Good. I love you, even though I do not say it often," Kaldill sighed. "Sleep well, my youngest." Kaldill ended the communication.

CHAPTER 14

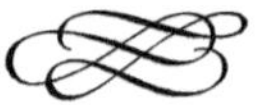

Campiaa had changed somewhat since I'd seen it last. Of course, Teeg hadn't allowed me to go out very often. People were everywhere. I made sure I didn't go into any business or casino where I might be recognized. Instead, I'd chosen one near the end of the half-moon shaped bay. Arvil hadn't owned that one. I wondered if Teeg were demanding the dues levied by Arvil in the past. I'd had to dig through everything in Aurelius' home to find the credit chip necklace that could be used on Campiaa.

"Three nights, please," I said to the hotel desk clerk. No need to make them think I only wanted the night before the summit. That might raise suspicions. I'd learned my lessons during my stint in the ASD. I wasn't helpless. Wounded in spirit and in my heart, perhaps, but certainly not helpless.

My knife was in my bag and a smaller one in my boot. Jes and I had a long talk. Eventually I sat down outside his cell and let him ramble. I'd learned a lot. Losing his family had harmed him. Jes was wounded, too. Only his had bordered on insanity. He wasn't willing to let anything else go that he cared for. And in some warped way, he cared for me. He was genuinely upset that I'd been harmed and my daughter killed.

Somehow, he hadn't reconciled my mother's death with my existence. He'd talked of the baby as if it weren't me. Jes was deranged in some way, and the condition had worsened since he'd met me. I couldn't help him now, and he'd have sentence passed eventually by the ASD. No longer my concern. I planned to heal Thiskil, if I survived the following day. Jes might not live over his crimes, but Thiskil stood a chance.

"Is there anything else we can get for you, Miss Largill?" The desk clerk asked, handing over a key chip.

"No, thank you," I said, lifting my bag. I'd used one of the many IDs Lendill had given me over the years. They were just as official as anything else I might use. My hair I'd also darkened with temporary dye—it was dark-brown, now. It matched the holographic photo of me on the ID.

"Then have a pleasant evening," The clerk smiled. I nodded and walked away.

Why wasn't I one of those lucky women who had a Larentii as a mate? They could provide a healing sleep better than anyone, or willingly trilled for their mates, achieving nearly the same result. Yet there I was, with two vampires—Gavril had been born vampire and Aurelius had been made so by an unnamed sire. One High Demon and a half-Elf. Not to mention the King of Karathia—a powerful warlock. Lissa had two Larentii. I hadn't deserved one, I suppose. Or a Falchani. I'd been so enthralled with that race when I was young. Lissa had two of those as well.

I shrugged into my leather jacket shortly after daybreak. I'd not slept much and felt worse for it. The meeting was about to start, and I figured if Nidris were going to make his presence known, it would be shortly before it started. At that moment, Campiaa's core was still intact—I could feel it if it had been tapped—the wrongness would make itself known. I was waiting for Nidris to tap it. That would confirm what Jes and I had determined—that Nidris would hire himself out to Teeg's enemies—the Strands. Nidris' loyalty lay with Nidris. If the Strands gained Campiaa, it would die within a decade. Nidris would get away soon, before the Strands would ever learn of his perfidy. I wanted Nidris. And the Strands, too, if they stood in the way of a peaceful transition to the Campiaan Alliance.

At the moment, it was still a large collection of self-governing worlds. By this afternoon, if things went as planned, they would be bound under a single set of laws. It might be similar to watching a difficult birth. Under other circumstances, I might have been awestruck at witnessing such a momentous occasion. Instead, I was struggling to keep it alive. My daughter's death fleetingly entered my thoughts, and the parallels didn't escape me. No, I wasn't willing to let this infant—the Campiaan Alliance—go. If it fell, I would fall with it. I clipped my knife to the waistband of my pants, squared my shoulders and skipped into the main ballroom at the San Gerxon Casino. I'd felt the tiniest bit of wrongness—Nidris was tapping the core.

"I want to thank all of you—and congratulate you as well—we will witness history today," Teeg San Gerxon announced to a capacity crowd. "In the coming months, we will pass laws and make adjustments until we have something that will bear the weight of the ages. My friends, we will depend upon our neighbors, just as they will lean upon us. We will conscript our armies and enforce the laws we forge together. Every citizen will be assured of equal treatment, no matter what world he stands upon within the Campiaan Alliance." Cheers broke out and every attendee stood and clapped. Just as five hundred Giffelithi mercenaries blasted their way inside, led by four warlocks.

I watched Teeg turn to mist as someone fired a ranos rifle at his head.

Nidris and the core would have to wait; even I had no idea that the Strands would hire hundreds of Giffelithi mercenaries. I might go down with the Campiaan Alliance after all. Furious at Nidris, the Strands and their mercenary army, I turned to full Thifilatha, as Astralan, Stellan and the others began hurling blasts at the invaders. I ran toward the army, screaming out my anger.

A ranos bullet pierced my right shoulder. I swept the shooter aside, burning his body and crushing his remains against a wall. Others fell beneath my feet and turned to smoking ash as I ran over them. Many of them were running—I think they weren't expecting something such as I. The Strands' warlocks were hurling blasts in my direction, but they were ineffective. I felt another bullet sting my side. The pain was inconsequential. I went after the ones who still held pistols and rifles.

~

Father, they're hitting Reah! Lendill sent desperate and frightened mindspeech. Lendill felt helpless, watching Reah go after five hundred Giffelithi mercenaries. He didn't have time to wonder at the expense of that—he had to do something. Pulling his pistol, Lendill began firing at the enemy.

Child, we are coming, came his father's mental voice. Lendill didn't have time to worry about it, he fired as quickly as his pistol recharged.

~

Garde, Tory, anybody, Gavril's being attacked, Lissa sent a mental shout. She and Gavin were already on their way.

~

I may have howled in anguish when the third ranos blast hit me in the left thigh. Things became complicated quickly after that, or perhaps I was hallucinating—I imagined that a hundred Elvish warriors appeared, armed with bows. What did they think to accomplish against ranos pistols and rifles, in addition to regular issue rapid-fires and other weapons? Nevertheless, those bows were aimed and none missed. It was as if the arrows were spelled to strike their targets.

Giffelithi were screaming and dying while more blasts came from Teeg's warlocks. I saw Wylend standing in a corner, surrounded by Erland, Wyatt and Ry. All of them were doing spellwork, killing with precision from afar. That's when I saw Nidris. He was glowing with the power he'd stolen from Campiaa's core. Anything aimed at him sizzled and disintegrated before striking his body. I saw him take aim at Wylend and those around him.

"No!" I shouted, flipping my wings out and leaping in his direction across the crowded, seething mass of people still trying to escape. My wings allowed me to glide overhead until I landed directly in front of Nidris. His spell was caught and deflected by my body as another spray of bullets hit me. Teeg was suddenly behind Nidris, lengthy claws out, eyes red and fangs showing. Nidris' head was lifted from his body so swiftly I barely saw it happen.

"Reah, get down!" Teeg shouted. I didn't. I couldn't. Teeg had his back turned and didn't see what I saw, since I was facing it and he wasn't. A ranos launcher. Aimed directly at him. Muting my ability to burn, I plucked Teeg off the floor and tossed him to the side while the launcher fired directly toward my chest.

"Wylend!" Erland shouted, preparing the spell and sending it on its way.

"No! In the name of the skies, no!" Wylend cried out, watching the launcher fire directly at Reah. Wyatt and Rylend grabbed him as Reah took the full blast of the launcher to her chest. The top of the ballroom was blasted away when Lissa, Gavin and three High Demons in full Thifilathi appeared, killing, burning and crushing their way through the rest of the mercenary army. Only moments later, when the entire army was either captured, subdued or dead, the ensuing silence was almost eerie. All of them turned to look as Kifirin, nearly twenty feet tall, his scales iridescent black, lifted Reah's lifeless Thifilatha from the ground and wept.

The End

www.ingramcontent.com/pod-product-compliance
Lightning Source LLC
Chambersburg PA
CBHW070526100726
47907CB00004B/994